D0909010

A
Garland Series

VICTORIAN

FICTION

NOVELS OF FAITH
AND DOUBT

A collection of 121 novels
in 92 volumes, selected by
Professor Robert Lee Wolff,
Harvard University,
with a separate introductory volume
written by him
especially for this series.

A ROMANCE
OF THE
NINETEENTH CENTURY

W. H. Mallock

Two volumes in one

Garland Publishing, Inc., New York & London

1976

Bibliographical note:

this facsimile has been made from a copy in the
British Museum
(12641.1.6)

Library of Congress Cataloging in Publication Data

Mallock, William Hurrell, 1849-1923.
    A romance of the nineteenth century.

    (Victorian fiction : Novels of faith and doubt)
    Reprint of the 1881 ed. published by Chatto and
Windus, London.
    I. Title. II. Series.
PZ3.M296Ro12 [PR4972.M5]   823'.8   75-1528
ISBN 0-8240-1600-9

A ROMANCE

OF THE

NINETEENTH CENTURY

VOL. I.

A ROMANCE

of the

NINETEENTH CENTURY

BY

W. H. MALLOCK

AUTHOR OF 'THE NEW REPUBLIC' ETC.

'DEFECERUNT OCULI MEI IN SALUTARE TUUM'

IN TWO VOLUMES—VOL. I.

London

CHATTO AND WINDUS, PICCADILLY

1881

LONDON : PRINTED BY
SPOTTISWOODE AND CO., NEW-STREET SQUARE
AND PARLIAMENT STREET

BOOK I.

CHAPTER I.

THE talents, the family, and the fortune of Ralph Vernon were all quite distinguished enough to make it worth the world's while to attend to him; and the result was that he was at once condemned and courted. This was not perhaps a matter that it is very hard to account for. His manners and his amusements led him to consort with the careless, whilst his deeper interests were really those of the serious; and thus, let him be in what society he would, he was always in a moral sense more or less an outsider. He had little of the gay good-fellowship which is the virtue most prized by the pleasure-seekers ; he was on the surface far too much of a pleasure-seeker not to irritate those who are busied with thoughts of duty : and his faults, actual or imputed, when they came to the general ear, repelled the one class without attracting the other.

It was supposed that he had trifled with the affections of numerous women ; it was supposed that he had wasted any amount of talent ; it was supposed that, from knowledge or want of knowledge, he was without any kind of Christianity, and that, from want of earnestness, he was quite unmoved by its substitutes ; he was supposed to have many friends warmly attached to him, and to be himself incapable of any warm attachment. And this marked want in him of all that is thought most lovable was made more marked still by his singular charm of manner, which, for the time being, was certain to win every one. Such was the general impression of him, which, whether true or no, was at all events not groundless ; and there was many a mother in London of the best and purest type who thought his character so cold, so unprincipled, and so repulsive, that he could atone for it only by becoming her daughter's husband.

The number of these mothers was at last reduced to one. Ralph Vernon became engaged to be married. The *fiancée* was young, clever, beautiful, and deeply attached to him ; nor in the case of most men would the event have seemed unnatural. But the general sentiment with regard to Vernon was merely wonder as to what could be here his motive : for most of the world thought what a rough-tongued cousin of his said, ' You may see me d—d if Ralph's ever in love with any one.' Let his motive, however, be what it might, his engagement caused, or was caused by, a very visible change in him.   All of a sudden he seemed to become serious ; and for many months one might have thought him a new man.   The father of the bride-elect was at the time absent in Afghanistan, and the marriage was put off till his return the following year.   Vernon, meanwhile, said good-bye to his idleness ; he was even not liberal in the days he allowed for love-making.   He devoted himself instead to his various county duties ; he studied such subjects as education and pauperism ; he projected the building of schools and cottages ; and he tried to become acquainted with the great mass of his tenantry.   Finally, when in 1880, came the renowned general election, he stood in the Conservative interest for his own division of the county, and lost the battle by less than a dozen votes.

This sudden devotion to public affairs,

however, was not construed altogether to his advantage. It was supposed to argue luke-warmness in love, rather than zeal in politics ; nor was the rumour at all wondered at that the lady took the same view of it. Vernon, it was said on all sides, was not behaving well ; it was added by many that he wished to back out of his engagement; and the latter opinion was certainly confirmed by the sequel. In due time the lady's father returned, and the various legal preliminaries were at once to be got over. What, then, were the feelings of all who heard it when Vernon insisted, as one condition of his marriage, that any children that might result from it should be brought up as Catholics ! The father and the family of the *fiancée* were all fiercely Protestant; and this move of Vernon's made an end of the whole matter. The rupture was abrupt and painful ; and he was himself severely criticised. That he had

any interest in religion was what nobody
gave him credit for ; and he was supposed,
in this case, to have used it as a last excuse
in his desperation.

His conduct directly afterwards did not
disarm the censorious. He was soon reported
to have formed another intimacy, and to
have given another lady a strong sentimental
claim on him. Then, the report went on,
he had repeated his former conduct, though
this time perhaps more judiciously. There
had been no formal engagement, the world
supposed ; there had been no need, therefore,
for any definite subterfuge. A simpler ex-
pedient had been quite sufficient : he had
buried himself somewhere in some retreat on
the Continent. This second drama had been
of a strictly private character ; but there are
acute observers who can pierce through any
privacy ; and the comments made on it were
not of a friendly nature. Indeed, when the

news was known that after all his mis-
demeanours Vernon was enjoying himself in
a charming Provençal villa, surrounded by
books, and supplied with a first-class *chef*, one
of the keenest and most discriminating of all
his feminine acquaintances was at last tempted
to speak of him as a voluptuary of the very
worst species.

In spite, however, of every ill report,
there were a certain number who always
stood up for him, and who maintained stoutly
that there were two sides to his character.
They could not deny that what the world
said was true of him ; they declared only
that it was not the whole truth. There was
one of these in especial—Alic Campbell
by name—who looked upon Vernon as the
best friend he had, and who knew much of
his inner history that was quite hidden from
others. When Vernon went abroad, he had
begged Campbell to go with him ; but

Campbell for certain reasons had felt constrained to refuse. Vernon had written from Paris to him, to renew his entreaties, but without the desired result. About a fortnight later he returned to the charge once more.

CHAPTER II.

'MY dear Alic,' he wrote, ' I am at last settled ; and I will now take no denial. You must and you shall join me. Could you only see where I am, I should have no need to implore you ; you would come instantly, and come of your own accord. As it is, I can only trust to writing; but you surely will not refuse me. Come to me do, if for no more than a week or two, and share with me this beautiful Southern solitude. Share my villa with its cool portico—a villa just large enough for two children of Epicurus. Share my garden with its myrtles, and its oranges, and the softly swaying gold of its great mimosa-trees. Yes, I am here in the South and the clear sunshine; and I am not, as you prophesied and as half my heart urged me, in any of the winter haunts of English fashion and frivolity; but I am embowered safely by myself on the greenest of all the promontories that Europe juts into the Mediterranean. I am settled at the Cap de Juan. I have, indeed, chosen a lovely spot, and already I love it tenderly. All day long, through the leaves of my dark evergreens, and through arched bowery openings, the sea shines and sparkles. You and I may change and grow weary; and we have both had much to weary us. But this bluest of blue seas seems to be always one-and-twenty; and as I breathe its breath, full of eternal freshness, the thrill and the dreams of youth once more revive in me. And ah, the view! In a vast majestic crescent the French coast of mountains curves away towards Italy, with its succession of pearl-grey headlands dying faintly and far off into the distance. Midway, about ten miles from here as a boat sails, a line of milk-white houses, Nice lies along the sealevel. Range upon range is piled up behind it, blue with far-off haze, or green with nearer olive-woods ; and bright over all, like the hills of another world, are the jagged Alpine summits with their white snows glittering. All day long the lights and the tints vary. New mists form and melt upon the mountains ; the sea changes from one glow to another. The wave-worn sea-rock, pierced with its clear shadows, has always new hues and aspects ; so have the silver gleams that sleep in the spreading stone-pines. The whole face of Nature is like the face of a living thing. It is the face of a Cleopatra.

> Age cannot wither it, nor custom stale
> Its infinite variety.

'Alic—you who are coughing, sneezing, and blowing your nose in England—will not this tempt you? Your first impulse will be, I know, to refuse me. You are not in spirits, you will say, for the sunshine; you have no energy left to make any exertion. I am quite familiar with the mood of mind you are in. You are like a man who is sea-sick at the extreme end of a steamer, and who yet will not move himself to make his way to the middle. You are arguing to yourself with the unique logic of grief, " I am comfortless, and therefore nothing shall comfort me." Let me try to move you to a brighter and a healthier mind.

' You are wretched, you tell me, because you want to marry a certain person, and because you find that, though she loves you as a friend, she will never love you but as a friend only. Now, I am going to speak very gently to you, and yet I hope convincingly.

I am not going to tell you any such idle lies as that your loss is a trifling one. I am not going to tell you that it is an atom less than you feel it to be; and you would, I think, injure your character by trying to undervalue it. No; I will not tell you to undervalue your loss. I will only show you—a thing you have quite forgotten—how to value your gain. Perhaps you will say I am not in a position to do so, for in some ways certainly you have been somewhat reticent. You have told me much about your own feelings, about your own devotion, and about the moral result that all this has had on you. But about the object of these feelings you have told me little. I know neither how you met her nor how you wooed her; nor anything about her character, except that her ways are simple. You have not told me even her name. But I don't think this matters. Let the difference between our two situations be what it may,

your case in many ways has been also mine ;
and I am going now to speak from my own
experience.

' I, as you know well, was not long since
to have married ; and during a good year's
novitiate I was preparing my whole being for
its solemn new condition.   My character
during that period underwent a profound
change.   My bright-coloured hopes and purposes lost their airy wings.   They fell to the
solid earth, and found for themselves plodding
feet.   I felt I was no longer my own.   My
life was owed to another ; and for the first
time there dawned on me the true sense of
responsibility.   But circumstances combined
to make my marriage impossible ; and after
I had already learned to mentally mix my life
with another's, our two lives were again made
separate.   When first I realised this, it was
like waking out of a dream.   I was conscious
of a loneliness I had never known before ;

and even now, with my shattered marriage prospects, my manhood seems to lie in ashes about me. But what do I find has happened? Something glad, strange, and altogether unlooked for. Out of the ashes of my manhood has re-arisen my youth—my youth, which I thought I had said good-bye to for eternity; and the divine child has again run to meet me with its eyes bright as ever, and with the summer wind in its hair. The sun has gone back for me on the dial. I am three years younger again. The skies seem to have grown bluer, and my step more elastic. Once more free and unfettered, I feel sometimes as if I were walking on air; and I have the delicious sense of having lost a burden, even though I may have lost a treasure as well.

' You will see my meaning better when I go on to tell you that, though I have recovered the buoyancy of youth, I have by no means recovered its ignorance. I still retain

a certain salvage of wisdom, sad and bitter
enough in some ways, and yet good for men
like us two to remember.   It is this—listen
patiently.   There is nothing in the world so
intensely selfish as a woman's deep affection ;
and the stronger and more single-hearted it
is, the greater becomes its selfishness.   A
man's passion is generous when compared
with a woman's love.   A man's passion, at
its worst, lasts but a short time ; even while
it lasts, its demands are limited ; and, what is
more than this, a good man will restrain it.
But the truer and more sensitive a woman is,
the more thoroughly will she let her love
master her ; the less effort will she make to
retain the least control of it.

'And what a master it is ! Its jealousy
is cruel as the grave, and its demands know
no limits but the imagination of her that
makes them.   A woman who loves thus is
not content with the chastest bodily con-

stancy; she is not content even with the constancy of an undivided tenderness. These she takes for granted: they are not the things she craves for. What she craves for is the constancy of your whole thought and intellect. You are to have nothing in your mind that you do not confide to her; you are to stifle every interest with which she cannot be associated. If you want any mental help, it is she alone who must help you; and she had sooner you were helped ill by her than well by another person. She will be as jealous of your friendships as she is of your affections, and as jealous of your thoughts and tastes as she is of your friendships. She cannot patiently conceive of you as in relation to anything excepting herself. She desires to absorb your whole life into hers; and the larger part of it, which she naturally cannot absorb, she desires to see perish. Her pleading, earnest eyes will be for ever saying

to you, " Entreat me not to leave thee.
Where thou goest I will go ; and go not thou,
my love, whither I cannot follow thee."

'What!—with all the world of thought
and imagination before us, are men such as
we are to be tied and bound like this ?   For
my part, the wings of my spirit seem to have
all the winds in them ; and I have a heart
sometimes likes a hawk's or a wild sea-gull's.
It is not a heart that is hard, or that does
not soften to companionship.   I could often
perch tenderly upon some beloved shoulder,
and bend my head to listen to words of
tenderness.   But if the hand that I trusted
but once closed to lay hold of me—dared,
from love, to use the least pressure to keep
me—I should start and struggle, and feel I
had suffered treachery.   I will stoop my
neck myself ; but no one else shall ever draw
it an inch downwards.   Why do we want
companionship ?   What is a man's need for it ?

Were my life really a bird's, I would gladly
have a she-bird to fly with me ; but I would
have her only because we were bound both
of us independently for the same resting-place.
That and that alone should be the fetterless
fetter we were united by.   But a woman who
loves deeply will never love like this.   She
has no wish to be your companion on these
terms.   It is not the common end that she
cares for, but the united struggle ; and she
reveres her wish to soar, chiefly because it is
an excuse for clinging to you.   Thus, on the
same principle, she will go nowhere in the
mental world herself unless you are there to
support her.   She thinks it a kind of treason
to you to try and walk independently.   She
cultivates her weakness, that she may be
always trusting to your strength ; and though
her weight might be dragging you to the
ground, she would never think of it, never
see it, but if possible she would only lean the

heavier. Was ever selfishness so pitiless and intense as this? And yet, by a strange magic, it looks so like self-devotion, that a man, if he be not a brute, can hardly fail to be crushed by it. Such love, Alic, may be a thing that suits some temperaments, but surely neither yours nor mine.

'And now I am once more my own. Ah, the sweetness and rest of this serene self-possession! But lately I felt, when I was looking even at the sea or the mountains, that I was not permitted to love them. The shadow of another would always seem to cleave to me and claim me; and I could no longer let my spirit, as I used to do, go floating on the lonely waters. But now I can look everywhere without fear. I can say to the sea, when it makes me in love with loneliness, "I violate no allegiance due to any companionship." I can say the same to the forest, when its leafy smells woo me, and the murmur of its brown branches. I can say the same in society, when bright eyes and alluring voices stimulate me, and I feel that many women are far better than one. Then, too—though I will not dwell upon this here—were there a God to turn to, I could turn to Him in solitude. And now in the morning, as I awaken, I often turn to my pillow, and kiss it, and say, "No head but mine can ever dare to press you." All the walls of my bedroom seem to smile kindly and quietly on me. By my bedside I see my dear companions, my books—so varied and so unobtrusive—that will themselves tell me all they can, and will ask for no confidence in return; and there, too, I see my letters, which have now the new charm for me, that no one but myself will ever want to open them.

'Yes; I have learned the truest secret of Epicurus, that the friendship of a man is more than the love of a woman. Friendship is always a free gift ; and it is always given readily because it is never owed.   Love, too, begins as a gift ; but a loving woman will never leave it so.   Before you know it, she will have turned it into a debt; and the more she loves the debtor, the more oppressively will she extort the utmost farthing from him.   But between friends, Alic, the intercourse is always free.   I could have no thought that it would be treason to conceal from you.   I could form no ties or friendships that would do you any wrong.   And yet—if I may alter Shakespeare in a single word—

> And yet, by heaven, I hold my *friend* as rare
> As any she belied by false compare.

'Come, then, and lay all this to your heart ; for your heart, I know, will assent to its truth as mine does.   Marriage would suit you no better than me.   It allured me first

with its many pleasing promises ; and in the
same way it is now alluring you.   It can give
much to numbers ; I do not deny that for a
moment ; but neither you nor I were made
for it.   In missing it, as I have said before,
you are no doubt a loser ; but my advice to
you is, do not brood over the loss ; think of
the gain, for the gain is far greater.   Recall
your imagination from the solace you would
have had in marriage, and dwell on the joys
and the freedom that you keep because you
are single.

'Freedom—yes, you have that still.   You
have not the caprices of any one else to bind
you.   My dear Alic, think of your priceless
freedom !   I say think of it ; but I want you
to use it also.   I want you to come to me,
away from your frosty England, and let me
see the Southern sunlight laughing in your
glad grey eyes.   If you will, all my house shall
welcome you.   My champagne is excellent ;

my cigars and cigarettes are excellent—I had them all sent from London; and my bookcases are well stored with poets, and with your own philosophers. At the end of one of my walks is a certain marble seat. You look straight down at the sea from it, and it is overarched with myrtles. There is a perfect wilderness of green shade behind it; and in the midst of this, like an enchanted lamp, is a great camellia tree, burning with scarlet blossoms. Close at hand there is a little table, just fit to support a bottle of Burgundy, and a quaint old glass goblet for each of us. It is an entrancing place. It is a bower after your own heart. And there we might sit together, in the calm, delicious mornings, talking or silent, just as the mood prompted us. Sometimes we might quote to each other our favourite poets; sometimes we might solve again the old insoluble questions we have so often discussed before, and which are still eating my life out; sometimes we might watch in quiet the waves and the rocks before us, and often, too, some gay, bright-coloured fishing-boat, floating lonely with its white plume of a sail, and its brown fisher at the stern bending over his own reflection. Yes, Alic, if you will only come out to me, we will contrive to elude the Furies. We will look into life together more clearly than we used to do; but it shall be a personal oppression to us no more than it used to be. We will only enter here on a new phase of youth. We will have free, cloudless days, and nights of moonlight. We will drive, and ride, and sail, and explore the whole country. We will know the folds of the hills grey with olive-trees; we will listen to the sound of mule-bells; we will see how the middle-age lingers in the wild hill-villages. Then, too, my own immediate neighbourhood—that is delightful also. The whole of my green peninsula is an

Eden of woods and gardens; and the life
that surrounds you there is like a living idyll.
Old brown crones crouching under the olive-
trees, the peasant proprietor tilling his small
field, the neatly dressed nursery-gardener
surveying his glass frames, the retired
domestic tradesman smiling over the gate of
his little villa-garden—these are the living
images that surround one, and that give to
one's thoughts such a quaint, delightful setting. A strange mixture, too, on all sides
touches one of homely plenty and of wild
luxuriance. Cabbages and palm-trees grow
in the same enclosure. Between beds of
kitchen stuff are strips starred with anemones,
and pink almond-blossoms tremble among the
apple-trees.

'Ah, my old companion, will not these
pleasures move you? Write, write to me
quickly, and say they will. Only in that case
I have something further to tell you. If you

would enjoy the seclusion I have described to you, you must come and enjoy it speedily : and for this reason. On one side of me is a beautiful marble villa, with immense gardens and long winding walks ; and on the other side, with immense gardens also, is a large disused hotel, whose proprietors last year were bankrupt. It is built like an old château. It has quaint vanes on the gables ; and flights of marble steps lead up to the doors and windows. It is just at the cape's point ; and its domain of gardens, with their long walks and terraces, and their arches of trellised roses, are bounded on three sides by the sea. Those gardens, silent and lifeless, not a soul but the gardeners now walks in them—the gardeners and myself, and, who should you think besides ? Poor Frederic Stanley—the cleverest of our Oxford idlers ; who, since we knew him, has been first a guardsman, and is now a Catholic priest.

How time does change some men! Stanley is here for his health : he is broken down with work. He looks, I fancy, rather askance at me ; but we have often little reserved conversations together.

' However I am wandering from the point. What I want to tell you is this. Up till now the hotel and the villa have been alike tenantless, and I have been able to use both gardens as my own ; but that happy period is now drawing fast to a close. Some English people, whose names I do not know, though no doubt I shall soon make their acquaintance, are coming, or perhaps have already come, to the villa. And as to the hotel, what do you think has happened ? Our friend the Duchess has taken it—it is still furnished—for the whole of next month, and intends having a large party there. So you see that very soon I shall be saying good-bye to solitude. This last piece of news

I have only this instant learned, and from the Duchess herself. I can't exactly say if I am glad or sorry. I shall have at all events a very enlivening neighbour; and her company always charms me. It is not the charm now, as it must once have been, of beauty and sentiment. It is what at fifty supplies their place, and rivals them; it is the charm of mundane humour. This bright, gay humour of feminine middle-age, it always seems to me, is a very rare gift. It is a highly artificial product, and is almost peculiar, I think, to one class of society. It requires to develop it a combination of two things in the past—the susceptibilities of the world of romance, and the indulgence of them in the word of fashion. However, be our friend's charm what it will, I am at this moment going to enjoy it; as in another five minutes I shall be at dinner with her.

And this at last brings me to a con

fession which will amuse you. Where do
you think I am writing you this letter? Not
in my philosophic garden, not in my quiet
study. All about me is gas-light and gilding,
and a murmur of garish life. The figures
surrounding me are gamblers and Parisian
cocottes ; and I am breathing, not the scent of
the sea or of flowers, but of patchouli and
faint stale cigarette smoke. I am in the
reading-room at Monte Carlo. I drove over
here this morning—or rather, my coachman
drove me—partly to try a new pair of horses,
and partly for the sake of the starlight drive
back again. The Duchess is staying for a
day or two at the hotel attached to the
gambling-rooms, and it seems she has a little
dinner party every night in the restaurant.
To-night the Grantlys are coming. You
remember Grantly at Oxford? He is now
in the First Life Guards ; and his wife is a
lovely American, whose face is even prettier

than her dresses, and, if possible, even more changing.

'*À propos* of the women here, there is one on the sofa opposite me, who is really divinely lovely. Whenever I look up from my writing, I am met by her soft large eyes, half sad and half voluptuous in their tenderness. She is as different from the women near her as day from night, or rather as the stars from gas-light. She is one of the fallen; I fear there can be no doubt about that; but refinement—even a sort of nobleness—can outlive virtue. There is not a touch of paint on her; and her dress, which fits her perfectly, is strangely simple. If I have any skill in reading the looks of women, there is something of a higher life yet lingering in that soft, pleading face, that she half hides from me by her large crimson fan. Some women have a glance that makes me long to talk to them, just as clear sea-water makes me long to plunge in it.

'Write to me soon.   I am obliged to stop now.

'By the way, besides the Grantlys, there is another guest expected, who is to me more interesting.   I mean Lord Surbiton.   He was the first man of letters I ever knew; and when I was seventeen, he seemed to me little short of a god.

'Good-bye; I must be going.   My fair one is rising too.'

CHAPTER III.

THE Duchess's stately figure was familiar at Monte Carlo, and many an eye followed her as she entered the gorgeous restaurant.

'Garçon,' she said, as she took her seat at the large table reserved for her, '*Pommery et gréno, extra sec*—the last champagne on the wine list. You must put three bottles in ice instantly, for in five minutes we shall be quite ready for dinner. And—wait, wait a moment, man, for I have not done speaking to you— we are not going to pay thirty-six francs again for a single dish of asparagus; so you will perhaps have the goodness to recollect that. And you must lay another place if you please, as we shall be five dining this evening instead of four.'

Captain and Mrs. Grantly appeared almost immediately, and with them was an elderly man in close attendance on the latter. The young guardsman and his wife were a very characteristic couple, and looked like a bright embodiment of the spirit of modern London. The appearance of their companion was very different. His dress was too showy for what is now correct taste, and his jewelled scarf-pin and sleeve-links were both of enormous size. But on him these splendours seemed to lose half their offensiveness. They were plainly the *fashion* of a past generation, not the *vulgarities* of the present one : they even heightened by contrast the strange effect of his face, with its worn weary cheeks, and his keen glance like an eagle's. This was none other than the renowned Lord Surbiton—the poet, diplomat, and dandy who had charmed the last generation.

The whole party had been winning largely at the tables, and their spirits were quite in keeping with the glittering scene around them. The crowd which filled the restaurant was to-night even more gay than usual. All the men were at least dressed like gentlemen, and most of the women were far more splendid than ladies. Fashionable exiles from the English world of fashion were detected in numbers by the amused eyes of the Duchess; and with them the fair companions who had caused their exile or were sharing it. It was said even that royalty was not absent, and that there thus was a divine element unrecognised in the midst of the human. Everywhere there was a flashing of restless eyes and diamonds; furred and embroidered opera-cloaks were being disposed of over the backs of chairs ; long gloves were being unbuttoned and drawn off; and white hands, galncing with rings, were composing deranged tresses. Above was the arched ceiling glowing with gold and pictures; and the walls, florid with ornament, returned every shaft of lamplight from the depths of immense mirrors, or the limbs of naked goddesses.

' Now, this,' said the Duchess, ' is exactly what I enjoy : charming company, a charming scene before one, and—let me tell you all, for I myself ordered it—a really excellent dinner. However,' she went on, as she unfolded her napkin, and looked with a slow smile at the *menu*, ' we must be temperate in the midst of plenty ; for remember, Mrs. Grantly, you and I and your husband are to go back to the tables again for one half-hour afterwards—only one half-hour, mind ; and then, as Lord Surbiton suggests—he is always, as we all know, poetical—we will have our coffee outside, and compose our feelings under the stars of heaven.'

'What!' said Mrs. Grantly, 'and is Lord Surbiton not coming back to the rooms with us?'

'Not he,' said the Duchess. 'He's not half a man at gambling. I don't think your poets ever are. But where,' she exclaimed presently, as she saw that a chair was vacant, 'where is Mr. Vernon? Has any one seen our Mr. Ralph Vernon? We can't possibly get on without our one unmarried young man; though, to say the truth, till this moment I had quite forgotten to miss him.'

'Mr. Vernon!' echoed Mrs. Grantly with a laugh. 'I'd advise you, Duchess, not to count upon him. I saw him on the hotel steps only ten minutes ago, and what do you think he was doing? Why, he was talking to that beautiful creature we were all admiring at the tables—the woman with the red fan and the long dark eyelashes. I don't know what she was saying, I'm sure, but she had her hand on his arm, and he was bending down to her.'

'Oh, ho——' began the Duchess, with a soft low laugh. But Lord Surbiton interrupted her.

'Vernon!' he said; 'can this be the Ralph Vernon that I once knew, some thirteen years ago—a dreamy eager boy, who used to come and show me his poetry?'

'To be sure it is,' said the Duchess. 'Poetry, painting, and heaven knows what else—I believe he has tried all of it.'

'Ah!' said Lord Surbiton; 'I once had great hopes of him. I once thought he was signed with the veritable sign of genius.'

'Well,' replied the Duchess, 'and he *is* very clever, I believe.'

'Men who are clever,' said Lord Surbiton

solemnly, 'we can count by millions: men
with genius we count by units. As for Vernon, his early verses were beautiful, in spite
of their crude language. They had the same
charm in them that his ideal eyes had—little
of the gladness of youth, but all its sweetness
and its hunger.'

' It seems,' said the Duchess, ' that this is
a young man who is very much to be envied ;
for in addition to all these charms, he has two
others that women think irresistible—a fortune and a history.'

' Yes,' said Lord Surbiton, with a wave
of his jewelled hand; 'women are always
attracted by a man with a history, because it
always means that he is to be either blamed
or pitied.'

' And what,' said Mrs. Grantly, ' may Mr.
Vernon's history be ? '

' Ah !' said the Duchess, ' that's just what
we don't know, and that's the very reason

why we find it so interesting.   Never be too
curious, my dear, about a friend's history ;
and then you can always stick up for him
with a clear conscience.'

'Look !' exclaimed Mrs. Grantly, 'here
the charmer comes.   I only hope he won't
be trying all his fascinations on me.'

Vernon was full of regrets for being behind his time ; but these he discovered were
met with nothing but laughter.   Mrs. Grantly
assured him at once that they knew all about
him and his doings.   'And this is the man,'
she went on—' now, I ask you all to look at
him—who says he has come abroad for the
sake of philosophic solitude !'

'And why not ?' said Vernon ; 'I think
I am quite consistent.   Solitude is my wife,
and society is my mistress ; and I like to live
with the one, and be always intriguing with
the other.'

'Well,' exclaimed Mrs. Grantly, 'since

we are your society for the moment, our collective place in your heart is, I must say, not very honourable.'

'Never mind about that,' said the Duchess. 'What my suspicions rest upon is Mr. Vernon's solitude—that retiring villa of his at the Cap de Juan : especially now we hear all this about red fans, and whisperings, and hotel door-steps, and long eyelashes.'

'My attentions on the door-step,' said Vernon, 'were of the strictly Platonic order. There is something rather touching in that woman, when one comes to talk to her.'

'Very likely,' said Captain Grantly drily ; 'there always is. *Touching* is the exact word for it. And what's her rank, Vernon ? Is she a princess or a duchess ? '

'If she's a princess,' said Vernon, 'she must have lost her principality ; for she was dreadfully in want of a thousand francs to gamble with.'

'Very likely,' said Captain Grantly ; 'they all are.'

The Duchess, meanwhile, was surveying the motley scene before her. ' I confess,' she said with a soft smile of amusement, 'this is hardly the place one would come to if one were in search of Platonic attachments. Now, look round, all of you, and take stock of the company. There are plenty of men one knows—of course, one expects that ; but the women with them—did you ever see anything like it ? Come, Mr. Vernon, you understand these things. Just observe the couple behind you—they can't talk English, so we needn't mind discussing them—are they man and wife, do you think ? Or that fine lady, with the hair sprinkled with gold-dust, whom Lord Surbiton seems to admire so—what relation should you say she was to the old Jew she is dining with ? Upon my word, Mrs. Grantly,' she added presently, ' I

don't believe that, our two selves excepted,
there's a single woman here you could possibly call respectable.'

'That's the very reason,' said Mrs.
Grantly, 'why I like being here so much.
It makes me feel like an angel. But talking
of angels, there goes a genuine one, if you
like, for you; there goes Colonel Stapleton.
Oh my! and isn't he grown fat and ugly!
You'd never have thought—would you?—
that that man was once the best dancer in
London. And, Duchess,' she went on, 'I
hope you admire the big checks on his coat.
'Twould take four of him, I guess, to play
one game of chess upon.'

Colonel Stapleton was a florid man of it
might be five-and-forty. Despite his incli-
nation to stoutness, he held himself well and
gracefully, and had an air about him of
dissolute good-breeding. He had one other
charm, too, of which Vernon was at once

made sensible—a taking and very musical voice, which, as he stopped for a moment to speak to a friend dining, could be heard distinctly at the Duchess's table. 'The one with the red fan?' he was saying gaily; 'yes, she, if you like it, is a regular out-and-outer. She's down here, so she tells me, with some fellow who belongs to the "Figaro."'

Vernon and Captain Grantly both overheard this. The former was somewhat annoyed, and the latter amused at it, though he was at the same time frowning over his wife's late observations. 'Poor old Jack Stapleton!' he said; 'Jessie can't bear him, though I'm sure I don't know why. He's as good-hearted a fellow as ever lived, and is nobody's enemy but his own.'

'To be sure,' said the Duchess. 'We all of us know Jack Stapleton. If he was a little bit thinner, your wife would be only too delighted with him.'

Mrs. Grantly, however, was by no means silenced.

'Look at his back,' she said, 'as he's sitting down to his dinner. Isn't selfishness written in every curve of it? The way'—she went on, as she leant over to the Duchess—'the way that man behaved to a young girl I know is something more than words can describe to you.'

'Jessie!' exclaimed her husband sharply, as if determined to change the subject, 'look behind you for a minute. There's the old hag—don't you see her?—who tried to collar your money this afternoon at the tables. It's worth while watching her just to see how she claws her wine-glass.'

'I hadn't observed her,' said the Duchess. 'Well, she at any rate has no compromising diamonds, and no wicked Lothario to attend to her.'

Mrs. Grantly's eye lit up with a sudden

laughter. 'Lord Surbiton,' she said, as she touched his arm with her fan, and pointed out the old woman in question, 'I guess I can show you one virtuous woman here. *Her* morals, I am sure, are strictly unimpeachable. I'll lay you six to one on them in black-silk stockings.'

Lord Surbiton eyed Mrs. Grantly with a look of somewhat sinister gallantry. 'If your feet and ankles,' he said, 'are as lovely as your hands and wrists, I shall proudly pay the bet, even if I have the sad fortune to win it.'

'In that case,' said Mrs. Grantly drily, 'I shall ask you to make your bets with my husband. If you will do so with him on the same principle next Ascot, we shall still manage, perhaps, to keep out of the workhouse.'

Mrs. Grantly, though she said what she chose herself, could always hold her own to perfection; and Lord Surbiton's gaze was now at once withdrawn from her. But a few minutes afterwards, when he again turned to her, there was a change in his whole expression that she was not prepared for. His worn face, as a friend had once observed of him, was like a battered stage on which the scenery was always shifting; and it now had a strange appearance, as of some ruinous transformation-effect. Every trace of its late look had gone from it: it gleamed, instead, with a grave uncertain tenderness, like a light from a lost boyhood; and even his artificial manner when he spoke did not destroy the impression.

'You have shown me,' he said, 'one virtuous woman. Let me now show you another. Do you see the two who have this moment entered?'

The eyes of all the party were turned in

the same direction.   There was no mistaking
for an instant who it was that had attracted
him.   Standing close to the door, and looking
about her in some uncertainty, was a tall
English girl, in company of an elder lady.
The two had apparently come there to dine,
and, being strange to the place, did not know
where to bestow themselves.   The girl's
hesitation, however, could scarcely be called
embarrassment.   The scene seemed to distress far more than to embarrass her ; though
it would hardly have been unnatural if it had
done both.   There was a proud reserve, however, in her graceful movements and attitude,
which, amongst such surroundings, sufficed
at once to distinguish her.   She was very
pale, with a brow and throat like a magnolia
blossom ;   only her lips, in the words of
Solomon, seemed by contrast 'a thread of
scarlet ;' and her large clear eyes were dark
as the darkest violet.   She stood there in

the glare and glitter like a creature from another world.

Lord Surbiton broke silence in slow, measured accents. 'It looks,' he said, 'as if an angel had descended in the midst of us, like a snow-flake.'

There was a pause. The apparition astonished the whole party. Vernon's eyes, in especial, were fixed intently on her.

'Angel or no angel,' said the Duchess presently, 'I can see, even from this distance, that she gets her clothes, not from heaven, but Paris : and nothing costs so much as well-made angelic simplicity. However joking apart,' she added, and more seriously 'upon my word I quite agree with Lord Surbiton. It is literally an angel's face ; and a very high-bred angel's into the bargain. But, good gracious !—what a place to bring her to !'

Suddenly the two strangers were observed

to move forward into the room, while the younger one first started, and then broke into a smile.

'Look!' said the Duchess with interest, 'they have evidently found some one they know here. Let us try and discover who **it is.**'

'Oh my!' exclaimed Mrs. Grantly, 'I can see who: and—would you believe it?—why, it's Colonel Stapleton! Duchess, you don't know what you missed. You should have seen how he jumped up when he saw them, like a beer-barrel on springs! And there's your angel, Lord Surbiton—there she is, shaking hands with him. Well, all I can say is, that I wish her joy of her company.'

'Come, Mr. Vernon,' said the Duchess, as dinner drew to a close, 'you seem very silent and abstracted. This interesting young lady has clearly made an impression on you.'

'Haven't you noticed him?' said Mrs.

Grantly; 'he's been watching her all the time; and I can tell by his face that he's jealous of Colonel Stapleton. However, Mr. Vernon, there is one crumb of comfort for you; she has not been dining at the same table with him.'

'No,' said Captain Grantly, 'but she's looked round and smiled at him every ten minutes. Keep yourself calm, Vernon, and don't go calling old Jack out for it.'

'I should think,' said Vernon, with a gravity he was quite unconscious of, 'that they are relations of some kind or other—cousins,' he went on meditating, 'cousins probably, or perhaps even niece and uncle.'

'Capital!' exclaimed the Duchess. 'He's thought the whole matter out to himself. Mr. Vernon, your tastes are, I must say, most versatile. You begin the dinner with Venus, and you wind it up with Diana. But tell me,' she went on, as she pushed her chair back, and sedately prepared to rise, 'are you a gambler as well as a lover? For if not, you will perhaps smoke here with Lord Surbiton, while we three go back to the tables for a little; and then we will all meet presently outside for our coffee.'

CHAPTER IV.

LEFT *tête-à-tête* with Vernon, Lord Surbiton fixed his eyes on him, drawing meanwhile from his pocket a gorgeous gold cigarette case. ' That tobacco,' he said solemnly through the soft smoke-puffs, ' which has the subtlest of all aromas, was grown amongst the haunted hills of Syria.' This probably may have been true enough : he omitted to add, however, that he had bought it himself in a spot no more haunted than Bond Street. But the old elaborate manner which had once impressed Vernon, now again arrested him ; though his eyes had still been straying in the direction of the fair stranger.

'It is a long time,' went on Lord Surbiton, 'since I last saw you; or to one, young as you are, it must seem long.'

'I like to be called young,' said Vernon, 'for I have at least one sign of age in me, and that is I am beginning to value my youth.'

'Happy philosopher,' cried the other, 'who can value the treasure while you still possess it! When last I saw you, you were just leaving Eton, and you had not learnt such wisdom then. You came to me one morning before luncheon, sad and eager, with some verses of yours, that you might ask what a poet thought of them. I suggested that you should read them aloud to me, but you were too modest to do so; so I took them myself, and read them aloud to you. When I had finished I looked up, and there were two large tears trembling in my young bard's eyes.'

'What!' exclaimed Vernon, 'and do you really remember that unfortunate boyish stuff of mine?'

'Boy,' said Lord Surbiton, 'your verses were *not* stuff; and there are certain things which *I* never forget—

> Oh Goddess, I am sick at heart, o'erworn
> With weariness,
> For the weight of life is bitter to be borne
> Companionless.

That is how your verses began: you see I can quote them still. Professedly, they were a sort of prayer to Diana: but really they were far more than that. They were the voice of youth that is heard through all the ages—youth crying in its solitude for some high companionship. There is nothing, Vernon, so unutterably melancholy as a boy's passionate purity: and for me you were then the symbol of the eternal longing of boyhood.'

'How well,' said Vernon,' I remember that little poem of mine, though I confess I am surprised that you do! I remember the day I wrote it, and the sound of it still rings in my ears; but there is one thing wanting— one thing quite gone from me—and that is the sort of longing I meant to express in it. My thoughts and my aspirations of those days have become a mystery to myself. I am startled to find sometimes how utterly I have lost the clue to them.'

'That is always the way,' said Lord Surbiton, 'when life is still developing, and one form of eagerness succeeds and dispossesses another. It is in virtue of this process that you now see your youth to be valuable. In the middle age of your boyhood you longed sadly for the unattainable; in the boyhood of your middle age, you idealise the attainable. Happy philosopher, I again say to you—philosopher, lover, poet, and man of the world in one!'

'I doubt,' said Vernon smiling, 'if I now idealise anything; and I fear, Lord Surbiton, that you idealise me. I am no longer a lover, nor even a would-be poet.'

'Not a poet on paper, it may be; but a poet in the way life touches you, and in the demands you make on it. To be a poet in this sense, you need never have written a line; and yet the name may fit you, without any violence to its meaning. The imagination is for every man the co-creator of his universe, and those men are poets whose imaginations create most gloriously. And yet, my dear Vernon, you say you no longer idealise! I shall as soon believe that as that you are no longer a lover. Why, within this last couple of hours, you have been making love to one lady, and longing, we all thought, to make love to another.'

'Ah!' said Vernon; 'but the excitement of making love is very different from the still devotion of loving. What I have ceased to be capable of, what I have lost even the power of imagining, is a single passion that shall sway or fulfil one's life. Love seems to me now to be very much like temper. Your dearest friend can irritate you into the one; the most commonplace woman can trick you into the other: and you adore in the latter case, and you accuse and abuse in the former, in a way which by-and-by you can only stupidly wonder at. I do not want to speak cynically about this. A cynic is a foolish fellow who either is ignorant, or pretends to be, of a good third of an average man's motives—those that are not contemptible; and I know that love, as a fact, can be pure and true and faithful, and that it is really to many the one thing worth living for. I only speak for myself; and all that I can see in

it is a passionate perversity both of judgment and of feeling. It exaggerates the
value of the special individual, just as
cynicism does the opposite for the race in
general. The concentrated praise is as false
as the diffused censure. Each is equally
silly to the eye of the calm judgment. My
wish now is for no emotion but such as
I can master. I wish to possess myself,
not to appropriate others ; and with regard to
women I agree with the poet Donne—

> I can love her and her, and you and you ;
> I can love any, so she be not true.'

' I did not expect,' said Lord Surbiton,
' when I called you a lover, to find you still
content at thirty with the intangible charms
of a moon-goddess. As we live on, we are
obliged to take the attainable, and do our
best to idealise that. You say you are not
constant. Well, no true artist is ; and you
have the artist's temper, I see, just as you

have the poet's—two things which by no means always go together : indeed to unite them is a rare triumph of character. Many poets perhaps might have drawn a Desdemona : only an artistic poet could have drawn an Iago also. What marks the poetic temper is the intensity of its sympathy ; what marks the artistic is the versatility. The artist not only feels much, but he also feels many things ; and in this way he always preserves his balance. Every one at the beginning has had the makings of several characters in him. The artist has the makings of an indefinite number. Most men, farther out of their possible characters, harden or settle down into one, but the artist never does ; for character is nothing but prejudice or trick grown permanent, and the artist has no character, just as the chameleon is said to have no colour. Thus when vulgar critics declare with regard to some artistic

writer's creations—as often and often they
have done with regard to mine, for instance—
" Here are his own feelings ; he has drawn this
man from himself," they are at once right
and wrong. He has not only drawn *this* man
from himself, but he has drawn all ; for he
becomes himself some new man to be drawn
from, every time he suppresses some newly-
combined nine-tenths of himself. This, Vernon, is the true artistic versatility ; and her
Grace—who by the way is an uncommonly
shrewd woman—at once saw you possessed
it. You can respond in the same half-hour,
she told you, to the beauty of Diana and of
Venus. Such versatility is the true elixir of
youth ; it makes even the wisdom of age
supple. My dear fellow,' he said, somewhat coming down from his pedestal, ' constancy, though we know its value for most
men, is the elixir of middle age. It makes you
five-and-forty at once, and it keeps you there.'

Vernon at this moment let his eye wander, and a sudden exclamation broke from him which at once put a stop to philosophy.

'Damn it!' he said, 'we have been talking of dead Dianas; and meanwhile the living one has taken flight, and deserted us.'

Lord Surbiton turned his head, and saw that the fair stranger and her companion had gone. Where feminine beauty was concerned, he was always prompt and practical; and he at once set about rising, though his movements were somewhat slow.

'She can't have gone far,' he said. 'We shall be sure to see her again somewhere; and her Grace, or Captain Grantly, will find out all about her for us. Or failing these, there is that fellow, Stapleton.'

He took Vernon's arm with a sedate and leisurely dignity, and the two left the restaurant. They paused in the cloak-room which is just outside, and Lord Surbiton was being helped by a garçon into a magnificent sable overcoat, when a female figure appeared, with a look that at once attracted him. This was none other than the lady of the red fan. She had come for her opera-cloak; and before Vernon was even aware of her presence, Lord Surbiton, with as quick a gallantry as his years permitted him, was arranging it tenderly for her, over her finely-shaped shoulders.

He was sufficiently delighted with his performance thus far; but a still greater pleasure awaited him. The lady cast a glance at him with her soft, appealing eyes, and murmured, '*Merci, milord.*' She did not blush, but she looked much as if she wished to do so. Lord Surbiton at once laid his hand on his heart, and was begging to be told how he was honoured by madame knowing him. 'Ah!' she replied, 'and need

a renowned man ask ? Why, the poems and
the romances of monsieur are as much read
in Paris as in London.' Here she caught
sight of Vernon; and, with the quietest
smile in the world, ' I am going,' she went
on, ' once more to the tables. Will not you
two come, and join your luck with mine ? '

Lord Surbiton was completely charmed
with her, and regretted not a little that to do
this was impossible. He was almost aware
of a slight pang of jealousy when she bid
Vernon to put in more securely a diamond
pin that had become loose in her hair.

Vernon's hands lingered over the soft
brown plaits. ' You are very lovely,' he
said, ' though, of course, you don't need to
be told that ; and my morals will let you
play with my heart, though my prudence, I
fear, will not let you play with my fortune.'

He was in the middle of uttering this,
when he glanced aside for a moment, and his

eyes met those of the girl to seek whom he had just risen from the dinner-table. It was but a glance she gave him ; and then her fair head was averted : but the glance and the gesture were only too expressive to him. She seemed at once to comprehend and be surprised at the scene he was taking part in, and to turn away from it with contempt, pain, and aversion. A disagreeable sense of shame at once came over him ; nor were his reflections made pleasanter by what he observed next moment. As the girl, with her companion, was quitting the cloak-room, he was just able to see her face light up for an instant; and directly afterwards Colonel Stapleton entered.

The Colonel seemed almost as versatile as Lord Surbiton himself ; for he was quite as familiar with the fair Aspasia as he had been a moment before with the pale and virginal stranger. Vernon and Lord Surbiton had been conversing with the former lady in French; and his lordship, who was somewhat deaf, had pronounced her accent perfect. The Colonel, however, to whom she turned instantly, composedly addressed some chaff to her in the homeliest English possible; and she with an equal fluency, though with a strong foreign twang, replied, 'If you don't look out, I shall smack your nasty little head for you.'

Vernon started at this astounding utterance, as if an adder had stung him. 'Good Heavens!' he exclaimed to himself, 'what an absolute fool I am!' And not without some *brusquerie*, which the fair one mistook for jealousy, he succeeded in withdrawing Lord Surbiton, and making a hasty exit. 'Her French,' he muttered, 'may be the French of the Faubourg, but her English is very certainly the English of Regent Street.'

Lord Surbiton, however, had completely

missed the above piece of *badinage*; and pausing on the hotel door-steps, and laying his hand upon Vernon's arm, ' What a woman that is!' he exclaimed, with a slow gravity. 'It is in her class, after all, that the soul of the old world still lives on, with its passion, its grace, and its intellect; and we, in our barbarous virtue, actually affect to look down on her. A woman like that ought to have lived at Athens, and have had a Pericles for her companion, and a Socrates for her pupil.'

Vernon made no response to this. His thoughts were still busy with those clear eyes that had humbled him. ' So much,' he said bitterly to himself, ' for a woman's power of insight! She looks nothing but scorn at me, and yet smiles like a sister at that fat, sensual beast there !'

Before long Lord Surbiton began again, as they went in the direction where they expected to find their party. 'Ah, my dear Vernon!' he said, drawing a deep sigh that made his satin necktie creak, 'it is the artist's gift——' Here he paused for a moment to eye critically two young ladies who passed him. 'It is the artist's gift,' he resumed, 'to discern between good and evil; it is his doom to be the servant of neither. He surveys life as a Cæsar surveyed the circus: and the affections and lusts of men can say nothing to him but *morituri te salutant.* He belongs to a middle race who are neither divine nor human, and he cannot really ally himself with any human being. This is why, when he dies, there are no flowers strewn on his tomb—no rosemary for remembrance, or pansies for tender thoughts; but only the bloomless laurel—the leaf, not of love, but of homage.'

'Lord Surbiton'—it was the voice of the Duchess—'when you've done quoting poetry, you'll find us all here, ready for you to discover us.' She was seated with the Grantlys outside the café, at a round table laden with cups and liqueur-glasses. 'See,' she went on, 'we have ordered everything, and we have been so thoughtful that we have even kept chairs for you.'

'It seems to me,' said Lord Surbiton, 'that your Grace has kept two a-piece for us.'

'Ah!' said the Duchess, laughing, 'those two other chairs are for some particular friends of mine, whom I asked just now to come and have their coffee with us. Now, Mr. Vernon, here is a riddle for you. Who should you think these particular friends are? Why, your fair paragon of the restaurant, and the old lady, her aunt. I met them five minutes ago, as we were coming here from the gambling-rooms, and it flashed on me all of a sudden who the aunt was. You, Lord

Surbiton, will remember her.   She's the
widow of Sir Edward Walters, who was our
Minister for so many years at Stuttgart ; and
the girl—I remember her too quite well now—
is that beautiful Cynthia Walters, who was
made such a fuss about in London three
seasons ago, and then got ill, and has never
appeared since.   Her home, it seems, is now
with her aunt in Florence.'

'Look out, Duchess,' said Captain Grantly.
'Here they are coming.'

CHAPTER V.

LADY WALTERS was a woman of great sweetness of manner, yet with a touch now and then of subdued humour. She produced the impression that she had once known the world, but that she hardly knew it now; for knowledge of the world can be forgotten like other knowledge, and from certain gentle natures it slips away easily.

She and Lord Surbiton had an extremely friendly greeting, and settled down at once into a talk over old days. As for Vernon

his position was less comfortable. The
Duchess introduced him to Miss Walters,
who had at first been unaware of his presence:
but the instant she recognised him the smile
died on her lips, and she acknowledged his
bow as coldly as any young lady of fashion
who seems to deny an acquaintance in the
very act of formally making it.

Vernon felt utterly worsted by her perfect
savoir faire; and what added not a little to
his suffering was that the Duchess should
witness his discomfiture, without knowing
what he felt sure was the cause of it. Too
proud or self-conscious to risk any further
repulse, he listened silently to the girl's
answers, as the Duchess put her through a
rapid catechism. 'We have taken,' she said,
'a villa beyond Nice, in the country. We
arrived but three days ago, from Florence.
We came over here this afternoon for the
music; but missed our train back again, and

so had to remain for dinner. I don't know what we should have done if Colonel Stapleton, whom I have known from a child, had not secured a table for us. I think this place horrible. I was here once before, and I detested it.'

Vernon watched her intently as she was giving these answers. The moments were few; but to him they were like a long dream. He seemed to become familiar with all the folds of her drapery, and each outline of arm or figure that her dress revealed or hinted at. There was a subtle air with her of fastidious fashion, from her hat to her pointed shoes and the long black gloves concealing her dainty hands. But this was not all, or at any rate Vernon thought not. She seemed not only a woman of fashion, but a woman of fashion who had the soul of a sibyl in her; and her clear eyes seemed touched with some high wistful melancholy.

The impression she made on the Duchess was different. Her Grace had found Miss Walters somewhat chilly in manner; so she brought her questions pretty soon to a close, and addressed herself to Mrs. Grantly. Vernon hoped with trembling that now might be his chance : but no, it was not to be. Miss Walters turned away from him, and seemed lost in the scene before her. That scene was one which is certainly unique in Europe, and it was now wearing its strangest and most striking aspect. The large *place*, with its gleaming buildings round it, was a lake of transparent shadow, dotted with countless gas-lamps, and full of the vague whispers of fountains and human life. On one side flared the hotel they had lately quitted ; on another the great casino, pale like a skeleton from globes of electric light. On another, where the buildings were lower and more broken, tall palms might be seen, with their plumes in the clear sky; and beyond were balustrades of marble, and spaces of dark sea: whilst behind and in grim contrast rose the barren towering mountains, and dwarfed the world at the foot of them into a small cluster of fire-flies.

Lord Surbiton had been on the watch to attract Miss Walters's attention, and he now saw his opportunity.

'This place,' he said as he fixed his eyes on her, 'always seems to me like the moral sewer of Europe—a great drain's mouth open at the foot of the hills. There is a tragic irony even in its loveliness.'

'Tragic or not,' said the Duchess, 'we have had a most amusing dinner here; haven't we, Mrs. Grantly? Though I'm sure I've forgotten by this time what it was we were talking about.'

'A proof,' said Lord Surbiton, 'of how well your Grace was conversing. True conversation is like good champagne. It exhilarates for the moment, but next morning we feel no trace of it.'

Vernon here broke silence. 'If true conversation,' he said, 'is like good champagne, true love is like bad. False and true love may seem just the same when we taste them. We only detect the true when we find that our head aches afterwards.'

'That,' said Lord Surbiton, still looking towards Miss Walters, 'is why a serious passion is so great an educator. But its work only begins when the pain it causes has left us. Strong present feeling narrows our sympathies ; strong past feeling enlarges them. Thus a woman of the world always should have been, but should never be, in love. She should always have had a grief : she should never have a grievance.'

'Why,' asked Miss Walters coldly, 'do you say this of a woman of the world especially ? '

'Because it is only in the world, or in what we call society, that intercourse with our fellows is really a completed fine art. It there *is* what elsewhere it only pretends to be. Men who profess to think gravely or to have grave ends speak of society as the type of what is vain and frivolous. Perhaps they are right— who knows? Yet society is the logical end of the whole of this world's civilisation; and of all the follies that I ever set any store by, fashion is the one I could still find most to say for. Fashion,' he continued, 'is the daintiest form of fame, and sometimes of power also; and were it only as wide and lasting as it is delicate, it would unite in itself the objects of all human ambitions.'

'Are the objects of ambition,' said Miss Walters, 'the chief objects of life?'

'Men in general,' said Lord Surbiton, 'are the puppets of three forces—ambition, love, and hunger; but love destroys the appetite ; ambition destroys love ; and fashion absorbs, or at any rate sways, ambition.'

These general maxims did not much delight the Duchess, and she betrayed at this juncture that her thoughts had been somewhat wandering.

'Captain Grantly !' she exclaimed, ' I wonder whose are those horses that are waiting there at the door of the casino— the pair of greys, I mean, in that rather smart-looking carriage. I watched them drive round, five minutes ago ; and the near one, do you know, is really a first-rate stepper.'

This profane nterruption put a stop to Lord Surbiton s eloquence, for Miss Walters turned round, and began to look at the horses : whilst her aunt, hearing a railway whistle, consulted her watch, and said they must soon be moving. 'However,' she added, ' there must be plenty of time yet, as

Colonel Stapleton said he would come and see us safe to the station.'

' I, too,' said Vernon, ' am reminded to think of moving ; for I see my carriage is already there waiting for me.'

' What ! ' said the Duchess, ' and is that fine turn-out yours, Mr. Vernon ? Well, here's luxury for a young man of thirty ! '

' By Gad, my dear chap, you *are* a swell,' said Captain Grantly, putting his hand on Vernon's shoulder.

Wealth has a certain power over those even who are least touched by it. It calls their attention to the man possessing it, if only to make it worth their while to despise him ; and Vernon knew in an instant that Miss Walters turned to glance at him. Once again he was about to attempt speaking to her, when he was interrupted by the arrival of Colonel Stapleton.

' Here's a go ! ' cried the Colonel, panting

and out of breath, ' I've been looking for you,
Lady Walters, for the last twenty minutes ;
and now your train's gone, and you must stop
the night here.   If you'll let me, I'll get you
rooms directly at the Hôtel de Paris.   The
Princesse de —— and the Prince for the time
being have just cleared out unexpectedly ; so
I know they can take you in, and we'll show
Miss Cynthia a little more of the life here.'

' If you stop, you know,' said the Duchess,
' there is my maid who can look after you.
I can lend you almost everything ; and you
can buy a tooth-brush here.'

Miss Walters turned to Colonel Stapleton
with a hasty frown.   ' No—no,' she said ; ' let
us do anything rather than that.   This place
is perfectly unendurable.'

Vernon observed her closely, and with
extreme surprise.   She spoke in a manner
that would have been rudeness to any common
acquaintance even of long standing, but the

Colonel, strange to say, was not in the least abashed by it ; he only eyed her with a look of quiet amusement. 'Come, little vixen,' he whispered, 'don't be naughty. I'm sure Aunt Louisa will give her vote for staying.'

But Lady Walters wished to do no such thing ; and she was already inquiring nervously if there would be any difficulty in getting a carriage. 'Come,' said Miss Walters, taking hold of Colonel Stapleton's sleeve, 'be good, and go and tell her about it. We mean to go somehow, so you may as well make yourself of use to us.'

He was forestalled, however, by Captain Grantly, who had at once volunteered to go off to the livery-stables, and was just starting when he was recalled by the practical Duchess. 'You may as well find out first,' she said, 'where it is Lady Walters wants to be driven to ; for at this time of night they will often refuse to take you.'

'Oh!' said Lady Walters, somewhat troubled by this, 'it is to the Cap de Juan. It is a long way by the road, I'm afraid. Perhaps, after all, we had better remain here.'

Vernon felt all the blood rush at once to his face; and for a moment his heart stopped beating.

'The Cap de Juan!' exclaimed the Duchess; 'why that settles everything. Come Mr. Vernon, now is your opportunity. My dear Lady Walters, here is a young man with a carriage and horses ready, who is only too anxious to take you back to your very door-step.'

A rapid look of annoyance passed over Miss Walters' face. 'We couldn't think,' she said, with a cold politeness, 'of taking Mr. Vernon's horses so great a distance. He is hardly aware, perhaps, of the journey there is before us.'

'On the contrary,' said Vernon, 'I am

particularly well aware of it, for it is the very journey that is also before me. If I am not much mistaken, we are all but next-door neighbours. Your house, I think, must be the Château St. John ; and, if so, our two gardens touch each other.'

After this there was nothing more to be said. Circumstances had at length played into Vernon's hands ; and another caprice in his life was to be at least partially gratified.

' Well,' said the Duchess, as the carriage drove off, ' I'm glad Mr. Vernon has got what he wanted, though Miss Cynthia, at first, was, I must say, very snubby to him. However, one can never judge by this. Perhaps, when we go to the Cap de Juan, we shall find them an engaged couple. Who knows ?'

' I know,' said Mrs. Grantly, ' and I'll bet you anything we shall not. A man like Mr. Vernon will never marry. He's exactly,' she added, dropping her voice, ' like a younger edition of Lord Surbiton ; and I guess they're a couple of shams—the two of them.'

'I think,' said the Duchess, 'that Mr. Vernon is charming.'

'Yes—to know,' said Mrs. Grantly, 'but not to depend upon.'

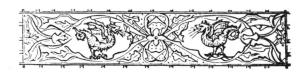

CHAPTER VI.

VERNON and his friends were meanwhile hastening homewards. Lady Walters had addressed to him a few kind civilities, eyeing him the while with a look of trustful friendliness; but her niece had hardly said anything, and the three soon sank into silence. Every influence, indeed, seemed to persuade to it—the easy motion of the carriage, the rhythmic tramp of the horses, the soft fanning of the night air, and the pageant of sea and mountain that was sweeping past them like a dream. Here was a gaudy villa, surmounted by a huge coronet, the home of some Russian gambler ; here, with domes and minarets, a dwelling yet more fantastic. Scents of flowers blew down to them from the gardens ; and over the garden walls hung spiked aloes and cactuses. Then presently the scene grew wilder. On the right, wooded gorges slanted up into the mountains ; and on the left, the sea below them broke into fairy bays. All this seemed to absorb Miss Walters ; and her eyes being thus occupied, Vernon was able unobserved to observe her. He had once remarked in one of his more delicate moods, that a woman whose dress is the perfection of fashion, is never herself the perfection of real refinement. But he now felt inclined to modify this judgment. The vanities of this world seemed, on the girl before him, as natural as its own petals to some delicate hot-house flower ; so that she was as little troubled by their possession as the saint is who has renounced them.

'The effect of her presence,' he wrote that night in his diary, 'was at once charming and singular. It did not at first concentrate my thoughts on herself; but it moved like a wind amongst them, and stirred them in all directions. Vague aspirations of many kinds awoke in me. I longed in grotesque rotation to make poetry, to ride hard, and to pray; and when something roused the aunt, and between two sleeps she talked a little to me, I was annoyed and jarred by having the silence broken.'

Lady Walters, it is true, had begun somewhat abruptly. 'What a pity it is,' she said, as though following up some train of thought of her own, 'that poor Jack Stapleton never married! He is naturally such a kind, good creature. It is self-indulgence that has ruined him.'

'And do you think,' said Vernon, 'that marriage will always save a man?'

'Not always,' she said, 'and it never affects a man as it does a woman. Yet some men, Mr. Vernon, are ruined for the want of it—often those with the warmest and sweetest natures. You know the man that his friends call a *good fellow*—who, like a sunflower always turns towards happiness. If such a man has a wife he cares for, he will live that he may make her happy ; but if left to himself, shall I tell you what will happen to him ? He will live, not to give pleasure but to find it ; and to like consorting with happy people is a very different thing from trying to make people happy.'

'Perhaps you are right,' said Vernon with a slight involuntary sigh. 'But how should you say that marriage affected women ?'

'Ah !' said Lady Walters, 'in another way entirely. When a woman marries with affection her whole character changes. She grows absorbed in the things that absorb her husband ; and, through him, they become really a new life to her.'

'If I thought of marrying,' said Vernon, 'it would be with a different hope. I should hope to find a wife, who, if she had my tastes at all, had had them before she knew me ; and that her already possessing them were a cause of her sympathy ; not that her acquiring them for my sake were the signs of it. I should like her life to stand on its own basis ; and in her pursuits I should like to have a constant rival, that should keep my affection fresh with a kind of stingless jealousy.'

Lady Walters smiled at him incredulously, with half-closed eyes. 'I am afraid, Mr. Vernon,' she said, 'you've never been in love yet.' Then the conversation dropped ; and it was soon evident that she had again fallen asleep. Vernon was pleased to have been able to talk in Miss Walters' hearing, since he found her so difficult of direct access; and he now fancied that she looked a little less coldly at him. Presently she asked him of her own accord the name of some place they were passing. He answered her question; but he found he could get no farther. In spite of himself he was still embarrassed in her presence. The remembrance that her first sight of him had been in the middle of his foolish scene with the Frenchwoman, abased him in his own estimation: he was in a thoroughly wrong position. He leaned his head back, and looked up at the stars, and was soon completely lost in another deep reverie. All of a sudden the tenor of his thoughts betrayed itself. He broke out aloud with a single line from *Hamlet* :—

Oh, what a rogue and peasant slave am I !

He spoke the words abstractedly, and for a second or two seemed not to know he had uttered them. Then he recollected himself, and there might have been an awkward moment, if Miss Walters with ready tact had not come to the rescue.

' I know that line so well,' she said ; ' but I can't remember where it comes from.'

' It is from *Hamlet*,' said Vernon, ' a play I know by heart ; and I often catch myself repeating bits aloud from it.'

With this there ensued a little conversation about Shakespeare, then about poetry generally ; and matters very soon were proceeding more smoothly. Vernon had once again found his footing. His thoughts, his feelings, and his words began to flow freely as usual ; and when he looked into Miss Walters' eyes he found she did not avert them. The character of the drive in a single instant changed for him ; and it quickly became as delightful as it had been disappointing hitherto. To all intents and purposes he was alone with this fair stranger ; and she

was visibly now beginning to take a certain
interest in him.   Gradually, too, he became
aware that her presence had some magnetic
effect upon him.   Her hand, her lips, her
eye, even the soft furs on her jacket, and
the faint perfume from her handkerchief
touched his being, and made the blood in his
veins tingle : whilst at the same time all in
him that was most refined or delicate, seemed
suddenly to be coming uppermost under the
attraction of her presence.   The moral recoil
from the low and frivolous to whatever was
pure and delicate, was in itself a pleasing shock
to the intellectual voluptuary : whilst the
sense that he had to efface a bad impression
gave double earnestness to his efforts to
create a good one.   To a man of Vernon's
temperament an experience of this kind was
a luxury.

And yet, on his part, there was no acting
or insincerity.   His goodness, to say the least

of it, was as genuine as his evil ; and his voice, his look, and his manner, as he now spoke to Miss Walters, were all instinct with a chivalrous and a quite natural reverence.

'I am so glad,' he said at last, 'that I happened to have my carriage, and was able to take you away from that horrid place there.'

'If you think the place horrid,' she said gently, 'why do you go yourself to it ?'

'One might ask, I am afraid, that question about many things. I went there to-day for distraction—to escape from my own company. It did well enough to distract me : but one wishes to shake the dust off one's feet afterwards.'

'Like my question,' she said, 'that will apply to many things. But are you living quite alone out here ?'

'Yes,' said Vernon, 'with no company but my books and thoughts ; and, though I came here on purpose to be with these, I am glad sometimes to escape from them. I had hoped to have brought a friend with me ; indeed, perhaps he may still come. The best escape from one's thoughts is a friend one is really fond of.'

'That is hardly a flattering light,' she said, 'in which to regard a friend. There are some unhappy people whose only chance of peace lies in forgetting themselves ; but such people, I believe, have made themselves unfit for friendship. I look on a friend as a person who will help one to find, not to lose, oneself. If you want to lose yourself, you should always live in society, and agree with Lord Surbiton that life's highest reward is fashion.'

'Are you then,' said Vernon, 'not fond of society ?'

'Of course for happy people society is a healthy thing ; but how one mixes in it depends on one's own character.   One can be the fashion, and yet not be oneself a fashionable, as one sees in the case of many of the greatest people in London.   I may myself have been less in the world, perhaps, than most women of my age ; but still I have seen plenty of smart society ; indeed, I have several relations who seem to live for nothing else : and, so far as I can tell, nothing hardens the heart like fashion.   To a genu- ine fine lady—who is a very different person, by the way, from a *grande dame*—it is a thing next to impossible to value character rightly.'

'And yet many of the qualities,' said Vernon, 'that secure most applause in society, are the fruits, as Lord Surbiton told us, of some deeper life in the past.   Take singing, for instance : what an effect real expression has !—and to express feeling in song, the singer must himself have felt.'

'Perhaps so ; and for that very reason

the most touching singing has sometimes
almost disgusted me.   What a use to make
of some buried and sacred sorrow, to conjure
its ghost up that it may secure a drawing-
room triumph for us !'

‘ One may, of course,’ said Vernon, ‘ exaggerate views like these, till they become
false and fantastic.   But I am quite sure
you are right to some degree.   To be
always in society is to be always with mere
acquaintances, and with acquaintances who
like you for your least genuine qualities.   I
have met many a man, staying in country
houses, who must have been sickened, as he
went to bed, by what he had said or laughed
at in the smoking-room ; and yet the night
after he has done just the same.   To be
always in this way with the world, is to be
always estranged from oneself ; and one's
true self, like other sensitive creatures, will in
time die of neglect, or at least be ruined by it.

'Do you remember,' said Miss Walters, 'what I said just now—that a true friend is a person with whom we can find, not lose ourselves? I,' she went on, with a sigh and a slight shudder, 'have had friends of two kinds —true and false; and they have both done all they could for me.'

She shuddered.

'Are you cold?' murmured Vernon, leaning forward and looking at her. 'Let me put that shawl over your shoulders for you.' No lover could have done the office with more tenderness, or at the same time with more respect. Then for a moment he laid his hand upon hers, and asked, 'Are you warmer now?' The look, the touch formed a new crisis in their relationship; and they both grew aware of this by a new tone in their voices. Vernon himself was surprised at what had passed. He had never thought she could have so softened towards him;

but he knew that it was so by her two words as she thanked him. And now with a soft sensation, he felt his heart expanding ; and grave and secret thoughts welled up to his lips, and began to demand utterance. Should he go on and utter them, fixing his eyes on hers ? To do so, he knew, would be an exquisite self-indulgence. It would be like a passionate mental kiss to the beautiful creature opposite him. But for a moment he vacillated ; and there was a short moral struggle in him. Had he the right intention that could make that kiss lawful ? Might not the very feelings he wished to express be wronged by his then expressing them ? Was such mental passion as this, with its spasm of self-abandonment, in reality much better than its coarser physical counterpart ? Conscience, however, was weak, and was swept aside by impulse.

'Shall I tell you,' he said, 'why I have

come out here ?   I have lost my self, and I
wish to find it again.   I wish to see how I
stand with my conscience, and to know what
I really value.   This is a task in which no
friend can help one ; one must enter into one's
own chamber and be still, for it. At present,
it seems to me sometimes that I hardly have
a self ; but I feel, like a man in a dream, that
I am being swept passively through changing
states of consciousness.   Some may be
pleasant enough, some dull and dreary ; but
they are all shadowy things ; I have no
abiding part in them, nor is one bound by any
chain to the other.   I seem to be swept
through them, just as we in this carriage are
being swept through this ghostly landscape.
What I want is, to wake myself from this idle
dream of the world, and to get back again to
the realities I was once familiar with.   Such
a waking is a long, weary process ; and a
friend's presence may soothe one in it though

he cannot help it forward.   Is that,' he said,
looking at her, 'is that a wrong view of
friendship ?'

'It is not my view,' she said, 'but no one
can answer for another.   If I had to seek a
self that was lost, I should like to have a
friend with me.'

'To encourage you, yes : but not to share
your labour.   You, for instance, could not re-
arrange my life for me ; and yet it is a great
help to me, even this little talk I have had
with you.   You and I are near neighbours
now.   Do you think we shall ever become
friends ?'

She gave him for the moment no direct
answer, but murmured half abstractedly, 'I
wonder how far you have wandered.'

'That,' said Vernon, 'is what I want to
find out myself.'

After this there was a pause, whilst the
two sank back into their own reflections, and

the changing fields and trees, as the carriage hurried onwards, surrounded and swept away from them.

Miss Walters at length began again. 'Perhaps you are surprised,' she said with a faint smile, 'at hearing me talk so decidedly about the world, and society, and friendship.'

'You certainly talk,' said Vernon, 'as if you had had experience.'

'I *have* had experience,' she said. 'I have had much—too much—of it. I have been a gambler, amongst other things. I won more than two thousand pounds once at *trente et quarante*. Do you think that was very nice of me?' And she fixed her eyes on him with a look which he could not fathom. 'You see, if I hate Monte Carlo, it is not because gambling has ruined me. And now,' she went on, 'I am going to say one thing more, which sounds also like the maxim of a rather experienced person. It is an answer to what you asked me just now. I have little belief, as a rule, in friendships between men and women—I mean when both the people concerned have youth and imagination. One or the other gets generally more or less than was bargained for.'

' I shall be thankful,' said Vernon, 'for the very least you will give me. You would find me a very safe person. A man's days of friendship begin when his days of love are over ; and I,' he went on, knowing that he was making love all the time, 'am in my days of friendship.'

' You and I then, perhaps, are exceptions to the general rule. There are exceptions. I can at least say this much for myself, that I am far more likely to be a friend than to have one.'

She said this with a curious unconscious bitterness that perplexed and startled Vernon.

'You must let me show you,' he murmured, 'that you are wrong there.'

She paused, and then said abruptly, 'I hope you didn't mistake me. I didn't mean that I thought you would fall in love with me. Perhaps you are just as safe from that sort of thing as I am.'

'You are very young,' said Vernon, 'to be talking in that way.'

'Youth and age,' she said, 'should not be counted by years. No nun dying a living death in a nunnery could be more shut out from all danger of love than I am—from all hope and from all fear of it.'

After this there was silence, till Lady Walters woke up, and Vernon soon afterwards was saying adieu to his friends on their own door-step.

But the night was not yet done for him. He had refused to enter ; he was anxious to be by himself again ; and, having sent his carriage away, he walked back through the gardens. In his own lamp-lit villa a delicate supper was prepared for him, but he did nothing more than taste it, and he went out again into the mellow night air. He was like a man who had eaten a sort of moral opium, and his breast was full of a sweet, fantastic tumult. There was a magical resurrection in him of the wild romance of boyhood. He leaned his elbow on a pale glistening balustrade, and looked out over the sea. 'Sea of Romance,' his unuttered thoughts began in him, 'once again you have your old charm for me. Inarticulate whispers of ambition, of passion, and of music float up to me from your enchanted surface. Sea of Southern moon and of Italian twilights, what eyes of famous lovers have looked out on you! The most musical of the world's love-songs have mixed over you with the vesper breezes! Pale, restless waves, rocking under

the stars of midnight, the limbs of the mermaids know you: the nautilus floats upon
your bosom! Yes, and in me, too, up from
the depths of my being, thoughts and longings
are rising that sing like mermaids. What do
they sing of? Is it of her eyes and lips?
Are they singing to her spirit that it may
stoop down to mine?' He turned back to
his garden. That, too, was enchanted. Were
Oberon and Titania holding revel there?
Bush and blossom seemed populous with
airy presences. Every passion, every pleasure of his life, became a separate fairy,
with its body some faint perfume, and its
dwelling-place some half-closed flower-bell.
In luxurious agitation he again returned to
his sea-view. Far away over the waters the
lights of Nice were glittering fair and distant
like a braid of golden stars. On a little
headland near him, covered with myrtles,
another light twinkled, solitary, dim, and only

just distinguishable. It came from a shrine of the Virgin, and his wandering gaze fixed on it. Suddenly into his dream-world there floated scents of incense, glimmering altars, and sounds of imploring music. ' Star of the sea,' he murmured, ' star of the morning, refuge of sinners, pray for me ! '

Going indoors, he sat down to his desk and wrote his diary of the day's proceedings. Miss Walters filled up a large space in it, and a fragment of what he said about her has been already quoted : but so hard is it to be honest to even a piece of paper, that he made no mention whatever of his qualms of conscience or his own self-accusations.

BOOK II.

CHAPTER I.

WHEN Vernon woke next morning some unlooked-for news awaited him. A fresh, delicious air stole through the open window, and fanned his cheek delicately as he lay thinking. He was enjoying the memory of his last night's adventure, which seemed to promise him a new life in his solitude, when his eye caught something which showed him he had overslept himself. This was a pile of letters on a table by his bedside ; and on top of the pile was one in the handwriting of Campbell. What was his astonishment when he found that it was dated ' Cannes '!

' My dear Vernon,' ran the letter, ' when you see where I am, you will of course set about being angry with me; and at first sight no doubt I seem to deserve that you should be. A month ago, when you begged me to come abroad and to take a villa with you, I refused you steadily, once or twice a little brusquely; and this with no better excuse than that very poor one—my feelings. I said I did not feel up to it, and upon my word that was true, Vernon—bitterly, deeply true. I had no heart to travel, and, though you may smile when I say so, the wretchedness I then suffered was crushing me. But I am better now; life has been going a little more kindly with me. I can enjoy my dinner again sometimes; I can laugh at a joke sometimes. My pleasure in my books and pictures is returning to me; and now it has actually happened that you find me abroad as my best chance of happiness. Here I am, doing the very thing by myself that I refused so churlishly to do with you. But I am coming over directly to see you, and make my peace with you; and you will perhaps put me up for a night. You will forgive me, I think, when I tell you all my story.'

Vernon was easily roused into the brightest animal spirits; nor did such sentiment as that of the night previous at all tend to interfere with them. Campbell's letter was like a burst of sunlight to him, and he smiled and whistled in his bath like any happy schoolboy. He immediately telegraphed, 'Come at once. I and my carriage shall fetch you at two o'clock.' He ordered his breakfast in the open air, at his favourite spot under the myrtles; and as he sat there with the liquid morning round him, food, he thought, had never tasted so well, nor nature looked so beautiful.

The friend he was thinking of was a very different man from himself. What had at first attracted the two was a certain delicate dilettanteism, and an indifference to the games and sports by which so many men's leisure is occupied. But deeper down in their character this likeness ended. Whereas Vernon was restless and loved the world, Campbell was shy and restful and inclined to solitude; and whereas Vernon had played with his affections, Campbell had kept his laid up in a napkin. There are passions, however, that lie near affection, although they are always ready to ruin it; and to these Campbell had yielded with a quite sufficient openness. He had even treated the questions involved in them with a certain ruthless humour, which was as coarse as that of Rabelais, and had in part been borrowed from it. But there had been a flavour of innocence even about his vices. They had never approached his heart near enough to corrupt it; and now that at last it was really touched and troubled, he had told the fact to his friend with a simplicity almost childish.

This frankness and depth of feeling had been something of a riddle to Vernon. He had been not long quit of his own engagement when he heard of Campbell's love affair ; and he had pitied his friend sincerely. He looked on him as caught in a trap he had himself just escaped from : and when he found that Campbell the lover interfered with Campbell the friend, the above feeling was intensified. But now as he sat at breakfast, with a volume of Horace beside him, he was happy in the thought that the lover's days were waning, and that the friend would be again restored to him. He had just lit a cigarette, and with a lazy smile was watching the silvery-blue smoke-wreaths as they rose and melted over him into the green myrtle shadows, when he heard on the gravel the sound of a firm foot-step, and, looking up, he saw Alic Campbell before him.

Nothing human could be brighter than a pleased greeting of Vernon's ; it had all the quick radiance of a pool in morning sunlight : and he felt as happy at this moment with his old friend as a child is with a new plaything. Campbell, too, for his part was glowing with glad excitement, though there was a pathetic tone in his voice, if Vernon had cared to note it. Campbell was, however, extremely hungry ; he was by no means in-different to the minor pleasures of the table, and Vernon's breakfast was excellent. Food had the best effect on the lately dejected lover ; his laugh came gaily, his eye gleamed with humour. There is many a heartache that can be made to cease on occasion by the modest soothings of a good *pâté-de-foie-gras.*

'Here,' cried Vernon at last, 'are two disciples of Horace; we have tried many philosophies, but we return to this at last.

> Huc vina et unguenta et nimium breves
> Flores amœnæ ferre jube rosæ,
>   Dum res et ætas et Sororum
>   Fila trium patiuntur atra.'

Campbell smiled, and asked for some more Burgundy.

'My dear Alic,' Vernon went on presently, 'I wrote you a letter only yesterday, full of advice and prophecy: and now, strange to say, before you have got either, you have taken the one, and fulfilled the other. I described to you, too, all the charms of this nook of mine, but now, look about you, and enjoy it with your own eyes.'

Campbell looked about him in silent, but evident, admiration. He had been a considerable traveller, and his eyes had known the world's fairest and most famous prospects; but he admitted frankly that till

now he had never seen such a paradise.
Vernon was delighted ; and filling a glass
with wine, ' It will be a little island in our
lives,' he said, ' the enchanted time we will
spend here.   We have both had our troubles
it is true, but, after all, we are still young :
and it seems to me on a day like this as if
life could have no sorrow except from want of
power to be happy enough.   Look between
those two palm trees at the hills with their
misty amethyst.   See the astounding blue
above us against the green of the stone-pine !
See how the living azure is cut by the yellow
mimosa-blossom !   The beauty of all this
goes through and through me like some notes
of a violoncello.   It is a cry, like certain
dance music, after some consummation of
pleasure unknown to us.   You can kiss, you
can embrace a woman ; and she can love you
back again.   But nature—you can't kiss the
sea ; you can't embrace the mountains.   If

one could only see God, and break one's
heart in praising Him, that perhaps might
ease one.'

A servant here made a moment's interruption, carrying Campbell's only luggage—
a hand-bag—and asking to know if it should
be taken upstairs to a bedroom. 'Of course,'
said Vernon ; and then turning to Campbell,
'My dear Alic,' he went on, 'it is indeed a
delight to think you are really here. It is a
pleasure beyond hope. But tell me—is that
little bag all you have brought over with
you? You couldn't travel with so little
luggage if you were married.'

'I admit,' said Campbell, smiling, 'that
freedom has its advantages. One would lose
a great deal in losing it.'

'One would lose,' said Vernon, 'all that
makes life bearable, as you would soon have
felt had your affairs gone otherwise. But
about the rest of your luggage, if there's not

a very great deal of it, we might drive over to Cannes this afternoon, and bring it all back in the carriage.'

'My dear Vernon,' said Campbell, 'I have got all I want for the night; and I must be returning to Cannes to-morrow. Don't let us waste our one day in driving.'

'Our one day!' exclaimed Vernon. 'God bless my soul, what do you mean by one day? Why, you are going to stop here at least three weeks with me.'

'My dear fellow,' said Campbell very slowly, 'God knows I should like to stay with you; but it is not to be.' And he fixed his eyes upon Vernon with a wistful, serious tenderness—it might almost be called solemnity. It was quite plain that he was resolute.

This to Vernon was like a thunderbolt out of a clear sky. He was at once startled, bewildered, and disappointed.

'Not stay with me!' he exclaimed.

'Why, what on earth do you mean, Alic?
Even if you are still a little melancholy, as I
can well believe you are, you will be surely
far better here than moping about in holes
and corners by yourself. Why can't you stay?
—tell me?'

When Campbell answered, his voice had
almost sunk to a whisper, and he looked at
Vernon with eyes that begged for sympathy.
'Because,' he said, 'I have to go on to San
Remo. I have to be there to-morrow.
Vernon, my—my friend is there. This is
the reason why I have come abroad. I may
see her to-morrow evening; I think, at
farthest, the morning after : and at one time
or the other I shall receive my life or death
at her hands.'

A sudden unwelcome light at last broke
in upon Vernon. '*Her*—her!' he said.
'Why, what on earth are you talking about?
It surely can't be true that I have taken your

letter wrongly? I thought, when you told me your case was mending, that you simply meant that you had fallen out of love again, and that you saw that the marriage state was not a thing worth sighing over.'

Campbell eyed Vernon for a moment or two with a curious, sad amusement. ' You're an odd creature,' he at last said, smiling. ' You know something of the world ; at least you have seen many men and women : and do you think that a man who has really loved a woman, can cast his love to the winds in the course of a single fortnight? What a strange notion you must have of the nature of human affection ! '

Vernon, who had not only conceived such a thing quite possible, but who had in this case actually taken it for granted, received a sudden check from those grave words of his friend. He was not embarrassed by what he had said himself—he knew Campbell far too well for that; but he felt that to Campbell's mind he had betrayed a singular ignorance; and the first thing that struck him was the absurdity of his own situation. A look came into his eyes that fully confessed his fault; but it was the gleam of humour rather than a tear of contrition; and his expression was not unlike that of a naughty child's, who has been caught for the fifth time committing some minor mischief. Campbell understood the expression perfectly; but it neither pained nor chilled him.

'I don't mind you laughing,' he said. 'True feeling can always stand being laughed at. Vernon'—and here his own voice sank low again—'this love of mine has lain down with me and risen up with me for a whole year. I have become a new man since first it took possession of me.'

'So it seems,' said Vernon, 'and a very much unhappier one.'

'Yes,' said Campbell simply, 'it has made me very miserable.   I was ill for several weeks.'   His lips quivered a little, and he raised his clear eyes upwards.   His look, thought Vernon, was like a young saint's in meditation.   Something seemed in his mind which he was a little timid of uttering; but at last he again turned to Vernon.   'I think all this trouble,' he said, 'has been bringing me nearer God.'

Vernon now began to realise that Campbell was really changed.   Was this the Campbell who, but a single twelvemonth back, delighted to dwell laughingly on the coarsest side of passion, and used God's name rarely except to give point to an epigram?   Vernon saw the change, for he had keen moral perceptions; it oppressed him, and at the same time he respected it.   Still, however, a faint hope lingered in him that Campbell might not be beyond repentance.   He repeated all the arguments he had before used in his letter, and added others of a more homely and practical nature. 'You have often told me,' he urged, 'about your own circumstances. You are a rich bachelor; you would be a poor husband. I have seen myself that you have always lived in luxury; and you have always travelled whenever the fancy seized you. Marriage would therefore mean to you, on your own showing, the complete loss of all your personal liberty. You would be fettered in every movement and almost in every thought of your life.'

'I know well,' said Campbell, 'all I should have to give up; and I value it as much, or nearly as much, as you do. I should have to give up many, many luxuries, which to me in my self-indulgence have till now seemed necessaries—mental necessaries as well as bodily. I should have to think about all sorts of little expenses—a thing I hate doing.

As you say, my wings would be clipped for travelling. I could no longer drink the best Burgundy, or smoke the best cigars, or buy books with fine engravings in them. I should lose all this; but what I should gain would far—far outweigh it. All this is a riddle to you, Vernon; for you have never known affection.'

'You wouldn't say that, I can tell you,' replied Vernon, 'if you had seen me last night.' And he gave a short account, in a tone of reserved banter, of what he called his adventure with Miss Walters.

'Adventure!' repeated Campbell. 'Yes —that is just what you consider a love affair. With you, it is a little incursion into an enemy's country; and your aim is presently to get back safe again. But when any man loves truly, does he act or think like this? Was it an *adventure* for the Dolorous Mother when she saw her son die on Calvary?'

His high-strung state of feeling betrayed itself in every accent; and Vernon at last realised that his friend was beyond his arguments. He put his hand kindly on Campbell's shoulder, and in a tone of compassion that was trying to rise to sympathy, 'My dear, dear fellow,' he said, 'whatever you wish for yourself, I wish. I should be very glad for you to be happy, even though I lost your old *you* by it.'

'Thank you,' said Campbell, smiling; 'but, as time draws on, my hopes get very shadowy. I build only on some slight expression which my friend let drop about me to a third person, and it is more than possible that I quite deceive myself. I feel, in going on to San Remo, as if I were going to my own execution. By this time tomorrow perhaps I shall be the forlornest creature imaginable.'

'And in that case,' said Vernon, 'what

should you do then ? You would come back to me, wouldn't you, and let me cheer you up a little ? '

Campbell's whole expression altered ; the lines of his mouth hardened. ' I know exactly what I should do,' he said. ' I have already faced the alternative. If necessary, I shall go straight off to Vienna, and shall find distraction in a complete course of sensuality. I am told that for a life of pleasure Vienna is the best of capitals.'

' Nonsense,' said Vernon sharply. ' You would do nothing of the kind.'

' I should,' replied Campbell. ' I was never in my life more serious. I have already settled the exact route I should travel by, and the hotel I should first put up at. I am a man of strong animal passions. I can easily make a complete beast of myself. Nothing in the world could deaden mental pain like that.'

'Damn it!' exclaimed Vernon with a sudden angry energy. 'For God's sake, Campbell, do talk like a rational being. It makes me sick to hear you speak in that way. A moment ago I had begun to admire and to envy you; and now you have spoilt all. Because some woman, it chances, does not love you, is that any reason why you should cease to respect yourself? Affection, you say, raises the soul to God; and, for aught I know, it may very possibly do so. But if you are crossed in love, does that make God valueless? Are your views about God dependent on a girl's views about you? If your passion really raises you, it cannot let you plan debasing yourself. If in cold blood you can thus plan debasing yourself, then all I can say is, that I don't think much of your passion.'

'You would not be so hard,' said Campbell meekly, 'if you had ever felt as I feel.

What a lover plans is never in cold blood.
Half the vice in the world, Vernon, is caused
less by sin than by sorrow. However,' he
went on, his tone again softening, ' I didn't
come here to croak my woes to you. Let us
think about other things, and let us explore
your paradise.'

CHAPTER II.

VERNON was charmed to escape to more indifferent subjects, and by a quick reaction Campbell became cheerful. The friends found plenty of small things to amuse and interest them. They went over the villa; they inspected books and etchings; they scrambled about on rocks; they walked through olive-groves; they climbed up a wooded hill, and examined a quaint old chapel. The chapel suggested a sudden thought to Vernon. 'Come,' he said, 'and let us look up Stanley.' The news that Stanley was in the neighbourhood was a fresh distraction for Campbell, and for the

time seemed quite to banish the unfortunate
thoughts that saddened him.   Stanley was
living at a small, somewhat rough *pension*,
that was not far from Vernon's villa.   They
learnt that he was at home ; and a prim little
white-capped maid left them to announce
themselves.   They found him upstairs, in a
small, bare sitting-room, bending over a table,
writing.   His face was fine and delicate ; but
had contracted now a slightly stern expression,
and suggested at once thought and physical
suffering. When, however, he saw who were
his visitors, his eyes lit up with a smile of
such frank and surprised pleasure, that for a
moment the sternness vanished ; and Vernon
presently, though not without some misgiving, asked him if he would come to
dinner. To his surprise Stanley accepted
gladly ; but added, ' If I come this evening, I
must send you away now ; for I have certain
work which I am obliged to finish to-day.'

'Poor Stanley!' said Vernon, as he and Campbell walked away together. 'How delighted he was to see you, Alic! and I don't think he much minded seeing me.'

'On the contrary,' said Campbell, 'I thought he seemed particularly pleased at it. Why should you think he minded it?'

'I don't know; but I always vaguely fancy, if I haven't wanted to see a man, that he hasn't wanted to see me. Besides, I haven't the least doubt that he thinks me rather a brute.'

'Do you mean to say that's the first time you've ever been to call on him?'

'I'm afraid it is,' said Vernon. 'But I shall go again now. Do you know, it almost made me cry to see the pleased way in which he smiled at us. I am always touched when a man who looks stern is really made glad by a trifle. But I'll tell you, my dear Alic, what our present business must be. We must order

some specially nice things for dinner this evening ; and I think, in spite of everything, we
shall have a very happy little symposium.'

Nor, when dinner came, was this anticipa-
tion falsified. The unlooked-for re-union of
the three old friends produced in each of them
a genial glow of spirits. Stanley, whatever
might be his private habits, betrayed at Vernon's table no trace of asceticism. He was
naturally a moderate man ; but to-night at
least he ate and drank what he wanted, and
in a quite natural way he remarked that the
champagne was good. Talk flowed freely
about the early days at Oxford ; and memory
lit up all of them with the reflected sunshine
of youth. The only one whose spirits were
at all forced or uncertain was Vernon himself.
The thought that Campbell was resolved not
to stay with him vexed him with a suppressed
persistency ; and with this presently another
began to mix itself—the thought of Miss

Walters, and the strange charm of her presence. It thus happened that at moments he would appear absent. But wine came to his aid whenever his will failed him, and drove his straying wits back to his guests and table.

When dinner was over, the three adjourned to the library, and Stanley and Campbell fell to discussing one of their college tutors. This was a man of great beauty of character, who, though somewhat rough externally, had had upon all his pupils the most powerful moral influence; and the mention of him led the talkers to other serious matters. Vernon at the beginning had occasionally put in a word or two; but he had relapsed gradually into a mere listener—a listener at first attentive, then a trifle drowsy; till at length, by gentle stages, he had sunk off into sleep.

The tone of the others presently dropped lower.

'Look!' said Stanley, as his eyes fell
upon Vernon, 'what a curious expression in
repose he has! He is the most careworn
sleeper I ever saw, and yet of all waking men
he is the most careless-looking. Do you
think he is happy?'

'He has his troubles,' said Campbell, 'no
doubt, like the rest of us. To make him
happy, he wants one or two things—he should
have less of a heart, or more of one. Somebody, I remember, once said of him bitterly,
that he got more love from his slightest friend
than he ever gave to his greatest. Perhaps
there is some truth in that: and yet, though
the man who said it is one of the most staunch
of creatures, I could depend on Vernon in
some ways more surely than on him. Were
there any urgent need, I could ask Vernon to
take any trouble for me. He would hate the
trouble, yet all the same he would take it;
and he would serve you better, when the

service was only a nuisance to him, than
many men would who might feel it a genuine
pleasure.'

'That just fits in,' said Stanley, 'with
what I heard the other day about him, from
an old woman here, whose cottage I sometimes visit. This woman had a poor, lame
child, who was taken out in a mule-cart, with
some of its brothers and sisters. The cart
broke down, and could not be brought home
again ; and the little crippie was naturally in
great distress. Vernon that moment chanced
to be passing by. He at once took it up and
carried it two miles, to its home, and the day
after ordered a boot with steel supports for
it, which the surgeons declare will give it the
use of its legs again. I happened to meet him
just after he had done carrying it, and he said,
" Don't shake hands with me ; I've been
touching a beastly child ! " '

'Have you ever looked at his books ?'

asked Campbell presently, as he glanced round him.

'No; I have never been in this room before. He asked me to breakfast once, but I was unable to come, and I gathered by his manner that he thought he had done his duty by me.'

'His library,' said Campbell, 'made me smile rather. A good half of it consists of dry treatises on theology. Look at his writing-table,' he went on. 'Do you see those three books on it—one on top of the other? I took them up before dinner, and they are "Horace," "The Spiritual Combat," and "Lord Chesterfield's Letters."'

'I remember that at Oxford,' said Stanley, 'he would continually talk of theology; but it was never with any reverence, though sometimes with thought and knowledge.'

'Yes; religion with him,' said Campbell, 'is merely an intellectual question—a tiresome riddle, that piques him because he can't answer it.'

The conversation continued for some time longer, whilst the subject of it still slept heavily. At last Stanley, who kept early hours, declared that he ought to go. ' But I won't wake Vernon,' he said. ' Poor fellow, he looks tired enough. You shall say good-night for me ; and I hope, Campbell, that I may soon see you again.'

' I am going to-morrow,' said Campbell. ' I am obliged to go ; but, if you would be in, I might come and see you in the morning. I, too, have my troubles ; and I am afraid I have been boring Vernon with them.'

By and by Vernon woke up with a start, and asked where was Stanley. ' What a brute I must have seemed to him !' he said, when he knew that his guest was gone. ' I ask a fellow to dine with me ; then I sleep like a pig all through the evening ; and now

for my pains, I wake up with a splitting head-
ache. Let us go out—shall we?—and take
a turn in the garden.'

Vernon was somewhat silent as they went
through the moonlit walks. At last he said
abruptly, ' What made me sleepy to-night was
my having taken too much wine. I did it to
keep my spirits up, for I was gloomy about
your going. Of course Stanley wouldn't say
anything ; but I know quite well he must
have thought me a beast.'

' That,' said Campbell, ' I am quite sure
he did not, for just before he went he
was warmly praising you. He was telling
me of your kindness to some little crippled
girl.'

' My kindness to what ? ' exclaimed
Vernon. ' Oh, I know what he must be
thinking of. Poor little dirty brat—she literally reeked of garlic ! How the devil did
Stanley hear about it ? But now tell

me,' he went on, 'must you really go to-morrow? Is it all quite decided? Can't you stay even for a day or two, and let me show you my beautiful neighbour?'

Campbell shook his head. 'No, Vernon —no,' he said.

'But she is very beautiful,' said Vernon, 'and dresses exquisitely, and has all kinds of high-minded views about the hollowness of fashion, and about genuine friendship, and falling in love, and so on. I would let you flirt with her, if you wanted to.'

'You forget,' said Campbell, 'that I am leading a consecrated life.'

'Well, she won't un-consecrate you. She has done with love, she tells me : though I'm not sure myself if I quite believe her. Is it Sterne—or who is it?—who says, "Talking of love is making it?"'

Campbell was silent, and Vernon began again.

' I think my true *métier*,' he said, 'would be that of wooer-in-ordinary to my male friends. Whenever any one of them had set his heart on a lady, it should be my business to awake her love and tenderness ; to teach her lips to kiss, her breast to move with a sigh or two, and her eyes to look expressively. Then without any peculation I would transfer my complete prize to my client. Would you on these terms have made me your agent ? You may be sure when the time came I should have no temptation to cheat you.'

This was said with a smile ; but Campbell answered in a tone of unexpected seriousness.

'My dear Vernon,' he said, 'what a thoroughly immoral man you are !'

' Immoral ! '

'Yes ; you really are. I am not in the least joking. You are one of the most immoral men I ever knew. What you said just now is only another proof of it.'

' My dear fellow,' said Vernon, ' I was only chaffing you.'

' Yes ; but the man in jest is the key to the man in earnest. Besides, I didn't judge you merely by what you said just now. I have known you for ten years, and have been your friend ever since I knew you. I was looking only this morning at one of your early photographs, and since that was taken I can see how your face has changed. In some ways you have hardly aged at all ; you still look very, very young. But youth is sometimes prolonged by a sacrifice of all that is best in it; and ah, Vernon, there is one look gone from your face which that photograph reminded me was once there ! And shall I tell you what has destroyed it ? It is what I call your immorality. It is this perpetual trifling with your highest and finest feelings. That the feelings are high and fine I don't deny for a moment. It is in that that the badness lies. You are making a playground of what should be your holy of holies. You may not be indulging your grosser appetites; but you are making yourself incapable for ever of any earnest affection; and this is the surest way in which you can quench the Spirit. It is not eclipsing the light, as lust does; it is putting the light out. Pure affection can extinguish lust; but if you extinguish pure affection, what then? Would a man who has done that ever be fit for heaven, even though in the world's sense of the word he were as moral as any anchorite?'

There was something in Campbell's manner which, despite his plain speaking, made Vernon listen without anger or impatience. He seemed a little annoyed, however, and anxious to change the subject.

' Heaven!' he said wearily ; 'and do you, Campbell, really believe in heaven ?'

' More than you do,' said Campbell, with the same gentleness. ' I am not wanting to preach to you. I am only trying, like a friend that loves you, to show you the reason of your being so ill at ease. This is a delicate thing to do, and even a friend can do it only when he is himself feeling deeply. A year ago I could never have spoken like this to you. Perhaps six weeks hence I shall be again unable to do it.'

' I know you mean kindly, said Vernon. ' But, honestly, I didn't quite understand you. What on earth makes you think that I am ill at ease ?'

' You are, though you may not acknowledge it. I can see it in your face, I can hear it in your voice sometimes. With all your bright spirits, and with all your gaiety, you have done your nature a wrong which you feel in spite of yourself.   My own sins, God knows, have been many.   It is perhaps because of them that all this sorrow is come upon me.   But there is something worse, Vernon, than even the garment spotted by the flesh.   What is commonly called immorality, does indeed stain life ; but *your* immorality eviscerates it.   It leaves you a husk—a shell ; a tissue it may be of supersensitive nerves ; but with no true self within to be informed by them.   You have not arrived at that state yet, but there are moments when you feel or fear the beginning of it.'

' I may have causes for care,' said Vernon, ' other than you dream of ; perhaps, indeed, of an exactly opposite nature.   You tell me I do not believe in heaven, and perhaps I don't ; but at least I feel daily the want of a belief in it.   My unhappiness, if I have any, arises not from having no woman to love, but from having no God to believe in.'

Campbell looked at Vernon with a friendly incredulity. 'My dear Vernon,' he said, 'you are the most irreligious man I know. The same course of conduct that deadens human love deadens divine love also; nor indeed would you play with the first, if you had any real sense of the second. I know quite well that you think about religion, and read about it; but you know quite well also that it is not an active power in your life. It is nothing more than an abstraction. You have continually told me that nothing in life absorbs you, whereas religion, when a reality, is all an affair of loving.'

'Not of loving only, but of believing also. You can't love a being whose existence you are not sure of; and it is quite conceivable —I am not speaking about myself, for that, after all, is a matter of little interest—it is quite conceivable that affection may in many cases be chilled by want of belief, just as

belief may become useless for want of proper
affection.   Love robbed of belief is like a bird
whose nest has been stolen.   It tries every
tree, but finds no twig to rest upon.'   There
was a short silence after this ; and then presently Vernon began again.   ' In one point
at least,' he said with a cold laugh, 'you are
wrong, Campbell, in your judgment of me.
You said that religion had no effect on my
life.   It was a religious question that caused
the breaking off of my marriage.'

' If you had been very much in love, if
you had been very anxious to marry, would
that question have stood in your way ? '

' It would have stood in my way, I sincerely hope, in any case.   I can think of no
self-indulgence so wanton, so complete in its
cruelty, as bringing children into the world,
and giving them no faith to guide them.
It would indeed be making a tragic toy of
affection, to let it lead one into blowing soap-

bubbles of conscious fretful vanity. Happy unconscious matter! The man is worse than a murderer who informs it with aimless wretchedness.'

'And this,' said Campbell, 'is the religious man's view of fatherhood! My dear Vernon, you have much to learn yet.'

Vernon made no reply to this. He had seen that Campbell, in spite of a friend's fondness, had but a scanty faith in his conduct with regard to the breaking off of his marriage; and a feeling of not quite unnatural anger had begun to swell up in him. But 'He means well,' he almost directly said to himself, and he forced the anger down. Its only outer sign was a few moments' coldness; and when next he spoke, it was once more with sympathy.

'You have told me much about love,' he said, as they moved back to the villa; 'but you have told me very little about your own love-story. You met your goddess abroad; she has very simple tastes; "first she would and then she wouldn't," and now she is doubtful whether she will or no. I knew this much, but that is all. Do you mind telling me her name, and a little more about her?'

'Not to-night,' said Campbell. 'No—nor to-morrow morning, I think. Had I better or surer hope, I would dwell on and tell you everything. But I can't now. I can't go over those scenes again. I would sooner not even tell you who she is, unless I can tell you some day that she is or will be my wife. I shall know that soon. Ah, me!'

'And are you still resolved,' said Vernon, 'that Vienna is your only alternative?'

'Perhaps,' said Campbell sighing, 'I am not resolved that it shall be; but I know that it is.'

The conversation then turned to brandy and seltzer-water, and the two friends retired.

CHAPTER III.

AMPBELL next morning paid a short visit to Stanley, and in the afternoon he was gone. Vernon's last words to him were, ' If you are not successful, come back to me, and give up Vienna. You have told me pretty plainly that I'm not far off from a devil ; so if it's the devil you want to go to, you may at least choose one who is fond of you.'

There was more in his manner, perhaps, than he was altogether conscious of ; for this last farewell of his touched Campbell and set him for some time thinking. As for Vernon himself, his spirits at first sank low enough, and his villa looked very blank to him. But he was not a man tamely to sit down with dejection; and, having mourned his friend's loss for an hour or so, his imagination suddenly wheeled round to Miss Walters. The effect was as quick on him as that of a glass of absinthe. He would at once hurry off and call at the Château St. John; and such a thrill did the prospect send through him, that he felt his present solitude was not without its advantages. Even a friend like Campbell might have been perhaps a little *de trop* just then.

He had rung the bell at the Château; the hall door had been thrown open, and with a confident inquiry he was already on the point of entering, when the servant informed him that the ladies had left for Nice.

'Left!' echoed Vernon in astonishment.

'They left yesterday, sir,' said the servant; 'but they will be back early this evening, as

I believe they are expecting a gentleman here to dine with them.'

Vernon at once concluded that this gentleman must be himself, and he resolved to hasten home to inquire if no note had arrived for him. He was spared, however, this trouble by the servant adding the next moment, 'A gentleman, I believe, sir, who is coming from Monte Carlo.'

This simple announcement worked like magic on Vernon. A sudden twilight of jealousy fell on his whole soul; and at the same instant the stars of romance shone out again. The expected guest, he felt convinced, could be none other than Colonel Stapleton; and the thought that the beautiful Cynthia could be touched by so gross a rival, seemed to withdraw her to some untold distance. But such are the ways of certain kinds of affection, that this fancied distance only increased his longing for her. His impressions of her, mental or sensuous, became all more vivid than ever, and he was soon lost in a deep, passionate reverie. Her eyes, her lips, her hands, the texture of her cheek and throat, the feather in her hat, the tones of her voice, her gestures—all these in their several ways touched him ; and she dwelt in his mind as some strange, delicate mystery that he was resolved to make his own.

Having indulged to the full in this kind of dreaming, the thought of Campbell once more came back to him. He paced the same walks that evening that Campbell had lately paced with him ; and he attentively thought over their last night's conversation, and looked longingly in the direction of the Château St. John. 'Ah me!' he cried, 'and am I really the brute that Campbell tells me I am ? Am I really heartless and selfish, and with no health left in me ?'

He went indoors to his library ; and took

down a volume from his book-case of Latin authors. He sat for some time poring over it motionless ; but at last a low voice broke from him, and he began thus translating aloud to himself :—

'Highest and holiest, mightiest and al-mightiest, most pitiful and yet most just, un-seen and yet ever near to us, fairest and yet most firm, ever before us and yet past our studying; never new, never aging, yet renew-ing all things ; striking the proud with age, and they know it not: whose work never ceases, whose quiet is never broken ; gathering, yet nothing needing ; sustaining, replenishing, and protecting ; making, cherish-ing, and maturing ; seeking, yet having all things : Thou lovest, and passion stirs Thee not ; Thou art jealous, and lo! no care touches Thee ; Thou repentest Thee, yet Thou has no contrition ; Thou art angry, and yet Thou abidest calm ; Thou makest Thy

works change, but Thy counsel endures for
ever ; Thou findest what Thou hast never
lost, and Thou takest it back home to Thee.
Thou art never in want, and yet Thou art
pleased with winning ; Thou hast no covet-
ousness, and yet Thou takest usury.   Thou
art paid more than Thy due that Thou mayest
be made man's debtor ; and who has aught
that has not been always Thine ?   Thou
payest, yet owest no man anything ; Thou
givest gifts, and behold Thou losest nothing.
And what, oh, what is this that I say con-
cerning Thee, my God, my life, my holy and
sweet desire ? or what, when he speaks of
Thee, can be said by any man ? and yet woe
to him that speaks not, since even the dumb
praise Thee.' [1]

The book over which Vernon was bending
was the ' Confessions of Augustine.'   As he
read he felt his eyes moisten, and at last he

---

[1] *St. Augustine's Confessions*, book i. chap. iv.

started at a tear that dropped on the page
before him.

'What's Hecuba to me, or I to Hecuba?'
he exclaimed. 'Do I really mean that? or
is it only another form of self-indulgence?
My God, what am I? Is there anything in
me not contemptible?'

He hid his face in his hands, and remained
for some time motionless. When he moved
himself, he did so with resolution. He
opened a drawer in his writing-table, he took
out some paper, and after a certain further
hesitation he abruptly put pen to it.

What he wrote was as follows:—

'Why should a man wince at the sight of
his inmost thoughts? Is he not a coward, if
he does not dare confront them? Ah me! I
am a coward; I wince and I hold back; false
shame overcomes me. But my heart is
troubled; my spirit is bruised and beaten,
and courage at last has come to me from my

wretchedness. I may pretend I am happy; but, O my God, I am not happy! It is true that my friends or the delicious sunshine make my blood beat with pleasure, and many other such trifles excite me. I become excited childishly; and I forget myself into a bright false happiness. But all the while there is a worm gnawing at my heart, and whenever I am quiet I feel it. I have tried to deceive myself; I have tried to say this is not so. But I can deceive myself no longer; and now I will face the truth. I will see what I am; I will examine this mangled self of mine. Yes—I will put my thoughts into shameless black and white; they shall have a solid body that I cannot pretend eludes me. Quick!—though I am shuddering, let me get the icy shock over; let me plunge into confession. What should make me hesitate? No one will see these pages, with this blurred image of my soul cast on them.

Whenever I wish it the fire can keep my secret.

'What shall I say? Shall I speak as in reality my soul pines to speak? I will.

'O my God, holiest and mightiest, most pitiful and yet most just, what I pine for is to speak to Thee. Let me write Thy name—let me brand it in writing, not think it only in faint and fleeting thoughts. Let me rouse my ears with the sound of my own voice crying to Thee. O God, what I long for is to lay bare my soul—to open it, to disrobe it, to expose it naked before Thee; and to cry to Thee to have pity, to have pity, and to look upon me!

'And yet, how dare I, impure and faithless, loving nothing—so they tell me—and nobody? For Thou art pure and holy; and my very friend has told me that I am viler than most men. Am I so? Oh, teach me to know myself; humble my pride; enlighten me! My God, I am not mocking Thee. What I ask of Thee is what my heart is crying for. Teach me to know myself.

'And yet if indeed Thou hearest me, I must seem like one mocking; for Thou knowest how faith has failed me, and how bewildered and dark my mind is. Even whilst I am crying to Thee, whilst I am trying to open to Thee all my secret being, I know not, I am not sure, if you have any existence—you, the God I am crying to. Perhaps you are only a dream—an idea—a passing phenomenon in man's mental history. And yet surely, if Thou existest, Thou wilt not, even for this cause, turn away from me, quenching the smoking flax. May it not be that Thou art revealing Thyself to me, through my wretched sense of Thy absence?

'But from me why art Thou absent? Is

it through my sins, through my own loveless nature ? Have I nothing in my soul fit to offer Thee ? And for this cause hast Thou put me far away from Thee ?

'I may be evil now ; I may be in outer darkness ; but I know that I was not always. I was once near Thee ; I was once ever with Thee. That was when I was a little child. O my God, I will confess to Thee through my childhood.

'I was no saint, Thou knowest ; I was a little, worldly child, yet I will maintain even to Thy face that as a child I loved Thee, and with a child's frankness I was always in secret turning to Thee. I thought of Thee in my play ; I thought of Thee in riding my pony. Hardly an hour passed in which, without kneeling, I did not say some word to Thee. Nor did this end with my childhood ; for as I grew older, and as my thoughts multiplied, more and more in secret did they fasten upon

Thee. And I grew very greatly to fear Thee, and yet I was not afraid to love Thee ; for my own sins were small, and I washed them out with nightly penitence. Often hast Thou heard my childlike lips confessing them.

' But as I thought upon Thy perfections, and as I looked round upon the world, a new sense grew in me. It was a sense of the world's sin, and of how Thou wast being grieved and blasphemed everywhere. Of men's sorrow, and want, and poverty, I had not heard much. What touched me was the misery of the sin that they lay wallowing in. The thought of this was never quite absent from me. It haunted me day and night through all my later boyhood. It very often subdued me in my gayest moments. Thou knowest how for this reason a great city was hateful to me. In the same way, although I could see my schoolfellows unhappy, and be little moved by it; yet many a time when I have seen some young soul corrupting itself, I have said, " I would die, if he might be saved from sinning." O God, Thou hast heard me, if Thou hearest anything. Thou knowest, too, how my pillow has been damp with tears from my thinking on these things.

'Thus the time drew on when there was a new thing to happen to me. I was to draw near to Thee at Thy Son's altar. For this cause, I turned my thoughts upon myself more earnestly; and I cleansed my heart as I had never done before. And I received Thy Son's self into me with fear and trembling; and I was drawn closer, O Thou Holy One, to Him and Thee. And at the same time also my early life was expanding. My passions and the world's excitements began to stir me, and shot new colours into existence; and I hoped for love and for companionship, and I longed for beauty. The sadness and the rapture overcame me that together stir men to singing. But Thou, O my God, wert present in all this. If I longed for the love of a woman, it was that both our faces might turn to Thee. And I saw Thee, too, in the blue sky and in the sunset, and in the reedy river with the moon in it, and in the sea, and the sea-shore. And each year I was tempted with more and more temptations, but I still kept watch over myself, and always in my trouble I cried to Thee. I spoke to no friend about these things. I communed with Thee only, and I tried very hard to carry the cross of Christ. When I have been dining with gay companions I have seen His face before me, beyond the lights and glasses. I have seen Him worn and sorrowful, pleading with and reproaching me. He has often said to me in the midst of my laughter, "I have suffered so much for thy sake, canst thou not suffer even a little for Mine ? "

' I lived like this for some four or, it might be, five years, and then the time began when Thou wert slowly to be withdrawn from me. Why was this, my God ? Was it for my sins ? And if so, for what sins ? When, when did they begin ? For Thou wast not withdrawn from me through my forgetting Thee, but through my ever thinking of Thee. I studied much and many things; and whatever I studied, I applied it to Thy Church and Thee. And new lights broke on me, and new roads of knowledge ; and my soul suffered violence, and the sight of its eyes was changed. For by-and-by, though the change came very slowly, all that I had once been taught about Thee, the Sacraments also, through which I once thought I approached Thee, became to me like outworn symbols. I struggled to stay the change. I called to

Thee, Thou knowest how often, to keep it from me. Thou knowest how, as I felt my prayers grow faint, and their words lose their meaning, I still said to Thee every night and morning, " I believe ; help Thou mine unbelief." Thou knowest, too, when Thou gavest me no answer, how I tried to find help thus, " He that doeth," I said, " shall know of the doctrine ; " and I tried with fresh diligence to do my daily duties, hoping that in this way might my faith revive again. But it never did revive. On the contrary, all this while I was receding farther from Thee ; and the more earnestly I sought Thee, the less near did I seem to come to Thee, till at last I was like a blinded bird, I knew not whither even to try to fly; and this body of mine, this Temple of Thy Holy Spirit, has been left empty ; and vain thoughts and desires had been holding and still hold **festival in it.**

'O my God, if Thou art, why for me art Thou not? Why art Thou thus withdrawn from me? Is it because I have sinned? Can that be the reason? Surely this Thou knowest, that it was not what men call sin that made my eyes dim to see Thee. It was not the lust of the flesh, nor the pride of life, although both of these assailed me. And if since then evil things have had hold on me, I have sinned because I first lost Thee; I have not lost Thee through sinning. There is no man or woman that for Thy sake I could not renounce easily, reserving no more care for them than to work for their souls indifferently. No—what I have lost Thee by is not sin; it is rather the very things whereby I resisted sin; it is my reason, my intellect, and my longing for what is true. I have lost Thee, my God, through my earnest search to find Thee.

'And yet, for all this, do I dare to say I

am sinless? It may be that I am far worse than I think I am; for has not my very friend told me that I am viler than most men? Does he speak truth? Perhaps. For in many ways—it may be in all ways—he is a better man than I am. The ties and the affections of this life—those joys and sorrows with which Thou hast surrounded us—touch him, and take hold of him, and leave deep marks in him; but me they touch only as the shadows in a dream-night. Perhaps, then, here is the secret. Perhaps I am vile, not knowing it, because to renounce all for Thy sake would be so very small a pang to me, and a sacrifice to Thee is worthless of that which costs us nothing. What then? Must one love Thy creatures before one can love Thee? Must one not rather love Thy creatures because of Thee?

'Thy creatures! Were they Thine I could indeed love them. I should know that there was in them some eternal worth and value. But, without Thee, what are they more than shadows are? What are they more than I, who am the most frail and vain of shadows? They get no hold on me, nor I any on them. For a little while one pleases me, and then a little while and it does not please. It comes near me; presently it recedes again, and another is pushed into the place of it; and in me there is left no regret, nor any pain in my heart. And how shall this be otherwise? And what shall give these ghosts substance? Why, without Thee, what but a mere ghost is the universe, even to its farthest stars? Of the only cosmos man can ever know or conceive of, he is himself the co-creator; and with the ending of his consciousness the All ends also. It falls like a house of cards when one card is taken away from it. Such is it without Thee. And yet it is told me that if I loved my fellow-ghosts, above all if I would take to my heart some one of them, they would then be ghosts no longer; and that, they being thus made real to me, I should again discern Thee.

'This may be true.   There may be some philosophy in it.   By Love as well as by the Word, the Heavens are perhaps made.   But, O my God, wouldst Thou only reveal Thyself first to me, wouldst Thou only show me that Thou indeed existest, I would love all things then for Thy sake!

'And yet should I ?   I am not certain of that even.   For, my God, if Thou existest Thou lovest all Thy creatures, and they are all infinitely precious.   How, then, am I to inflame or influence my heart, that I should permanently love some one of these more than I love the others ?   I am perplexed, I cannot tell.   Yet I know—even my common sense tells me—that it is only in this way that loving men do love.

' Nay, this, too, Thou knowest of me, that I have, as a fact, striven to love in this way. I sought to marry, and to be faithful all my life to another; and I trusted that with another's eyes I might again discern Thee. But even this hope failed me. For what return did she whom I chose make to me? She gave me no help that I needed; but proffered me comfortless comfort, and help that I had no need of. Instead of showing me *Thee*, she turned away and prepared to worship *me*. She would have made me into *her* God, instead of guiding me to *mine*. And for a time this consoled me a little; but I soon grew weary of it, and more restless than ever. For how should this blind passion satisfy me? I did but blind her to Thee. She did not show Thee to me.

' It seems, then, that I have tried everything. And now, my God, what remains for me? How shall I plant my foot firm in this

land of shadows ?   I am not in pain.   Ah,
if I were in pain there would be more hope
for me!   I would not complain to Thee that
I did not feed upon roses, if Thou wouldst
vouchsafe only that the thorns might wound
and tear me.   And yet, O God, Thou knowest I am distracted still by trifles, by pleasures
that are no pleasures, and by pains that are
no pains.   And Thou hast given me high
spirits, and Thou hast hidden my soul in a
raiment of light laughter, and in what, even
to me, sometimes seems contentment.   But
my brain is empty ; I know not where to
turn.   To this thing and to this thing I would
apply myself; but whenever I begin to stir
myself, the reason which Thou hast given me
plucks me by the ear, and hisses in a whisper,
" To what purpose ?   Are not all things
vanity ? "

'And what is this I say ?   To whom am
I speaking ?   I am speaking to One of whose

very existence I am doubtful. I am not certain if I would stake a hundred pounds upon it. Oh, my forlorn hopes! My reason trips me, I am entangled and thrown down. Fool that I am—wretched, wretched fool! And yet, though I am thus lying prostrate, thrown abject and confused upon the ground, I will not be hindered. O God, I still will speak to Thee. I will call Thee to witness that at least I *have* been near Thee, that I *have* known Thy presence, and that, far away though I be from Thee now, though this world of shadows may now blind my eyes to Thee, there nothing is in it anywhere that I have longed for as I have longed for Thee, there is nothing I have desired in comparison of Thee. Thou hast been to me my all, my life, my light, and my salvation. Thou hast been the one wealth of my soul— its one and only fire; and all that has hidden Thee has been but as burning ashes.

'Am I mad ? Am I a hypocrite ? Am I dreaming ? Am I lying to myself, as I write thus ? Am I playing a part before myself to deceive myself ? O my God, after all, is it nothing but my own sin, my own lovelessness, that stands between me and Thee ? Dost Thou put me away, seeing how lightly I have esteemed Thy creatures ? Have I, as Campbell said to me, quenched Thy Spirit ?

'How odd Campbell's name looked, stuck in like that !

'My God—is it not possible that I may plead my cause thus with Thee ? May I not justify myself to Thee, and say, the worse I am now, the more does this show how I loved Thee ? Thou wast present in every affection, in every energy of my life ; therefore with Thy withdrawal every energy, every affection is ruined. Yes—I might say this, but for one thing. Ah me, my God, behold what is now happening to me! The desire of Thee has long made me miserable; and, ah, more miserable that I am! even my desire for Thee is now deserting me. My heart is ceasing to ache for Thee. A hateful peace is slowly soothing it to its death. My soul is getting colder and colder; warmth is leaving it, as it leaves a man who is dying. O my God, remain with me! Keep my pain and my desolation alive in me! If Thou wilt not fill the void in my heart that Thou didst once fill, let the void remain void, let nothing else fill it. Give me no peace, unless it be Thy peace. Torment me, but forsake me not. Scourge me, keep me wretched and restless till I find Thee! This is indeed a sincere prayer. O my God, is it a wrong one?'

Here he came to a long pause, and threw his pen down, as if he would write no more. He looked round the room wearily, and stared in a kind of stupor at the various books about him. At last his eye fixed on a volume of Herbert Spencer; and for many minutes he was motionless. Then, seizing the pen again, he rapidly added what follows.

'Our own inward condition—our own sins and longings, and the bitter strife between them—to the teachers of the present day what trifles do such things seem!—or at best, what a storm in a saucer! To the prophets of humanity, an unskilful bricklayer is a more tragic object than a ruined soul!'

Several times during the long course of his writing, Vernon had gone to the window, and peered out. He now went again once more, and the moon was setting—the moon, which during his after-dinner walk had been so high in the middle heavens. This showed him that the night must be far spent. Presently his eye fell on a small side-table, and there lay an object so common-place that it seemed to him like a spectre. It was a letter he had not before noticed that had come for him by the evening's post. The writing, which was large and decided, might have been either a man's or woman's; and he fancied it was familiar, though he could connect no name with it. He broke open the envelope, as if the sight of it half dazed him; and the first words he read sent all the blood to his cheek.

'Dear Mr. Vernon,'—began the letter, 'When I saw you the other day, I quite forgot to tell you that my very heart was broken. ('What!' thought Vernon, 'can this be from Miss Walters?' He went on reading.) 'And only a clever young man like you can be of the least comfort to me. My poor little darling sky-terrier Prinny—the thing on this earth I have loved best and longest —was run over and killed the other day by a young man with a tandem. Only conceive it—a tandem! And this young gentleman could have hardly held in a donkey. Had he been one of my own stable-helps, I should have known pretty well what to do with him. And now you—if you will, I want you to write an epitaph for me. My angel is being embalmed by a very accomplished bird-stuffer, and is to have Christian burial when I get back to England. Your verses shall have a most honourable place; so be a good man, do, and write them for me.' And then followed the bold signature of the Duchess.

With a tired, sleepy smile Vernon again sat down at his writing-table. A thought had struck him suddenly; and seizing the pen, he scribbled these hasty lines :—

> Thou art gone to sleep, and we—
> May we some day sleep like thee !
> Prinny, were this heart of mine
> Half so true, my dog, as thine,
> I my weary watch should keep
> For a something more than sleep !

Whatever besides sleep the exhausted writer may have longed for, sleep, at least, now unexpectedly fell upon him. His eyelids grew heavy like lead, the pen dropped from his hand, and, sinking back in his chair, he became lost to consciousness.

BOOK III.

CHAPTER I.

WHEN Vernon awoke it was already daylight : the Venetian shutters were barred with the red gleams of morning. His eyelids ached, and he looked about him bewildered.

'What has happened to me?' he said to himself. 'Am I awake, or is this a nightmare?'

He paced about the library, at first almost staggering ; but by-and-by he recovered himself. He mounted to his bedroom. It had a ghastly, alien aspect. There was his bed, cold, smooth, and unslept in, with his night-

shirt folded lying upon it. He ruffled the
sheets and pillow, that he might seem to his
servant to have passed the night as usual ;
for, as to lying down, it was the last thing he
now thought of. Then he tore his clothes
off and plunged into a cold bath. He re-
dressed himself ; he made a large cup of coffee over a spirit-lamp ; and having drunk it,
he softly stole out of doors.

The long shadows of the clear day in its
infancy made his garden wear an unfamiliar
face for him. But the living breath of the
air, fresh with the dew, and quick with the
smells of flower-beds, woke in him new pulses.
He paused and looked about him that his
spirit might 'drink the spectacle.'[1] The sea
was a pale sheet, sharply dark at the horizon,
where it washed with its long levels the red-
dening tract of sunrise ; and it was strewn

[1]   His spirit drank
The Spectacle.—WORDSWORTH.

with floating fragments of the crocus and the rose of the sky. The faint promontories of Italy slept in a veil of vapour. Inland lay the far hill-villages, white scattered specks on the huge slopes of the mountains ; and below them were sombre ranges of far-reaching mounded olive-woods. These were unchanging in their soft, impassive darkness ; but except on these the light was brightening everywhere : and presently, far beyond them, all the gigantic highlands flushed in an instant from grey to a shining rose-colour, as they caught the risen splendour on their bleak frosts or dews.

Vernon, as he looked, felt himself come to life again, but to a life of clear sensation rather than clear thought. Thoughts, however, of some kind must have begun to dimly stir in him ; for he soon found himself moving in a definite direction. It was the direction of the Château St. John. He passed through

a wicket, into a large open expanse studded
with heath and furze-bushes. The sea was
on one side of it ; it was traversed by several
paths ; and, for the sake of the air and view,
he had often before wandered in it. Here he
paused. Beyond were the tufts and plumes
of the luxuriant Château shrubberies, and
between these, by glimpses, the Château itself
was visible. Vernon's eye fixed on the line of
windows. The blinds were down ; the whole
house seemed slumbering. The path where
he stood led to. a marble gateway, through
which one entered the gardens and passed
into an avenue of orange-trees. Towards
this gateway, though he could not explain
why, he was, in another moment, moving.
Last night he could write his thoughts ;
now they were too vague for analysis.

He passed through the gates with a feeling of hope and peril ; he might have been
entering the charmed bounds of a sorceress.

And yet the place was already known by heart to him ; and only a week ago he had roamed at his own will in it. A maze of paths branched from the orange-avenue. He instinctively chose one that led far away from the house, and that brought him by-and-by to a long succession of gardens, terraced on the hill-side, and leading down to the sea. He stole on rapidly, past urns and statues, fountains and set flower-beds ; he descended by broad flights of steps from one level to another ; and he at last diverged into a steep winding path, which dived into a natural tunnel amongst certain fantastic rocks. This brought him presently, after several turnings, to the strand of a tiny bay. On either side was a curve of sheltering cliffs, not lofty but precipitous, and plunging straight into clear grey-green sea-water. The strand was a little platform, gravelled carefully, and backed by a bed of violets.

Here he paused, and at last began to meditate. Slowly his vague feelings turned into thoughts and images. His vigils of the night came back to him, with the strange projection on paper he had made of his own condition : and they took a ghastly aspect as the air of the morning breathed on them. Mixed, too, with these phantasmal memories were thoughts of a different order, which soon began to reveal themselves with semi-transparent bodies. They were thoughts of the clear-cheeked mistress of the grounds where he was now trespassing. No sooner had he become conscious of this, than a memory came back to him of certain sayings of Campbell's ; and he exclaimed to himself, with weary self-reproach, ' Do I think again of yielding ? What is it that has brought me here ? I do not love this girl. I have no wish to bind myself. All the fine and all the high feelings she stirs in me—they are not

serious : I attach no worthy meaning to them.
I am merely trifling with them in the very
way Campbell warned me of. Let me be
brave for once—let me make one sacrifice ;
let me call my imagination away from her.
And yet—ah me—those lovely, lovely lips of
hers ! '

At this moment a slight noise startled
him. He turned quickly round, and there, at
the distance of a pace or two, she was herself
standing before him. In an instant, like bats
from daylight, his scruples took wing, and hid
themselves. He was conscious of a shock, as
of all his will yielding. For a little while he
stood silent and looked at her, feeling nothing
but his own blood beating, and letting his
eyes rest on her. Seen thus in the dawning
she was a fresh surprise to him. His
memory, it is true, had retained her image
clearly ; but it had let the image tarnish, and
lose its exquisite delicacy. He saw she was

far more lovely than in his thoughts just now she had seemed to him. She was dressed in a way that, it was evident, was meant only for solitude. She had a long cloak on, with a border of broad sable. It was fastened round her throat, with additional closeness, by a small brooch of diamonds ; and below it descended a pale-blue satin dressing-gown. She had apparently taken what at waking she could first seize upon ; for on her slim shoes there was a glimmer of gold embroidery, and on one of her hands was a long evening glove. The other was bare, and held a pale, dewy rose in it.

Vernon's rapid glance took in all these details ; and the same impression was renewed in him that he received at first meeting her. Everything about her was dainty, almost *fine* in its daintiness ; yet, in relation to her, it seemed natural as her own complexion. And she herself, with the early

light caressing her—had that complexion
stolen a tint from morning? Had the dews
of night washed her violet eyes clearer?

Miss Walters was the first to speak; but
she only exclaimed, ' Mr. Vernon!' and he
for the first moment could only exclaim,
' Miss Walters!' He was not, however, a
man to remain long tongue-tied; and very
soon, with a smile, he was begging pardon as
a trespasser. ' Before you came here,' he
said, ' these gardens were a favourite haunt
of mine; and I thought that, under cover of
the morning, I might venture in, just once
more, undetected.'

' And I thought,' said Miss Walters, with
a glance at her own costume, ' that I might
be undetected also. I certainly did not come
out expecting to confront company.'

The soft, low voice in which these words
were murmured, showed Vernon that she was
not displeased at meeting him. Directly

afterwards she happened to drop her glove. She fixed her eyes on him smiling, and said, ' Pick that up, will you ? '   It was a simple request to make, but it had in it that subtle note of command, the assumption of which by a woman is one of the first signs of an understanding. Vernon realised this perfectly, and his heart swelled with rapture. He was fully launched now on the tide of luxurious feeling; and he murmured secretly, as his eyes met his companion's, ' My own ! my own !'   The consciousness of having even in thought applied such a phrase as this to a woman, might be to many men a sharp self-revelation ; but Vernon knew himself far too well for that.   No lover, however, of the most earnest and genuine kind could have put more tender expression than he did into his voice, when he asked her presently, ' Are you always so early a riser as this ? '

' No,' she said; ' but I slept badly last

night ; and the morning looked so beautiful. I huddled on these things, as you see— anything I could get together ; I stole out noiselessly, and found myself in a fairy-land of roses, silent and fresh with dew. I hardly know these gardens yet. They are all a wonder and delight to me. I had never explored that little tunnel before ; and you may judge how surprised I was when I found you standing here.'

'Let me show you,' said Vernon, 'the mysteries of your own domains. Let us go up again, and I will be your *valet de place.*'

She turned, and she went with him. His whole being was possessed with the sense of her near companionship. They wandered on together through the more sequestered walks, slowly and often pausing, for the sake of some sight or sound. Now it was a bird's song that arrested them, now a prospect—a fan-palm, an arch of roses, or the peaks of the distant Alps : and such things as these were for some time all they talked about. Impersonal, however, as the conversation seemed to be, a sense of mutual ease between them was growing under its kindly shelter ; nor was this to be wondered at.   Conversations which are impersonal in form, are sometimes intensely personal in spirit.   The subjects spoken about are like the masques worn at a ball ; and a passion can be declared plainly under the guise of praising a view.   Things on the present occasion had not come to this : but the conversation was full, on both sides, of oblique hints of feeling ; and the subtle response of Miss Walters to every sight of beauty revealed to Vernon new depths in her character. She saw a thousand minute things that his eyes had passed over, even to the play of the dewdrops falling from leaf to leaf ; and when he pointed out to her the wider and bolder prospects, the feelings they stirred

in her seemed to be more deep than his own.
She looked, he thought, amongst the dews
and the roses, like the spirit of the morning
facing its own creations.

Presently he was preparing to turn up a
certain path, when with a quick movement
she put her hand on his arm, and stopped
him. ' Not that path,' she said. ' It brings
us in full view of the house ; and to the
observation of the servants, I think, we should
be a somewhat mysterious couple.'

When a woman once shows herself conscious that she is doing anything clandestine, a
man can rarely avoid some slight change in his
manner towards her ; and Vernon now, as
they diverged into a different path, felt that
he turned to her with a slightly less disguised
admiration. Any such freedom, however,
spent itself like a relapsing wave, as his look
encountered hers. Hers showed no fear

of, or no offence at, him.   It was full only
of a sad, earnest inquiry, as though she were
wondering what were his feelings.   As she
thus regarded him, she betrayed something
he had not before noticed.   In spite of its
radiant aspect her face bore signs of weari-
ness, and under her eyes were streaks of
transparent purple.

'Yes,' she said absently, as Vernon remarked on this; 'last night I was very wakeful.   And you,' she added—'I think the same
fate must have been yours.   Why, Mr.
Vernon, how is it that this has escaped me ?
You are more than tired; haggard is the
only word for it.   Has anything painful
happened to you ?'

Vernon was silent for a few moments;
then he answered smiling, 'You make me
speak to you; your voice acts like a spell on
me.   I spent last night face to face with a
spectre.   I spent it face to face with that

dead self of mine which I told you I had come here to find again.'

'Yes,' she said; 'you told me. To some people your words might perhaps have had no meaning. But I understood them. I have seen and known things that made them quite plain to me. Tell me, then—have you so soon found what you were seeking for?'

'Not it—no; but the phantom of it. It was the piteous phantom, not the returning friend. At least I think so; for just now I can be sure of nothing. Some day, perhaps, I may be able to tell you better.'

'I, too,' she said, 'have something that I may perhaps tell *you*—some day.'

Vernon was silent for a moment; and then he said to her, 'Give me that rose as a pledge that you will keep your promise.'

'It is not a *promise*,' she murmured; 'it is a *perhaps* only.' But at the same time with a slow, regretful movement she gave him the pledge he asked for. As he took the flower from her, their hands touched; for a few seconds they lingered in light contact, and then gently, and with no resistance on her part, Vernon took hers in his own. As he held it, he looked into her face silently; by a slight movement he made her turn round to the sunrise, and raising the rose in his hand, he laid it against her cheek. 'And you are pale,' he said, 'like one of these creamy rose-petals. See what you have given me— it is your own image.'

Miss Walters made no answer, excepting with her eyes and with her cheeks, whose living rose-leaf flushed with a faint carnation. A pause here might have been not without embarrassment. Vernon felt this with the instinct of the true love-maker, and he lit on a new subject instantly. He saw that in her left hand she was holding a small volume,

and with a voice quite altered, he asked,
' What have you got there ? '

'You would hardly guess perhaps,' she
said, with a little, flickering smile. 'It is a
Bible. I always keep it by the side of my
bed, and I always read a verse or two in
the morning when I get up. I make my
selections in a way no critic would approve
of ; and I'm sure I can't explain to you what
my exact principle is. This morning I chose
—shall I tell you what ? Let us sit down
upon this bench for a moment, and I will read
it out to you. No—' she said, putting her
hand on his, ' you must not take the book
from me. I don't want you to see the con-
text. "Awake, O north wind ; and come,
thou south ; blow upon my garden, that the
spices thereof may flow out. . . . I sleep, but
my heart waketh : it is the voice of my
beloved that knocketh, saying, Open to me,
my sister, my love, my dove, my undefiled :

for my head is filled with dew, and my locks with the drops of the night." '

The selection of this passage was a slight shock to Vernon, or rather the fact that, having selected it, she should have thus read it to him. But so absent from her seemed all consciousness that it could have any personal application, that he instantly felt ashamed of so vulgar a suspicion of her.

' They are beautiful verses,' he said, ' and you read them beautifully. I am going to ask you an odd question, seeing that this is only our second meeting. Do you say prayers in the morning, as well as read the Bible ? '

' I am a person,' she said abstractedly, ' who has said many prayers—many, many, many. I have passed nights of watching, just as last night you did. But women endure and suffer with more patience than men do.'

'With more patience, yes; because they have less to suffer.'

'Do you think that is true?' she said, smiling sadly.

'Not of all women—no; but of women like you it must be. The sufferings we talk of are those of the heart and spirit. I don't know your history; your burdens may have been more heavy than mine; but they have been burdens of a nobler kind; they have been such as are laid only on those who are fit to bear them. It is far easier for the saint to carry the cross, than for the sinner to find or raise it again when he has once dropped it in the snow.'

Again she looked at him with the same sad smile. 'Do you think,' she said, 'that I am a saint, then?'

'No,' he answered; 'you are not a saint. But I think you are listening for the sounds that the saints hear.'

Presently he resumed. ' I might perhaps have thought you were a saint already, if it were not for one reason.'

' And what reason is that ? '

' Do I venture to tell you, I wonder ? It is entirely a subjective reason. Well—it is this. If I knew that you would never know it, or that, knowing, you would forgive or forget it, I feel quite sure that I should touch your lips with mine.'

As Vernon said this, he again put out his hand to her, but, instead of meeting it, she raised hers to her face, and for a moment hid her eyes with it.

' Remember,' she said presently, ' nothing like that must ever come into our friendship. I have set you apart in my own mind from all other men, and you must learn to think of me not as others have done.' She seemed to be half pleading with and half warning him ; and her words came with a singular soft solemnity which at once fanned his feelings and made him resolved to check them. 'You must think of me,' she went on, 'just as I am to think of you. I am your friend, or, if you like it, your sister : and near relations, you know, are only absurd when they are sentimental.'

Vernon could not understand her. She was evidently all in earnest ; but there was something in herself, some subtle power in her presence, by which her words were more than neutralised. 'Surely,' he thought, 'this is not the voice of a sister ; and when feelings are merely sisterly, it is never worth while saying so.' He was stung by a hybrid impulse—the wish to obey her words and the wish to yield to her fascination.

'I will think of you,' he exclaimed, 'in any way you tell me to : and you shall let me call you by the name you have yourself taught me—my sister, my love, my dove, my undefiled. May I call you that ?'

She made no answer, but she clasped her hands before her; he could see that she clasped them tightly: and she sat motionless with her eyes turned upwards. At last she said, 'Could you only call me that truly, I would give up everything!'

'What,' murmured Vernon, 'should hinder me? My love, my dove, my un-defiled, I shall always connect you with the clear dews of the morning; and your friendship will revive my life like a second baptism.'

'You are reckoning without your host,' she answered, still looking straight before her. 'You know nothing about me yet, nor who it is you are speaking to.'

'What is wanting in my knowledge,' said Vernon, 'is made up by my instincts. Think, we have only met twice; and yet already you are my friend and my sister, and you have already—at least, I think so—put a new life into me. I feel like a dusty flower that has had dew fallen on it.'

She rose from where they were sitting, and began to walk on slowly. He followed her in silence, watching her graceful movements. A long branch of roses dangled across the path. She drew it towards herself, and stood still, smelling one of the blossoms. Presently, not looking at Vernon, ' I think,' she said, ' you had perhaps better beware of me.'

' For my sake or for yours ?'

' Not for mine, certainly. There is little need for me to beware of anything.'

' Nor for me either,' said Vernon. ' You will not ruin my peace. I should perhaps be a better man if you were able to. Friendship is all I ask for. I neither expect more nor wish for it. As long as you care to meet me, let my heart throb as I think of you. If you withdraw your caring, no matter how capriciously—well, I will not reproach you.'

' I doubt,' she said smiling, 'if even I could take things quite so easily as all that.   However, we shall see—we shall see.   We shall have plenty of opportunities.   And that reminds me'—here all of a sudden her manner became conventional—' I fear you called upon us yesterday and did not find us at home.   It is my fault that you had your trouble for nothing. I had written you a note myself the day before, to say that we were called away, and to ask you in my aunt's name to dine last night with us.   But—you see this is what it is to be a methodical woman !—I left it on my dressing-table, and it never was taken at all.   You would have only met Colonel Stapleton.'

' What sort of man is Colonel Stapleton ?' said Vernon abruptly.   ' I barely know him to speak to.'

'Oh,' she said carelessly, 'you can see what he is in a moment. He hunts and shoots, and has travelled over half the world. I am fond of him, for I've known him ever since I was *so* high; but there's nothing whatever in him; and I don't know that you missed much in not dining with us.'

'The night before,' said Vernon, 'I had a little dinner of my own. My guests were an old college friend, who, I am sorry to say, is gone; and a poor Catholic priest, who is staying near here for his health—an excellent man, but a little depressing sometimes.'

'A priest!' said Miss Walters.

'Not one of these country priests. My friend is an Englishman, whom I once knew well—a fellow called Frederic Stanley.—— You seem surprised. Do you know him? He is stopping here at the *Pension.*'

'Know him!' she replied. 'He is a sort

of cousin of mine, and is the truest friend I ever had in the world. Mr. Vernon,' she went on, 'whatever relationship yours and mine may be, Frederic Stanley was *really* like a brother to me. I could once have told him anything ; I could have asked his advice in anything. But I shall never do that again. There is one thing gone from my life—gone like many other things.'

'Why,' said Vernon, 'should his being a priest estrange you ?'

'It doesn't,' she said. 'I was not thinking of that. That, in itself, would rather help to unite us. It is nothing that he knows of that divides us now. Perhaps you—but let me look once in your eyes again ; just look at me, please, for one moment steadily—perhaps you will know what it is some day. But about Fred Stanley,' she went on. 'I should like you very much to be friends with him ; I feel so sure he could help you. I have an instinct, in your case ; I have a power of divination which tells me so.'

' We are old friends already,' said Vernon ; ' we were at the same college together.'

' You are not yet friends in the way I wish you should be, or I am sure you would not have spoken of him as you did just this moment. You call him depressing, and I think I know what you mean by that. You remember him as he once was, full of feeling for art and poetry, and full of interest in everything from science to society ; and you misjudge the change in him.'

' In some men,' said Vernon, ' religion kindles poetry ; it seems to have quenched his. There is something now about him that is hard and prosaic.'

' If this is so, I can tell you the meaning of it. His right hand has offended him, and he has cut it off deliberately. There is no one who naturally is more alive to beauty, or

to whatever can flatter delicately ambition, intellectual pride, or the senses ; and under the
priest's surface, if you can only once get under
it, you will still discover the man of the world
and the poet ; only you will discover them
crucified. He has given his best as a sacrifice
to the God who, he thinks, loved men ; his
best, remember, not that which has cost him
nothing. You will detect his love for poetry
in his very silence about it. Try—to please
me, try—to make better friends with him.'

'I will try,' said Vernon, 'both for your
sake and for his. But tell me this, will you
—what you have just said makes me ask you
—are you yourself a Catholic ?'

'No,' she said with decision ; 'that is a
thing I never could be. I admire goodness,
and I hate evil—you might realise how
intensely, if you only knew my history ; and
amongst my Catholic friends have been the
best people I have known. But how, with

their eyes open, they can swallow so much nonsense—I suppose there is some explanation, but I confess it is quite beyond me.'

'What sort of nonsense?'

'Frederic Stanley, for instance, thinks he could absolve me from my sins. I confess to him, and then he wipes the sin out. That is his notion. Now he might advise me, were I able to take advice, how to avoid repeating my sins; but it is ridiculous even to fancy that he could relieve me of those I have committed.'

'It is quite as mysterious to me,' said Vernon, 'that God should forgive sins at all, as that He should forgive them through Stanley's agency.'

'It may be so,' she sighed. 'I don't know what to think about it. A God who is not merciful is a monster; a God who is just and merciful seems an impossibility. Perhaps, after all, there is no mercy needed except from one human being to another ; and as to what we do to ourselves, perhaps that matters nothing.'

Vernon looked at her in surprise. ' Do you really think that ? ' he said.

She cast her eyes down, and began to put on her glove. She seemed occupied with the beauty of her own delicate hands. Presently however, and not without hesitation, ' I'll tell you,' she said, ' what I really do think. Religion, when a good man is possessed by it, makes him unselfish, and eager to work for others ; but it makes a woman selfish. It centres her whole anxiety on keeping her own robe taintless ; and it is always sending her to her looking-glass that she may examine her moral toilette. In the language of religion, this is female virtue *par excellence.* Well, I can't help thinking—I hope you won't be shocked at me—that there are other virtues in God's eyes more important than this; and that it will be asked us first, what work have your hands done? not, whether we have kept them quite clean in doing it.'

'I have myself,' said Vernon slowly, and not without some surprise, 'been inclined to accuse Catholicism of the same fault in its teaching. But the fault—and I am sure it exists—is really not in Catholicism, but in certain times and teachers; perhaps, too, in certain pupils. What the Church teaches is, that we all of us, women as well as men, have two duties—one to ourselves, the other to humanity; and that these are like the two feet on which the pilgrim goes to God. It is easy to sneer at the self-regarding virtues; but the Church is a true philosopher when she insists to man on their necessity. Unless we work for others, we shall have nothing to offer God: unless we keep our hearts pure, we shall be unable to offer it.'

'Are you, then,' said Miss Walters, 'a Catholic?'

'I don't know,' he murmured, 'what I am.'

'Just now,' she said, 'you asked me a question, and I believe I evaded it. You asked me if I said my prayers. I am now going to ask the same question of you. Do you?'

'Very ill; but still I do say them.'

'Then if you do,' she said, holding out her hand to him, 'pray for me. Now, go. The clock is striking eight. I must get back to the house.'

Her hand was in his. He held it, and it was not withdrawn from him. Here again there was a sharp, distinct struggle in him. Should he do something, or should he forbear from doing it? Impulse urged him one way; conscience, with clear voice, the other: and in a few seconds again conscience yielded. Nearer and nearer to himself he drew his fair

companion. She, as if spell-bound, offered
no resistance. Presently he was sensible of
the warmth of her face close to him: a
moment more, and he had done what he said
he longed to do ; he had kissed her on her
sad, proud lips.

The touch recalled her to herself. ' Go,'
she said, ' go! You don't know what it is
you are doing to me.' And without another
look she was gone.

Vernon found his way homewards in a
new, confused excitement. A wild pleasure
was struggling with self-reproach, and he
hardly knew the exact nature of either. His
mind was a mystery to himself, like a magi-
cian's crystal globe. There seemed to be in
it a white vapour rising, which would take
presently some unconjectured shape.

CHAPTER II.

THE after-taste of the above inter-
view was to Vernon not without
bitterness. He was beset by two
reflections of an opposite nature, and each
in its own way annoying. One of these
was, ' I was a fool to kiss her.' The other,
' I was a still greater fool not to ask her when
I might be allowed to see her again.' He
had already made his formal call at the
Château ; he could not repeat it without some
sort of invitation ; and it might be a day, it
might perhaps be even two, before his new
romance could be proceeded with. Fate,
however, proved more kind than he had anti-

cipated; for in the course of the morning the following note arrived for him :

'Dear Mr. Vernon,' it ran, 'there is a little town among the mountains here called St. Paul du Var, which my aunt has seen from a distance, and much wishes to visit. We have some thoughts of going there this after-noon ; and if you have nothing better to do, it would give her great pleasure if you would come with us.

'Sincerely yours,

'Cynthia Walters.'

Then came the following postscript :

'Remember, if you are to be ever a friend of mine, you must never act again as if you were more than a friend.'

He seized a pen eagerly, and had begun to write an acceptance, when he was cut short by a very unwelcome interruption. The mother had arrived of his little crippled *pro-*

tégée, and was begging to speak to him about
her child's condition. 'Damn her!' was his
first exclamation ; and then to the servant he
said, 'Let her come to-morrow.' The man
closed the door, but in another moment
Vernon had recalled him. 'No,' he said ;
'you may tell her to come in now.' A breath
of garlic announced the old woman's advent.
Vernon forced a smile and held his handkerchief to his nostrils. The story was this :
the boot required altering ; one of the steel
supports grazed the poor child's ankle, and, so
far as Vernon could gather, she was in great
suffering. 'Let her take the boot off, and I
will come to-morrow.' It was on his lips to
say this, and to say it with some impatience.
But he happened to look into the old crone's
face, and his purpose altered. 'I will be
with you,' he said, 'in the course of the
next hour, and will take the child to Nice
with me, where the boot shall be refitted on

her.' Biting his lips with irritation, he wrote
Miss Walters an unwilling refusal, and started
presently on his distasteful work of mercy.
' I wish,' he murmured, ' the little animal was
at the devil. Here's another day she's spoilt
for me.' By-and-bye, however, he saw a
brighter side to the question. ' After all,' he
thought, ' it has perhaps turned out for the
best. Had I been with that girl, I should
have committed myself more and more. I
should have said much and meant nothing.
Or else—my God, what a brute I am!—I
should have been using the very thoughts
that I should like to hold most sacred as so
many dominoes in an idle game of love-
making. I have done that already this
morning. Campbell was right about me!'

Reflections such as these kept recurring to
him throughout the day ; but they were not
without their rivals. The memory of Miss
Walters—her beauty, her delicate feeling, her

strange, ambiguous phrases, and the touch of her hand and lips—these would recur also, and make him again long for her company. His business with the child detained him some hours at Nice, and it was latish when he got home again. But the events of the day had done little to calm his mind. Prudence, desire, and conscience still stung and distracted him.

When he entered his library, he found another letter awaiting him, in an envelope not unlike the one he had received that morning. But he was disappointed; it was not from Miss Walters. It would have told its own authorship, even without the Duchess's signature. 'I hope,' it ran, 'that you have composed me those verses. However, it is not about these that I am writing; and I shall not dun you yet. What I want to tell you is that old Surbiton is coming over to the Cap to-morrow for me, to give a proper blowing up to the head gardener at the Hotel there; and, as we all know how particular he is about his eating, I want you, if you will, to let him come to you for luncheon. If I may give you a hint, I will tell you he worships truffles. There's another man here—a good sort of creature in his way. You would perhaps, if he comes, let him trespass on your hospitality also.'

The prospect of any excitement pleased Vernon at the moment. He wrote out a telegram to the Duchess, that was to be sent the first thing next morning. He summoned his *chef*, and had a long conference with him about a luncheon: then, thoroughly wearied, he took himself off to bed; and Lord Surbiton, truffles, and Miss Walters in turn engaged his thoughts, as by dreamy stages they decomposed into unconsciousness.

CHAPTER III.

HE sent next day to the station to meet Lord Surbiton, who in due time arrived. He was not alone, however. The other man mentioned by the Duchess had escaped Vernon's mind for the moment; and it was with no great feeling of pleasure that he discovered it to be Colonel Stapleton. He had had a nodding acquaintance with the Colonel for many years previous; he had had a vague impression that he hunted, shot, and gambled; and he had had passing glimpses of him at various London houses. But as for thinking of

him for two minutes together, he had never done
this till the dinner at Monte Carlo.   Colonel
Stapleton since that evening had been a vivid
personality to Vernon, and a personality distasteful to him to a degree he could not
account for.   He was aware that in some
vague way he might regard the man as a
rival ; but his distaste was different from the
mere distaste of jealousy.   He grudged him
Miss Walters' acquaintance, not because there
was much that could attract her in him, but
because there was so little.   ' Brute !' he had
murmured several times to himself, ' how I
hate those swimming eyes of his !   I can't
bear to think that her eyes should look at
him.'   This, however, he had himself seen
they had done ; and whenever he recollected
how often and how smilingly, Miss Walters
seemed withdrawn from him to some mysterious estranging distance.   But that was
not all.   In the very process of this with-

drawal she became more alluring to him ; and he felt himself at such moments grow sick with a new longing for her.

The Colonel's reappearance made him again conscious of this ; and it required all his tact to prepare to receive him civilly. It was a moment's consolation to him, as he welcomed the two guests, to find that Lord Surbiton looked somewhat bored with his companion ; and Vernon at once, in his own mind, taxed the Duchess with the arrangement. Here at least he was right. Her Grace dearly loved arranging.

Matters, however, went better than he had hoped for. The Colonel's manner was one of extreme good breeding ; and his frank and evident shyness at intruding on a bare acquaintance, at once made Vernon genial without the trouble of trying to be so. Presently, too, at luncheon Lord Surbiton lit up into vivacity. All he had wanted hitherto had been some subject he could discuss strikingly ; and he soon found, in the science of good living, one suited equally to himself and his small audience.

'I often think,' said the Colonel, 'that the best meat I ever tasted was a piece of mutton in the desert, that was cooked for me by a young Coptic girl.'

Lord Surbiton turned to him with a keen glance in his eyes. 'The Coptic Church,' he said, 'shows a singular lenity, does it not, in its rule over the human affections ?'

'Certainly,' said the Colonel, 'when I studied its constitution, you could be married and unmarried by it, just as the fancy seized you. You could be married when you went to Egypt, and unmarried when you left it. What one gained by the arrangement was a wider field of choice.'

'But suppose,' said Lord Surbiton, 'one of these women became attached to you ;

might there not be some difficulty then in getting quit of a lawful union ? '

' I shouldn't think so,' said the Colonel, despatching a fine truffle. ' Besides, distance can divorce one, as well as the Coptic Church.'

Lord Surbiton sighed. ' I regret much,' he said, ' that I have hardly set foot in Egypt; and I have yet been a constant wanderer. Like Shelley's *Alastor*,

> I have known
> Athens and Tyre, and Baalbec, and the waste
> Where stood Jerusalem.'

Colonel Stapleton stared. ' I, too, have been in the East,' he said quietly. ' I was at Jerusalem only a year ago.'

' Not,' said Vernon, ' as a religious pilgrim, I suppose ? '

The Colonel brushed a speck of dirt from his finely-shaped finger nail. ' No,' he said ; ' but I went there with a remarkably unrepentant Magdalene. She had had something

to do with some one who had something to do
with India; and I came across her at a loose
end in Cairo. It was a curious thing to see
a woman of that kind amongst the sacred
scenes one has heard about, and all that kind
of thing. She, now—this woman—what
should you think her great wish was? Not
to see Olivet, or Jericho, or any of those
places. Upon my word I doubt if she had
ever even heard of Abraham. What she
wanted to see was a certain dance at
Damascus.'

Lord Surbiton's eyes shot with a fire of
intelligence, and his mouth emitted the ghost
of a hollow cackle. 'I know the dance you
mean,' he said. 'I've seen it myself several
times.'

'I mean this,' said the Colonel; and he
gave a minute description.

'I must confess,' said Vernon, 'that I
don't myself see the point of it.'

'Why, my dear fellow,' replied the Colonel in a slightly aggrieved tone, 'it's the most damned suggestive thing imaginable. Though, upon my word,' he went on, 'I don't know if it beats some of the plays in Paris. Have you, Lord Surbiton, seen—— ?' and he named a certain play and theatre. 'You have? Well, in the second act, did you ever notice how the women's dresses were cut?'

Lord Surbiton with regretful interest confessed that he had not. The Colonel at great length enlightened him. It was now Lord Surbiton's turn to impart instruction, and he repaid the Colonel in kind; it may also be said with usury. His vivid power both of imagination and description made most of what he said quite unfit to be chronicled; and the Colonel's eyes, as he listened, swam with attentive moisture.

By-and-by they all adjourned to the garden, where a table, under the myrtles, was set with wine and coffee. This turned Lord Surbiton's thoughts into quite a new direction, and, greatly to Vernon's pleasure, he began quoting Horace. Colonel Stapleton since he left Eton had been no great student; but the sound of the Latin tongue reminded him of one classical quotation. *Post prandia, Callirrhoe.* He had hardly aired this small fragment of learning, when his manner changed suddenly; and, slightly embarrassed, and not without some feeling of delicacy, 'That line,' he said, 'was not very well chosen by me, since, after Mr. Vernon's *prandium*, I have to call upon his next-door neighbours.'

'Confound him!' thought Vernon. 'What the devil does he come over here at all for?'

'But Colonel,' said Lord Surbiton, 'you are to help me as her Grace's emissary.'

'I will be back in half-an-hour, if our host will excuse me presently.'

An idea flashed upon Vernon. ' Will you bring your friends with you,' he said, ' and we will all see the Hotel garden together ? '

' Certainly,' said the Colonel, with gay good humour. ' I forgot to ask you if you had seen much of them, since that evening when you carried them off in triumph. I watched you as you drove away, and a fine, spanking pace those horses of yours went, too ? '

' Who are you talking of ? ' exclaimed Lord Surbiton. ' Is it that lovely Miss Walters ? By all means bring her, if such a goddess will deign to appear among us.'

' Upon my word,' said the Colonel, ' she is a nymph or a goddess. Did you ever see any one with a turn of the neck like that ? She's about the handsomest woman in Europe — Miss Walters is ; at least, that's my opinion ; and full of fun when you only get to know her as I do. Then, the dear old aunt too—what a capital old lady that is! I've the greatest regard for Aunt Louisa.'

'You, I suppose,' said Vernon, 'have known them for a long time?'

'God bless my soul, yes! Why, when I first knew Miss Cynthia she used to sit on my knees and kiss me. But'—the Colonel suddenly started, and his voice dropped with alarm—'who's this coming here? It looks, for all the world, like the parson.'

Vernon turned and saw it was Frederic Stanley. 'Well,' said the Colonel hurriedly, 'I'm off to the Château, and in half-an-hour I'll be back again.'

As for Stanley, he began with a quiet apology: 'Your servant, Vernon, never told me you had visitors; but merely said that I should find you here in the garden.'

'Sit down, my dear fellow,' said Vernon; 'I'm perfectly charmed to see you.' But

he felt, at the same time, that the priest
was out of his element ; and was a little
nervous when he made him known to Lord
Surbiton.

The event, however, set all his fears to
rest. Lord Surbiton's versatility was more
than a fancied gift in him ; and on Stanley's
appearance his entire demeanour changed.
His furrowed face invested itself with a look
of thoughtful gravity ; and in his tone and
gesture, as he acknowledged his new acquaintance, there was the most perfect mixture of
fitting respect and dignity. Vernon thought,
as he watched him, that he had never seen
a truer gentleman. Stanley too, in becoming
a priest, had by no means forgotten the
savoir faire of the guardsman ; and now that
the Colonel was gone, the trio were presently
quite at ease together. The picturesqueness of
the scene was such as to strike all of them.
The blue of the sea that glowed through an

arch of myrtles, the glitter of the glasses, the red flash of the Burgundy, and the gold of the piled-up oranges, not to mention themselves in the green shadow—all this to three graceful scholars again suggested Horace, and the calm of the Horatian philosophy. Lord Surbiton broke out into several apt quotations, which both the others would in turn either cap or continue; and he exclaimed presently with all his pomp of utterance, 'If every pleasure, as Epicurus said it did, springs somehow or other from some satisfaction of the senses, it is poetry, it is literature alone, that makes them last a lifetime.'

'Epicurus,' said Vernon, 'would, I think, have admitted that. He was the wisest, in his generation, of all the old philosophers; and the popularity of Horace is one of the best proofs of this.'

'True,' said Lord Surbiton. 'There is

something, to me, much finer in the Epicurean calm than in the Stoic fortitude. The man who is stern, is repressing his emotion ; the man who is calm has killed it. Think how the two schools looked on death, for instance. The Stoic looked on it with a defiant frown ; by the act of an iron will he resolved not to wince at it. He braved it—' and here in Lord Surbiton's eyes came a slight flash of the Devil—' as a clumsy but virtuous peasant might brave some wicked nobleman. But the Epicurean had no need of resolves, or for making heroic faces. He met death, as Metternich met Napoleon, with the reserved grace of a man who is the superior in all but power ; and who yet gives power its due. Horace, as you say, Vernon, is a proof of this. His odes show us more clearly than anything the pathetic dignity, the politely-concealed contempt, the easy self-possession, and the superb high breeding, with which the Epicurean poet greeted and treated death.'

'Whatever we think,' said Stanley, 'about the religious view of the matter, that sort of philosophy is now no longer possible.'

'Goethe's mother,' said Vernon, 'found it so; and so did our Charles the Second.'

'I was thinking,' said Stanley, 'not of death then, but of life. What I meant was that a life of the proudest calm, though enriched with all the pleasures that can stimulate mind or body, is an ideal that now no man of insight can be satisfied with. We hear much, it is true, about the sublime calm of Goethe. I have almost thought myself that that sublime was very near the ridiculous. But, even were it not so, we are in Goethe's age no longer. There is a new spirit now abroad in the world; we are becoming roused to the sense of a new duty. I am speaking of the modern conception of progress, and

the duty of each one of us to humanity.
Your Epicurean with his calm, in the face
of a thought like that, is like a man who
sits on his luggage when his train is leaving
the station.'

'Surely,' said Lord Surbiton, with a smile
of surprised courtesy, 'the Catholic Church
generally does not regard progress so com-
placently : and humanity as an object of
worship I should have conceived in her
eyes to be little better than Antichrist.'

'Do you remember the last words of an
expelled Pope on his death-bed, and the
answer his attendants made him—" Because
I have loved righteousness and hated iniquity,
therefore I die in exile " ?   " Because God
has given thee the heathen for thine inherit-
ance, and the uttermost parts of the earth
for thy possession, Vicar of Christ, in exile
thou canst not die."   Well, in the same way
one may speak of the Church always.   She

cannot be outside progress, because she herself is everywhere. What she rejects in the
spirit of Modern Secularism, is not its truths,
but its false and delirious expression of them.
The religion of humanity, the religion of
human progress—these are really implicit parts
of her system; and it is she alone that can give
them a reasoned meaning. Many people,
we know, think them to be new revelations.
Suppose we call them so. The life of the
Church is a series of new revelations. She is
human nature perpetually unfolding itself.'

'I should have conceived,' said Lord
Surbiton, 'that the Catholic type of sanctity
was a thing fixed for ever, and that it could
make no terms with progress.'

'That is true,' said Stanley, 'in one sense,
but it is not true in another: for change and
fixity are not of necessity incompatible. The
type of a perfect soldier may always remain
the same; but it includes a change of conduct

according to changed conditions. His part
may be sometimes action ; sometimes a mute
vigilance : and it is the same with the saint,
in the world's changing ages. Myself I fully
recognise that we are now being swept
onwards into an era of new duties, and that
Almighty God may be demanding a larger
service from us.'

'I, too,' said Lord Surbiton, 'can tell that
a change is coming. You and Vernon will
see it ; but it will find the eyes of me and my
generation closed.' He was silent for a
minute or two, whilst he lighted a large cigar.
'I am not a Catholic, Mr. Stanley,' he resumed, 'but I am a student of human history ;
and, putting our obvious differences aside,
my view of the Church has been yours. I
am glad to find that I have so orthodox an
authority for it. She has seemed to me to
have embraced, and to have been the only
cause that has done so, all that the most

many-sided genius ever could or can be busy with. She was at once a perfect Saint, and a perfect woman of the world, and she could understand all man's lowest impulses, and yet still for ever lead him up to the highest. Me,' he went on sighing, 'she has taught at least one lesson—that there is little in this world worth a regret on losing it.'

'You are the last person, my lord,' said Stanley with politeness, 'one could expect to hear say that. You have fame, position, fortune—all that the world can give you.'

'It is these blessings,' said Lord Surbiton, 'that have made my heart so teachable. It may be wisdom to despise the world ; but to despise it thoroughly you must first possess it.'

These words were uttered with a ghastly kind of impressiveness, and received the reward they courted—a moment's complete silence. This was ended presently by sounds of a new quality. The music of female voices was suddenly heard approaching, and mixed with them came the Colonel's crackling laughter.

Vernon's heart had begun to beat quickly. He turned his head, and there was the group before him.

'You see,' said Lady Walters, 'we have come to return your visit ; and we hope you will show us your villa, as well as her Grace's gardens.' But Vernon had little time for thinking of Lady Walters. Her niece was there, standing side by side with the Colonel. She had just, as she said presently, been driving her pair of ponies ; and she still had on a tight-fitting cloth dress, beneath which protruded the tip of a varnished boot. The slightly masculine air which her present costume gave her, made a piquant mixture with her natural grace and softness. It seemed to hint to Vernon of some new side to her character; and it touched him, he knew not why, with a quick twinge of jealousy. The way she greeted him did not dispel this feeling. She was perfectly frank and friendly: she was, indeed, too frank. He sought in vain from either her eye or hand any sign of their strange, secret intimacy. 'Good heavens,' he thought, 'and it was but yesterday that I kissed her!'

In an instant, however, he was distracted by another scene enacting itself. Stanley, hearing strangers approaching, had withdrawn to a little distance. He had not even heard that the Walters were at the Cap de Juan; and he now first learned the fact by finding them there facing him. Vernon narrowly watched Miss Walters, as the meeting was taking place; and he saw how truly she had spoken when she called Stanley a brother. 'I had been meaning,' she said. 'to have sent you a note yesterday: but now to-night you

must come—won't you?—and dine with us.'
Stanley assented, and directly afterwards
withdrew himself.

The next step with the others was now
to see Vernon's villa; and Vernon in showing
it began to feel more prosperous. The
Colonel, it is true, showed a wish to engross
Miss Walters; but events at present would
often stand in his way. She was anxious to
be told about various books and pictures,
and on these points she could only appeal to
Vernon. Indeed for a good five minutes he
was almost *tête-à-tête* with her, as they turned
over together a portfolio of old engravings.
During this time their eyes met once; and
for a moment hers softened as if in recogni-
tion of their intimacy. Directly afterwards,
however, came an odour of Ess bouquet, and,
looking up, Vernon saw the Colonel behind
them. 'Fine engravings,' said the latter,
' some of those, I should think.' And then

in an undertone, when Miss Walters' back was turned, 'And devilish free, too, a lot of those old plates are.' He said this with a smile, and a glance at the closed portfolio.

Vernon answered him with extreme coldness. 'There is nothing, you may be sure, that is free in that portfolio; or I should not have been showing it to Miss Walters.' But the Colonel was quite unwounded. He only glanced over his shoulder to see that they were unobserved, and pulled from his pocket a small morocco book with a lock to it. 'If you want,' he said, 'to see modern art, just look into that. I got it at Nice this morning.' Vernon looked, but it was for an instant only. The contents were a series of photographs, such as in England the police would seize upon; and he gave it back with a curt 'Thank you' to the Colonel.

The above incident, so far as Vernon's peace was concerned, was the worst prepara-

tion possible for what was about to follow.
The party presently set out for the Hotel
gardens ; and, during the short walk thither,
kept more or less together.   The head
gardener was summoned.; the directions of
the Duchess were given, and the little group
was on the point of moving on again.   Vernon
looked towards Miss Walters, hoping she
might fall behind with him.   A look was
enough ; he did not repeat it ; in an instant
he felt what had happened—she was attached
to Colonel Stapleton.   Step by step did these
two separate themselves, letting the others
go on ahead of them, and pausing at times
on pretence of examining something, that
they might keep or increase their distance.
Vernon's heart was full of pain and bitterness,
and he walked almost silent by Lady Walters
and Lord Surbiton.   Suddenly a surprise
was caused by the sight of another party,
which made his lordship exclaim, 'It's lucky

that her Grace isn't here!' The trespassers proved to be a certain set from Nice, amongst whom Vernon recognised a few of his own acquaintance. Of this number was a certain Mrs. Crane, one of the fairest and freest of the married women of London. She not only knew Vernon, but his companions also; and, quitting her own party, she advanced to meet the others, whom a halt had again united.

'I'm dying,' said Mrs. Crane, 'to get out on that reef of rocks there, but the people I'm with have not got a spark of enterprise; and my boots have such high heels that I daren't venture alone.'

'Let me be your guide,' said Vernon; 'I know the way perfectly.' And he fixed his eyes on her with a look of shallow tenderness.

'I,' said Miss Walters, 'should like to come too. I have often watched those rocks and wished I could get out to them.'

The instant she spoke Vernon turned

sharp round to her. Mrs. Crane noticed the movement. But the impulses of the jealous reverse themselves in a flash of lightning, and the eager gesture was followed by the coldest of tones. 'The walk is perfectly easy,' he said, 'if Colonel Stapleton will give you a hand now and then. I have been there myself continually.'

Both the elders declined so rough a pilgrimage, and the two younger couples set off by themselves, Miss Walters still with the Colonel, and Vernon with Mrs. Crane.

'Well, Mr. Vernon,' said that lady presently, ' I've not seen you since that charming Sunday last summer, when we went down together on the drag to Maidenhead. At least I have seen you, though you were far too well occupied to take any notice of me. I saw you at Monte Carlo, and I saw, too, who it was you were talking to. However,' she added, as she glanced behind her towards

Miss Walters, 'you've a prettier one now to play with—that is, if Colonel Jack will allow you.'

'What has he got to do with it?' said Vernon, a little brusquely.

'What has not he? There he is now side by side with her. My good friend, don't you wish you were in the shoes of one of them?'

'Upon my word,' said Vernon, 'I can't say I do. If ever I want Miss Walters she is my next-door neighbour, so I could well spare her for an hour or two, even if all my heart were set on her. Besides, at the present moment, how could I even wish to better myself? You're very pretty, and I'm very agreeable; and when there's nobody better to hand, you know quite well that you have a *caprice* for me.'

Love and its kindred feelings can make the wisest men like children, and when it does not make them children in the best sense

of the word, it will often make them childish in
the worst. It can not only bring back the
simplicity, but also the tempers, of the nursery.
Of these last, one of the least lovely forms is
a sullenness towards one person, expressed
by effusion towards another. It was this
form of temper which now overcame Vernon.
He could not spend his day in making love
to Miss Walters, so he resolved to spend it
in making love to Mrs. Crane. Nor was
Mrs. Crane in the least displeased at
this. It was strictly true that, amongst
a hundred other *caprices*, she had one
that she could quite distinguish for Vernon ;
and as all that she demanded of most
of her male friends was, not that their
devotion should be constant, but only that it
should recur on occasion, no jealousy of a
rival made her in the least cold or *difficile*.
Vernon and she were thus soon on the
tenderest terms, as they had often been before

for five or six hours together; and by the
time they had reached the special rock they
were making for, they were pretty well advanced in a very unmasked flirtation. This
was just what Vernon in his present mood
wished for; and when the two others joined
them, and the four sat down together, he hoped
that his conduct would not escape Miss
Walters. This was a child's bit of temper, but
he had a man's self-possession in showing it.
He betrayed no sullenness to the person he
wished to wound; he addressed her instead
with an easy, genial indifference, which he
knew would be more effective; and an in-
tuitive sense thrilled him that each of his
smiles was freezing her.

At first, however, when she looked about
her she was lost in the lovely prospect. He
could see how its beauty sank into her, like
a stone into a clear well. 'What a contrast,'
she said, 'between that grey cliff and the

water!   And how one little plume of foam
tosses over the sunken rock!'

'Yes, beautiful,' said Vernon civilly, with
a slight, fatuous laugh.   'It's all as charming
as can be; though, for my own part, the love
of scenery is one of the many things I have
outlived, I think.'

Mrs. Crane patted him with her pretty
gloved hand, and said, 'You tell that to your
grandmother.   Don't flatter yourself, my dear
man, that you've outlived the sweets of life
yet.'

'You are right,' said Vernon, as he looked
at her; 'for I have not outlived you.'

Mrs. Crane acknowledged the compliment
with an impertinent little grimace, that became her admirably; and then, turning sharp
to the Colonel, she made an observation on a
slight red mark on his temple.   'What on
earth have you been up to?' she said.   'Has
Colonel Jack been fighting?'

'Upon my soul,' cried the Colonel, 'it was something rather like it. What made the mark was a pistol bullet.' This announcement created the right surprise, but the Colonel plainly was talking with no eye to effect; nor was there the least bravado in the way in which he told his story. He had been sleeping, it appeared, the preceding night at Nice; and, arriving late there from Monte Carlo, he had walked to his hotel from the station. In a lonely place he had been beset by two men, it seemed with the intent of robbing him. 'One of the fellows,' he said, 'a little chap, I knocked down in a moment. The other fired a pistol at me; and then, not seeing me fall, he bolted. There have been several cases of the same sort this winter; and for the future,' he went on, producing a revolver, 'I shall not go out late without this.'

The weapon was a small one, finely

chased with silver, and Mrs. Crane inquired
if it would really kill a man.

'It's killed two men already,' said the
Colonel. 'If it hadn't been for that, I should
have been a dead dog at Alexandria five
years ago.'

The tone of the speaker was in all this so
modest, that Vernon was conscious of a kind
of grudging respect for him ; but what most
amazed him was the aspect of Miss Walters.
She was staring at the Colonel, not with the
least interest or anxiety, but simply as if his
face fascinated her. As for him, he was
guiltless of any wish to be serious ; and
his next observation showed it. 'Bless me,
Miss Cynthia,' he said, putting his hand on
her arm familiarly, 'what a knowing coat
you've got on to-day ! Just turn my way and
let me look at it. How many inches round
in the waist does that make you ? '

She at once roused herself, and with a

smile and a frown together, 'Two inches more,' she said, 'than I should be without it.'

There was nothing in her manner that could be set down as coquetry; yet Vernon, whose perceptions were in a super-sensitive state, detected something in it that made him turn sharp away from her. Presently they all rose, and began to set about returning.

Mrs. Crane, though she was not piqued on account of Miss Walters, was far too true a woman to be able to keep silent about her; and as she and Vernon were descending the rocks together, she again opened the subject.

'Come,' she said, 'and tell me honestly how you like her.'

'I hardly know her,' said Vernon drily.

'Exactly; and I doubt if you ever will. I've seen her at Florence before now; and all the foreigners were at first sight in love

with her.　But it was at first sight only.
She's as cold as ice afterwards.　Every man
I've heard speak of her, has told me the
same story.'

'That fellow Stapleton,' said Vernon,
'seems to get on well enough with her.'

Mrs. Crane broke out into a little, malicious
laugh.　'My dear man,' she said, 'I saw all
along you were thinking so.　I can see when
a man's jealous as plainly as I can see what
his necktie is.　But you must be a goose if
you're jealous of fat Jack Stapleton.　He
was a dangerous man once, I grant you ; but
if he wants any conquests now, he has to go
rather farther afield for them : and, from my
own little observations at Monte Carlo, I
suspect he goes farther afield pretty often.
Besides, as for that girl there, he might just
as well be her elder brother, or her uncle.
He must have grown tired of kissing her
before she was well out of the nursery.　Just

listen now, how she chatters to him. That's not the tone of a lover.'

Miss Walters' voice, it is true, was at that moment raised slightly. She was preparing to cross the last piece of broken ground ; and Vernon distinctly heard her, as she declined the Colonel's assistance. ' Thank you,' she said, ' I can get on quite well by myself. Really, my dear Jack, there's no need for you to be so affectionate.'

Vernon knew not why, but he uttered an inaudible oath to himself.

When they regained the gardens, Mrs. Crane found her own party had flown, and Lady Walters announced with a smile that Lord Surbiton had done so likewise. He had been carried off by a fascinating Polish countess. ' Why, it's the very woman,' said Mrs. Crane, ' that my own husband's in love with. And of course he's gone off too. Now, isn't that like a husband ? '

'My dear,' said Lady Walters, 'you needn't put yourself out.   You know the train that they are going by, and I said that I would send you in our carriage to the station.   Or if you like to wait for dinner, we should be very happy to see you.   These gentlemen too, in case they have no other designs for themselves—we should be exceedingly glad if they would enliven us with their company.'

She looked round with an inquiry at Vernon and Colonel Stapleton.   The latter at once assented ; Vernon declined, having business, he said, that evening.   'Very well then,' smiled Lady Walters, 'we will hope for you at some other time.'   He trusted that Miss Walters would take notice of this refusal ; but he found she was standing even more near to him than he thought she was. The branch of a rose-tree had caught itself in her hat, and he heard her, in a constrained voice, asking him if he would disengage it for her. He was startled by her tone, and still more by the look she gave him. There was something in both of them, timid, piteous, and appealing. She reminded him of some wounded animal. He was in no mood, however, to be moved by impressions of this kind. He did the service she asked of him with the same easy politeness as heretofore; but when in the process, by accident, his hand touched her shoulder, he recoiled from it as if he had touched hot iron.

He discovered, the moment after, that Mrs. Crane as well as himself had declined Lady Walters' invitation; and a new inspiration seized him. 'Why should Lady Walters,' he said, 'be at the trouble of having her horses out? I can see Mrs. Crane to the station, if she has no objection to waiting here.'

Mrs. Crane's eyes flashed with a pleased intelligence ; and the matter was so settled.

'In that case,' said Miss Walters, 'we may as well be going back.' And the parties prepared to separate. As she took leave of Vernon, her voice seemed still unnatural, 'And are you *never*,' she murmured, 'coming to see me again ? ' This was not, however, the last thing he heard of her ; for turning to her aunt she said, 'We may as well dine punctually, as Frederic Stanley does not like late hours.' These simple words had a sudden effect in one quarter. Colonel Stapleton with a frown drew Miss Walters apart a little ; his face changed ; he had evidently lost command of himself. 'What ! ' he exclaimed in an undertone, 'and is Mr. Stanley going to dine with you ? '

'He is,' she answered coldly. 'Do you happen to have any objection ? '

'Objection!' cried the Colonel, still between his teeth. 'My dear girl, are you an utter, absolute idiot? What the Devil's the good of my coming, if you've got that confounded parson with you?'

END OF THE FIRST VOLUME.

LONDON : PRINTED BY
SPOTTISWOODE AND CO., NEW-STREET SQUARE
AND PARLIAMENT STREET

A ROMANCE

NINETEENTH CENTURY

VOL. II.

A ROMANCE

of the

NINETEENTH CENTURY

BY

W. H. MALLOCK

AUTHOR OF 'THE NEW REPUBLIC' ETC.

'DEFECERUNT OCULI MEI IN SALUTARE TUUM'

IN TWO VOLUMES — VOL. II.

London

CHATTO & WINDUS, PICCADILLY

1881

LONDON : PRINTED BY
SPOTTISWOODE AND CO., NEW-STREET SQUARE
AND PARLIAMENT STREET

BOOK III.

(*continued.*)

CHAPTER IV.

'NOW,' said Vernon to Mrs. Crane, 'we will come in and have some tea together; and you must give your own orders as to when you will have the carriage.'

Mrs. Crane was a woman who, as had once been said of her, could kiss with her eyes almost as unequivocally as with her lips. Several times during the afternoon she had already done this with the former; and they had not many moments been left alone with the tea-things before she repeated the operation with the latter. She was lying back in the depths of an easy chair, and seated on one of its arms, Vernon was bending over her.

'If you were nice,' she said presently, 'you'd ask me to stop and dine with you. If the others wouldn't wait for me, I don't see why I should go hurrying after them.'

'Very well,' said Vernon, still smiling down at her.

She pulled a peacock's feather from a vase beside her, and began to touch his face with it. As she continued looking at him, he felt he was becoming magnetised. His face was drawn down to hers, and once more he kissed her. 'Naughty boy!' she murmured, patting his cheek tenderly. Vernon now felt as if a net had been thrown over him—a net of the coarsest kind, and yet he could not escape from it. 'Don't you think you're a naughty boy?' she went on after a moment's silence; and then contemplating him, she uttered his

Christian name. ' Ralph,' she said. ' That's what you're called, isn't it ? Ralph—little Ralphie—is that what Miss Walters calls you ? '

A shadow at this juncture flitted across the window. Vernon sprang from his seat, Mrs. Crane recovered herself like an expert, and her husband, a few seconds after, was ushered into the library. He was a small dissipated-looking man, and was apparently in very bad humour. ' So here,' he said to his wife, after a word or two for form's sake to Vernon, ' so here you are, are you ? Why the deuce you must go off to those rocks is more than I can tell. We've returned this way, which we had not meant to have done; so you can come home with us after all, and your friends need not be at the trouble of sending you. It's lucky for you, Mr. Vernon,' he went on, with what was meant to be pleasantry, ' that you've not got a wife.

They lead one a pretty dance, I can tell you.'

Mrs. Crane and her husband were gone. Vernon clasped his hands on his forehead; he drew a deep sigh of relief; and hurrying upstairs to his bedroom, washed his face in cold water.

' Oh that beast of a woman,' he exclaimed, 'and more beast I to talk to her!'

The relief he felt, however, was only comparative. The reflections he was left with were composed of many disquietudes. His thoughts first went straying towards the Château St. John; and he was restless with conjectures as to what was now passing there. For a moment he repented that he had refused Lady Walters' invitation; but he was still aching with jealousy, and so this feeling was only momentary. Had he really gone, his mind might have been somewhat tranquillised. The Colonel's behaviour at dinner was subdued, indeed almost sheepish; and he left directly afterwards, by the earliest train available. As for Miss Walters, her ways had had a sad touching softness in them. She had done her best to harmonise the Colonel and Frederic Stanley; and, finding the former quite unresponsive, had given most of her conversation to the latter.

The Colonel's departure, however, produced a strange effect on her. She all of a sudden became constrained with Stanley, instead of, what might have seemed natural, becoming more at home with him. She did not, it is true, relapse into reserve or silence; on the contrary she talked on with a kind of nervous persistency, and seemed anxious to keep her aunt a party to the conversation. But her ease of manner had altogether quitted her, and was replaced by a liveliness that sometimes verged on flippancy. Stanley, though not on the outlook for any behaviour

of this kind, still could not fail to be slightly
struck with it; but it was not till later in the
evening that he gave any serious thought to
the matter.   By-and-by, however, as her
custom was, Lady Walters went to sleep by
the tea-table; and her niece, whose boudoir
opened out of the drawing-room, took Stanley
to inspect it and its contents.   It was pretty
enough, but as yet was in some confusion;
though even the confusion was not without signs
of taste in it, especially when seen as now under
a lamp with a shade of rose-colour. Some rich
oriental stuffs had been thrown over ugly
sofas; some flowers and palms had been
already arranged effectively; there was an
easel in one corner, with a picture of some
sort resting on it, and every table was littered
with books and bits of bric-a-brac.   It was on
the books that Stanley's attention centred.
He was far too wise a man to be always or
even often moralising, or to think he ad-

vanced his faith by referring to its claims perpetually. None the less, however, was it a
part of his very life ; by a process he was
often unconscious of, it coloured his view of
everything ; and his zeal for souls, though
many might see no trace of it, was still and
silent, not from sleep but from watchfulness.
When therefore on running over Miss Walters'
books, he found volume after volume of the
most pronounced sceptical literature, it was
but natural in his case to revert to her altered
manner, and, at least tentatively, to put two
and two together.

Something of the truth, it seems, was
divined by Miss Walters, for she said presently, 'I'm afraid, Fred, you won't much
approve of my library. I suppose you think
it is wrong to read Strauss and Renan, and
books about geology and evolution.'

'There is hardly a book here,' said Stanley, 'that I have not read myself, and I don't

think that wrong in me.   The wrong or right
of a book depends on what the reader gets
out of it, and out of modern science one may
get good or evil, just according to the condition that one approaches it in.'

'Well,' said Miss Walters, 'don't let us
talk religion, please, this evening; for you
know quite well that we shall never agree
about it.   Tell me, if you're not above gossip,
a little about Mr. Vernon.   It was from him
I first heard you were here, so I know he's a
friend of yours; and as he's our next-door
neighbour, it is only natural that I should be
a little curious.'

'Did you never,' said Stanley, 'meet him
before in London ?'

'No,' she said, 'though of course I had
vaguely heard of him.   What I did hear I
confess I did not much fancy; though there
were always people, I think, who believed in
his good qualities.'

'Once,' said Stanley, 'I used to see a good deal of him ; but that was before things had changed with me. Since he has been here, I have often walked and talked with him ; but it was some time before he ever thought of calling on me; and as, from his point of view, all the advantage to be gained was on my side, I did not like unasked to inflict my visits upon him. This last week, however, the ice has been broken ; and now we are good friends again. Poor fellow !—it makes me rather sad to hear of him, and I don't wonder if he is looked at in many different lights.'

This conversation put the two on an easier footing. Miss Walters lost her flippancy and became soft, grave, and natural. Stanley went on to praise Vernon in many ways. 'Naturally,' he said, 'he was a man of the finest feelings, and I think of the most generous aspirations. But there is something wrong in him, I can't tell what.   He was like a peach-tree : always blossoming, and being always nipped with frost.   He can do a kind thing, which would make one love another man ' (and he here told the story of the little crippled peasant-girl), ' but he does it as though he were anxious to disarm affection. Perhaps it is the craving for pleasure and the exactions of a brilliant vanity that have been eating his heart out silently.   And yet even on this view he puzzles me.   I have seen him in scenes of pleasure ; and yet pleasure has hardly pleased him.   He has taken it as a man might who was looking for an angel, and was consorting meanwhile with the publicans.' Miss Walters was quite silent and Stanley resumed sadly, ' And yet the world—not only its sins but its vanities—has a power we little dream of.   With quiet unobtrusive persistence, it can work miracles of evil on us.   It was only to-day, as I listened to Vernon talking, that I thought there was a remnant in him of what might once have made him a saint; and two lines of Dante flashed across my mind as I looked at him, " If vain thoughts had not been a petrifying fountain to your soul, and pleasure as Pyramus to the mulberry tree." What a true, what a perfect simile! I know nothing in any poetry that can equal it. Pyramus, do you remember, was killed at the foot of the mulberry tree, and it was his death-blood that stained the fruit red. It is pleasure, and dying pleasure, you see, that stains the whole fruit of life.'

Stanley had been looking towards Miss Walters, but not at her, while he was speaking. She, however, had had her eyes fixed on him, glazed with mute attention. When he ended she still said nothing, and her silence made him at length turn to her. She was pale as ashes, leaning back in her chair, and was now staring straight before her.

'Is it not very hot?' she gasped.
'Would you mind opening the window a
little wider.'

Stanley rose to do so, and when he came
back to his place she had her handkerchief
pressed to her eyes, and was in a flood of
silent tears.

The subject of the above conversation—
at that moment how was he employing himself? He was again seated at his writing-
table, as he had been two nights previously;
and the pages of his confession were lying
open before him. He glanced at them, but
with no look of sympathy. His mouth, which
could smile so softly, had a hard, unpleasant
curve in it; and, as he took up his pen negli-
gently, there was a shadow of a sneer about
his nostril. When he began to write, this
expression deepened; nor was it out of
keeping with the following deliberate sentences.

'I am a brute—a dolt—a hypocrite. If I met my own double, how my gorge would rise at it! "For God's sake," I should say, "keep that filthy beast away from me." And yet, upon my word, I am wiser than some of my betters, I think. Were I the Deity that I addressed the above whimperings to, I should —supposing my own existence—make short work of the whimperer. I should first kick, then kill him. Can I believe it? But two nights since I thought I would lay my mind bare to God! It seemed then to me a little rose-garden of delicate scented sorrows. I forgot, I suppose, that if the scented sorrows were there, there was an open sewer stagnant side-by-side of them. Ah, the shattered fabric of my whole moral existence! If a man can't respect himself, there are but two escapes from torture—to die, or to respect nothing.

'Wretched, wretched me, will no one

redeem or comfort me ?   No—no one ; and
indeed I do not deserve it.   As I look round
my heart there is nothing but unreality everywhere—selfish sham affection, a profanation
of what might have once been highest in me ;
and this, when thwarted, turning—ugh !—to
ill-temper and appetite.   Good heavens—it
was the other day only that I sat in judgment on Campbell when he told me what he
should do in his misery : and here have I
been doing the same thing ; or if I haven't it
is through no merit of mine—the same
thing—but not with the same excuse for it.
What my poor Campbell dreaded was a pain
that only his own truth made possible.   My
pain was only a wretched, diseased petulance.
And yet—am I right there ?   Oh, my Cynthia,
have I no true feeling for you ? '

Here he paused, and laid his pen down
suddenly.   The fact of having written her
name sent a quick shivering thrill through

him, and her image came before him with a strange painful vividness—her image, and that of the Colonel close to her. Then all the events of the afternoon repeated themselves, in a series of sounds and pictures. Not only did her laugh come back to him, the clear colour of her cheek, and the curve of her vestal lips, but a number of trivial details also —the feather in her hat, her slightly soiled grey gloves, and her sleeve-links, shaped like a horse's curb and snaffle. The impression she made on him was, he came to see, a complex one. She was instinct, as when first he saw her, with an air of high refinement; but there was a something about her too that was not quite in keeping with this. What was it? He could not tell; or he could tell one thing only. It was connected with that side of her character which made her tolerate Colonel Stapleton. The remembrance of this man gave Vernon a sick sensation—a man, so it seemed, with a wholly corrupted mind, utterly past the power of thinking a clean thought. This was Miss Walters' friend—her intimate chosen comrade. Vernon was not now jealous of him ; indeed such an emotion would be, he felt, ridiculous ; but there was something inexplicably tragic in that clear-eyed girl's familiarity with him ; there was something horrible in her want of horror of him. The eyes of the Vestal looking full into those of the Satyr, unknowing of the beast's nature ; his oily laugh mixing itself with the ripple of hers ; his coat-pocket in her very presence bulging with his hateful photographs—these images stung Vernon as they presented themselves, and filled his heart for Miss Walters with a strange passionate solicitude.

Again he had recourse to his pen and paper. He continued on the same sheet ; but it was not now to accuse himself.

'Cynthia, my darling,' it was with these words he began again, 'I am sending a mute voice to you from my dwelling to yours. You have moved me—you have moved me : I feel your life upon mine, and a longing, intense to bitterness, is stirring me now for your sake. Is it love, my Cynthia ? It may be, but I can't vouch for that. It seems to me like a wish on your behalf, far more than on my own. And yet I still would wish you in some way to open your heart to mine. I should like to have some possession in you. Keep one look in your eyes for me, and for me only ; and, ah, your lips !—shall I dare to breathe of them ? Whenever I think of you, I think of a " garden enclosed," my love, my dove, my sister, my undefiled. I think of dews, and roses, and of grey wet aloes, and of sleeping morning seas, and purple borders of cinerarias. Has the spirit of the morning passed into you ? or has your spirit passed into the sights and smells of the morning? Cynthia, you are also a mystery. I cannot yet understand you. We have all had our troubles. We have all done things to be repented of. Oh be true, my lovely one, to your own noblest self; and may our holy God keep guard over you!'

Vernon cast his eye back again over this and his previous pages. The whole of his manuscript was written without break or date, and, so far as appearance went, might have passed for a coherent composition. As he looked he smiled—not with a sneer now, but with a sense of soft whimsical humour.

'I begin,' he said to himself, 'with an address to God; and I end it with a note to Miss Walters. I am like a girl I was once told of, who used to dose over her evening prayers; and who caught herself murmuring as a conclusion to "Our Father," "I am very sincerely yours, Kate Dixon."'

The bitterness of the earlier evening had by this time passed away from him ; and he closed his eyes that night a little more in peace with himself ; although for many causes he was still sad and feverish.

CHAPTER V.

B Y the following morning, whether through self-knowledge or self-deceit, he found he had settled with his conscience to pursue Miss Walters' acquaintance, and to become her friend in the closest degree possible. It was not therefore without some palpitation of the heart, that he received a letter brought to him, in her own hand-writing. It bore the date of the preceding night; and he was still in bed when it reached him. Why was it sent thus early? What could she have to say to him? Would she decline his future acquaintance, and express contempt and anger at him? His conscience was by this time smiting him, and reminding him of Mrs. Crane. His courage failed him; and it was some minutes before he broke the envelope.

' You will be surprised at hearing from me,' the letter began abruptly, ' especially, I think, after the last few hours we spent together. You were angry with me, I do not know why. But let that pass; I am not going to reproach you with it. Reproach you! I can't help laughing at having written that. What earthly right should I have to reproach you? And yet, I am going to do something even stranger. I am going to presume farther on our short, our very short acquaintance. I am going to break through every rule of common sense, of common etiquette, of common everything. I hope you will not think me a mad woman. I hope you will understand me. I hope—I believe you will.

I am acting on a perception sharper than
common sense, which I do not think is
deceiving me. And shall I tell you what
makes me bold to do so? When I met you
the other day in the garden, I hinted that I
had had my sorrows. Now I tell you the
fact plainly. I won't beat about the bush
any longer; I am miserable. Sometimes my
misery is good enough to keep its distance
for a little; but before long it overtakes me;
and I live in a helpless terror that it may add
to itself. It has overtaken me now—yes
now, within the last few days, since I have
been here, since I have known you. To-
night it has become unbearable; and I can't
help writing to you. But why to you—you of
all people? Oh, I can't explain; but I think
you will understand why. You have had
your sorrows also; and you have told me
you have. You are looking for a something
you have lost, and that you long to find

again. So far, you are a faint, faint image of me. A faint image only—I don't wrong you for a moment by thinking you more than that. But even that gives you sympathy; and what I want is a friend. Will you be a friend to me? Will you treat me as a woman who you know wants help and tenderness? I am utterly lonely; I shall die if I am not supported.

' And now, listen. I don't want to alarm you. I am not inviting you to a series of confessions, scenes, and hysterics. Don't ask me about my unhappiness; it would do you no good to hear about it; but be my friend. Talk to me as if you trusted me; try to talk to me as if you respected me, and believe me I long intensely to do and to be good. Try to know me—will you? You have not to come far to see me. I am not asking very much of you. Indeed, Mr. Vernon, why should I be mock-modest? As I write, I

am sitting opposite to a looking-glass : and
that reminds me that many men would come
much farther for my company. It is not a
thought that I have any reason to be proud
of. What I want to remind you of is, that if
in the end you should not care to help me,
you will at least have had a little amusement
in finding that I am not worth helping.

'One word more. When next we meet,
don't allude to this letter. Act if you will,
upon what I have written ; and form your
own conjectures from it ; but as for itself, let
us consent not to mention it. So much
depends, in the building up of a friendship,
on what is said, and on what is not said. A
thought understood, or written, may help to
produce intimacy ; when the same thought
uttered would produce only embarrassment,
and perhaps estrangement. I think when
you have read all this, you will see I am

using something more than a conventional form, when I sign myself, very sincerely yours,

'CYNTHIA WALTERS.'

To this was added a postscript, that had been written the next morning. 'I am very unwell. I have passed a wretched night : but unless I am unfit to appear, my aunt, I know, means to ask you to dine this evening. She is devoted to you. Don't answer my letter, unless no invitation comes for you. If you dine with us, I can draw my own conclusions from you !'

As Vernon read this, a new life seemed breathed into him. The disappointments and the barren self-reproaches of yesterday were dispelled by a tumult of anticipations, and his whole being expanded. As for Mrs. Crane, she was quite forgotten. His late conduct with her ceased to give him any uneasiness. The memory of it fell off him like a cloak, and seemed so little a part of himself, that he needed no repentance to get rid of it.

The day, however, proved a weary one; till at last, about five o'clock, the invitation to dinner came. The long blank suspense had made his expectations keener, and by the time he came to dress his agitation was almost painful. His hands shook as he forced his shirt-studs into the button-holes; and he murmured to himself as he was tying his white neck-tie, ' I feel for all the world as if I were just going to my dentist.'

Never till this evening had he entered the Château St. John. A long corridor led from the hall to the drawing-room ; and as he followed the servant over the noiseless carpet, he could almost have thought he trembled. Much to his relief, when the door was flung open, Lady Walters was alone down to receive him; and he was thus able to recover himself before Miss Walters entered. The old lady was full of a pleasant if not a wise kindness. Age seemed to have mellowed out of her all the suspicions which give chaperons a practical value; and Vernon saw that whatever intimacy he might contract with the niece, the aunt would accept it on trust as the fittest possible. Her niece, it was evident, was in her eyes nothing short of perfection. Vernon remarked on the taste with which the drawing-room had been arranged. 'It is all Cynthia's doing,' said Lady Walters. On the chimney-piece were two delicate minia-tures. 'They,' said Lady Walters, 'were painted by Cynthia. They are her father and mother. That screen, too, is hers also, with the panel of lilacs and laburnums. But she has most of her things in her boudoir, which I have no doubt she will show you afterwards.'

'Miss Walters,' said Vernon, 'was, I think, only in London for one season, and I was at that time out of England.'

'Yes,' said Lady Walters, 'only for one season. But I hope she will go back next year. She is so much stronger now than she has been ; and it is a pity that a girl, so young and beautiful as she is, should see so little of the society of her own country. She hates society, so she says herself ; but I don't think that such hates are the right thing at her age ; and whatever they may say, young people don't really feel them.'

Just at this moment a door opened. There was a soft rustle of skirts, and then Miss Walters entered. Her appearance might well have justified her aunt's last observation. It would have been hard to imagine a form that seemed more made for the world, or who could have added a tenderer charm to its most delicate pomps and vanities. She was all in creamy white, with but two touches of colour upon her—a red rose-bud in her hair, and a red rose blown upon her bosom. Her whole toilette, as she softly advanced forwards, was like the art of a Greek sculptor, translated by a Parisian *modiste* ; and with its double air at once of fashion and simplicity, it deepened the rapt expression of her dark regretful eyes.

All Vernon's embarrassment again rushed upon him at the sight of her ; but it was not of long continuance. There are certain difficulties in which a woman is always a man's superior; and this was one of them. In Miss Walters' manner there was no trace of consciousness or of confusion. Her greeting was the perfection of calm high-bred gracefulness. Not by a glance even, or a gesture, which should be visible to him only, did she seek to allude to the smallest understanding

between them; and Vernon himself could
hardly believe it possible that this was the
same woman who had appealed to him so
passionately only a few hours before. One
good actor, however, sustains another. He
felt instantly that he was in stronger hands
than his own; and this girl who had been so
lately asking for help, had already been first
to give it. He was restored to ease by her
almost in spite of himself. All his appre-
hensions were replaced by a delightful form
of excitement: and he often thought, during
the course of dinner, that he had never in
his life felt so strong a stimulus to talk his
best, whether about grave things or gay. In
the presence of those two companions it
seemed as though a new home were receiv-
ing him: nor was this charming sensation to
be wondered at. He had fair reason to be
certain of two most flattering facts, that the
young lady admired, and that the old lady

was fond of him; and he, in especial, delighted himself at every proof of the latter, because it seemed to reflect upon him a softened pleasure from the former. Thus, impatient though he was in general of any personal catechism, he bore with positive pleasure Lady Walters' numerous questions. Many of them would have been irritating from their mere generality, if they had not expressed an interest to which he attached a value, and if Miss Walters had not been present to make it worth his while to answer them. He was questioned about his tastes, his books, how he employed his time, and if he had ever been in any service, diplomatic or military; and finally, if there were any pursuit to which he meant to give himself for the future.

'When Goethe,' said Vernon, 'was about my age, he called it a solemn period. He was able by that time to take stock of his

powers and character ; and he renewed his
resolves and deliberations as to what use he
should put them. I am by way, here, of
doing the same thing, and all my longings are
leading me towards some kind of public life.'

Lady Walters smiled, and shook her head
at him. 'Take my advice,' said she, 'and
keep clear of that. Political ambition is as
cruel a passion as gambling. It takes just as
much out of your life, and adds just as little
to its pleasures. A man with a good position like yours is far happier when he is
content as he is. I should envy a country
gentleman more than a prime minister.'

Vernon smiled softly, and turned his
eyes to Miss Walters. 'The public life,' he
said, 'that I am dreaming of, might perhaps
have no connection with even the wish for
office.'

Miss Walters answered with a look,
which said, 'you will explain afterwards.'

For purpose of explanation there was certainly no lack of opportunity. In the course of the evening, as had happened before with Stanley, Miss Walters took her guest and showed him her own sitting-room ; whilst her aunt meanwhile closed her eyes peaceably. At the prospect of another *tête-a-tête*, Vernon's shyness was again returning ; but when he found himself alone with Miss Walters, he saw that his fears were groundless. So complete was the nerve and tact with which she managed the situation, that any awkward scene, or *éclaircissement*, was quite out of the question. It seemed as though she had given him a kind of mental chloroform ; and that she had, while he was under it, done in a day the work of weeks on him. He felt that between them there were now no formal barriers ; by some noiseless magic they had all been swept away ; and he could speak his mind to her with a calm but entire confidence. He had no spasmodic wish to extort or to make confessions; but her presence seemed to act on his thoughts as the moon does on the sea it illuminates. They moved under her influence, and stirred with a new life in him; and he had the delicious fearless sense that when he spoke he should be understood by her.

'See,' she said, 'here are all my books, and the signs of how I employ myself. That picture over there is of a nun praying. Some time or other I will let you see it by daylight. Frederic Stanley, I fear, looked rather askance at my library. It made him think that I was very wicked. It will make you think I am very *blue*. Which of the two faults do you think is the greatest shock to a man? However,' she went on, 'I have not done my reading out of *blueness*. I had my reasons for it.'

'What reasons?'

'I was brought up chiefly among Catholics, and I once had thoughts of joining the Church myself. Thoughts!—I was on the very point of plunging. I was on the brink of a precipice, and the sea of faith was under me. The longing to throw myself off was thrilling up my back bone, it seemed: but something held me back, and I regained my senses. Well—since then, I have been trying to see more clearly what an impartial world has got to say on the matter; and I feel now that I have been saved from a mental suicide.'

'Which is the best,' said Vernon, with a half-serious smile, 'to kill your own thoughts, or to be killed by the thoughts of others? Will the Professor save you any more than the Pope?'

'You,' she said abruptly, 'don't believe in the Pope, do you?'

'Once,' Vernon answered, 'I was engaged

to be married; the marriage was broken off, and for this reason—I insisted that my children, if I had any, should be brought up Catholics.'

'Yes,' she said, 'I had heard that much about you; and had I been the lady in question, I should have acted just the same. I could never—no matter how much I loved a man—I could never bind myself at the altar, that I could rear my children upon a lie. But that is a question,' and she here smiled softly, 'that a brother and sister can have no need to quarrel over.'

'To me,' said Vernon, 'it is the only question of interest; and I want you to tell me this. Have your books of science and history led you to anything better than Catholicism?'

'It is not a question of *better*, if by *better* you mean more comforting. If that were all, you would have found me in sackcloth long ago. Could I only with my eyes open believe the Church true—were it on one side not so ridiculous—could we only discover some new proof of its authority——'

'That,' said Vernon, 'you may be quite sure we never shall : and if the Church on one side is ridiculous, so is every grave conception of life. If we cannot be persuaded by the proofs that are now before us, we should certainly not be even if one rose from the dead. It is we ourselves that must be changed, not proofs that must be multiplied. It is not the pole, but the needle, that needs to be re-magnetised. A fact, or a thought may in itself be single ; but its relations to men and women may be infinite.'

'Talk low,' said Miss Walters, 'for my aunt must be still asleep.' The doorway into the drawing-room was only clos'd by a *portière*. She rose, and pulled this aside for a moment. 'Yes,' she said, 'she is sleeping. She has

been very tired to-day.   Go on, Mr. Vernon;
only speak softly.'

Vernon went to the window and opened
it without noise.   A breath of the night air
came in, warm and scented, and the moon was
shining with a clear, unclouded brilliance.

'This,' he said, 'is the same moon that
all the world looks at.   But what different
thoughts it wakes nightly in a million hearts!
And it is the same with scientific discoveries,
and with thoughts and arguments.   If you
want another illustration, let us take our own
personalities.   You are one single soul, you
are one single human character; but are
there two other souls to whom you have ever
seemed the same?   Have you ever affected
anyone as you affect me?'

She had followed him to the window, and
was standing close beside him.   He had
obeyed her injunction to the letter, and he
certainly now spoke low enough.   She had

hung her head, as though the better to listen to him, but she now raised it when he finished, and fixed her eyes upon his.

'How do I affect you?' she said in a voice that had sunk to a whisper. 'So much depends upon that, that I have hardly courage to ask you.'

Vernon took her hand, he drew her towards himself, and slowly bent over her till his lips were approaching hers. For a moment or two she had remained passive, but she now gave a slight start away from him, though she did not withdraw her hand.

'Remember,' she exclaimed appealingly, 'what I have already said to you. Nothing like *that* must ever come into our friendship.'

Vernon made no answer; and as if by some silent understanding the two walked out together into the moonlight. They were both of them emerging also into a new period of their existence.

BOOK IV.

CHAPTER I.

WHATEVER might be awaiting them in this new period, the portal by which they entered it was one of unearthly beauty. The gardens lay before them in mysterious light and shadow, and seemed to lure them onwards. Distinct out of the mist of foliage rose the black spires of cypresses, and here and there an almond-tree, like a fountain of pink moonlight: whilst beyond, with a dazzling sparkle, the waves shook dreamily.

The window opened on a flight of marble

steps. They paused for a few moments, and then went down together. Miss Walters' last injunction had been spoken with an appealing emphasis ; but to any outside observer the result would have been hardly obvious. Her hand was on Vernon's arm, and seemed to lean on it ; and they were for a long time silent as only lovers can be. But though they were silent, the night was not silent round them. The green frogs made a chorus of soft innumerable murmurs ; fountains gleamed and splashed half-hidden amongst the orange-trees ; the roses trembled in the balmy moving air ; the leaves of the eucalyptus whispered ; and through all these sounds continuously came a yet gentler sound of the sea.

The hour filled them as it has filled so many thousand others, with a sense of dreamy spiritual voluptuousness : and secret thoughts in both of them came floating up out of their hiding-places, and gathered in soft impatience for the time when they should find utterance.

Miss Walters was the first to speak. 'You must tell me,' she began, 'about your public life, and the way you want to employ yourself. And you must tell me too,' she went on more tenderly—'you must tell me another thing, for I do not quite understand you. You believe in a God, don't you?—I think you do—and that it matters something whether we do right or wrong? Of course it matters to others, so far as our acts touch them. I know all about *organ and function*, which is the prig's duty to his neighbour. But I am not speaking of that. I mean as regards ourselves.'

'If I believe anything,' said Vernon, 'I believe that it does matter. If this poor human race of ours is worth a moment's unselfish care, it is worth it because we each of us have a soul to be saved or lost.   I have, and so have you.'

'Do you really believe that?' she said.

The question was put so earnestly that it a little embarrassed Vernon.   'You remember,' he answered, 'what I have said to you just now.   One may know that a proof exists, and may yet fail to be touched by it.   The soul may become demagnetised, and may cease to point to God; but one may know he is still somewhere, though one cannot tell where.   That is my condition, and the condition I am struggling to escape from.   I have come here as I told you, to arrange my plans for doing so.   It is a hard, hard work,' he continued presently, 'this piecing together of a broken self again.   I only see hope in one thing, and that, as I said at dinner, is public life.'

'And is your only hope then,' she said, 'in that kind of strong distraction?   Do you wish to forget your loss, not to retrieve it ? '

'You think of public life,' he said, 'in the same way your aunt does. You heard her advice at dinner to me : it was full of the old spirit of *goodness*. Rest and contentment, her moral was, are the truest springs of happiness. But the time for that teaching is gone, or is fast going ; even Frederic Stanley feels this : and though the spiritual air is growing each day darker about us, yet through the disastrous twilight burns the shape of a new duty—the duty to spend and to be spent for others. I call it new, but it is not. It only speaks in an ampler language. Look at me: I have wealth, and power, and I think some talents. It is to others that I owe these ; that is the sense that haunts me ; and the greater a man's power or place is, the greater, in God's eyes, is the number of his creditors. If I ever find God again, it must be with hands full of good deeds, not only clean of evil. Perhaps when I have something to bring him, he will again show his face to me. Such at least is my rather forlorn hope. It may turn out true, as I often used to say to myself, "He that doeth shall know of the doctrine."'

'You speak of work in the world. What sort of work are you thinking of?'

'There was a time when I actually made a beginning of it; but since I put my hand to the plough, I have looked back again; and I am in a worse state now than ever.'

'You stood for Parliament and you were not elected. Yes, I had heard of that; but that was surely no fault of yours.'

'No, and besides, that was merely a piece of by-play. I should have liked to have been in Parliament, certainly; but my wishes to do good did not stand or fall with my active part in politics.'

'Well,' she said, 'and have they been wishes only? Have you given the struggle up? Have you exchanged life in England for a dream by the Mediterranean?'

'One of the oldest,' he said, 'of all old mysteries is the division between will and wish. I have still the wish to act, but at present I have lost the will: and though our work may be all cut out for us, we can't do it if our arms are broken. I began my activity under a passing emotional stimulus; but that has now gone and has left me as weak as ever. For a life's work, unless one's own advancement is included in it, one needs some other motive than the strength of one's own conscience. On a night like this, alone, and with you beside me, what dreams I might fill my soul with, of deeds done, and of hope and faith recovered; but to see one's castle in a dream is one thing, and to build it with brick afterwards is quite another thing.'

Vernon felt on his arm Miss Walters' hand press heavier, and she looked at him with liquid eyes.

'Am I, then,' she said, 'any help to you in your dreaming?'

As she spoke they paused, and looked at the scene about them. They had just emerged from a walk of winding shadow, and found themselves suddenly face to face with the sea. It was close to them. They were on a long curved terrace, and the quiet ripples were lapping on its marble border. The sight for a moment held the two wanderers breathless, but presently they had to turn to a matter a little homelier. The air was warm, but Miss Walters shuddered slightly as a breath from the waves swept up to her. Vernon remarked it tenderly.

'It is nothing,' she said. 'However, just round that corner, in the boathouse, is a hat and a shawl of mine, which Jack Stapleton

left there.   I think I will go and fetch
them.'

They entered and found the things; and
again they paused together.   Into the dark
gloom of the boathouse ran the waves in
silver tendrils; the boat softly and slowly
rocked with its freight of shadow.   In the
course of a few seconds they could distinguish
the oars lying in it.   The same thought seized
both their minds simultaneously, and they
exchanged a glance in silence.   Vernon at
last said, ' Shall I row you ?'   She gave no
direct answer, and he had time to reflect a
little.   ' But what,' he added, ' would your
aunt say ?   It must be getting late by this
time.'

' Oh,' said Miss Walters, ' she never asks
me questions.   If I am not in the drawing-
room, she goes to bed without enquiring for
me ; and she will think that, to avoid waking
her, I sent you home through the gardens

not that she would in the least mind, if I were to stop out till midnight with you, except for my catching cold.'

'Come then,' said Vernon, and he drew the boat towards him; but she was still silent. He jumped in and began to arrange the cushions, and then in the shadow he held his hand out to her. At last by her movement he saw that she had consented. She gave him her hand, her form leant on his for a moment, and in a moment more they had shot out into the moonlight.

For the first five minutes or so Vernon pulled with vigour, and between themselves and the shore there was soon a good interval. Then his exertions lessened, the oars began to splash with a gentler dreamier cadence, and a consciousness of the situation dawned softly upon both of them. The imagination at times like these acquires stronger powers than ordinary; it transfigures places, and it does

what it will with distance.   It seemed to these
two that they had left the world behind them :
they were solitary adventurers on some far
enchanted ocean.   There awoke in both of
them a strange sense of exultation ; and at
last Vernon murmured, 'Listen, and I will
sing to you.' He seemed to have scarcely
spoken when the following song broke from
him :—

Hollow and vast starred skies are o'er us,
  Bare to their blue profoundest height ;
Waves and moonlight melt before us
  Into the heart of the lonely night.

Row young oarsman, row young oarsman,
  See how the diamonds drip from the oar ;
What of the shore and friends ? young oarsman,
  Never row us again to shore.

See how shadow and silver mingle
  Here on the wonderful wide bare sea,
And shall we sigh for the blinking ingle—
  Sigh for the old known chamber—we ?

Row young oarsman far out yonder,
  Into the crypt of the night we float ;
Fair faint moon-flames wash and wander,
  Wash and wander about our boat.

Not a fetter is here to bind us,
  Love and memory loose their spell !
Friends of the home we have left behind us,
  Prisoners of content, farewell.

Row young oarsman, far out yonder,
  Over the moonlight's breathing breast ;
Rest not, give us no pause to ponder,
  All things we can endure but rest.

The song ended ; but it had broken the spell of silence. Miss Walters murmured some vague words of applause ; and then said abruptly, though in a low voice like music, ' I want you to tell me one thing. You made a new start in life, under the influence of some strong emotion. What emotion was that ?'

Vernon smiled slightly. ' It was emotion,' he answered, ' connected with my plan of marrying.'

She smiled also. ' That is surely an odd way of putting it. Was it falling in love, then, that nerved you to do your duty ?'

' Indirectly you may call it that,' said Vernon naively. ' I realised that to marry was a very solemn step, and that it was the death-blow to everything that had hitherto made life enjoyable. It was as that I welcomed it. I would die through it into a new life. I resolved that thenceforward I would only live for duty. My personal interests would all be blighted; and I would lay up interests for myself that should be more than personal. I looked on marriage as a sacrament not of joy or rest, but of sacrifice.'

'How strangely you talk,' she said, 'it is not like a human being. You might be some cold sea-creature floating on its own element. What, if these are your feelings, made you ever think of marrying?'

'Perhaps,' said Vernon, 'I have given a wrong account of myself. It is not every one that can write his own history truly: our hearts and memories are littered with false materials. Some people think—perhaps you are one of them—that a man, with a will to do so, can of course confide to another his motives on any given occasion. But it is not so. There are actions we may account for in a dozen contradictory ways, and yet be doing our best, at each attempt, to be truthful. Try to catch on paper your own face in a looking-glass. Does the power to do that come to us for the wishing? It is as hard sometimes to describe your tastes or motives as to take a pencil and draw your own expression. Each is equally likely to elude your most painful touches. I perhaps made a wrong stroke just now. Let me rub it out, and see if I can't do better. Of course it was love that made me first think of marrying; but I don't think love acted well by me. He came like a porter, bearing a great pack of duties, which he left inside my door, and then he went away again.'

Miss Walters smiled at this whimsical simile. 'Then it was not true love,' she said,

' if it played you a trick like that. True love never goes away till you drive it.'

' No,' said Vernon, ' I suppose it was not true love ; and yet at the time it must have seemed very like it. However, the whole affair proved a *fiasco* in all ways. When I gave up my frivolous interests, I wished to live for larger ones. My wife that was to have been wished me to live for her. She used often to say to me, "Am I the chief thing in your life ?" '

' No doubt,' said Miss Walters, ' she would have been ready to live for you.'

' Only too ready,' said Vernon. ' But that was not what I asked of her. I wanted to find God, not to be made a fetish.'

' Still,' said Miss Walters, ' you are talking like a merman. Would there have been no help to you in the sense of her near companionship ?'

' If you mean by *her*,—the special person

I speak of, I doubt if there ever would.   It
it true that at one time I could honestly say
I love you to her.   But the love that I long
for is but half expressed by *I love you*.   One
must be forced to add, *You comprehend me ;
and you give a new life to my thoughts because
I can speak them freely to you*.   Or perhaps
this would be more accurate—*Because you
enable me thus to speak them, you are indirectly
creating them.*'

'And have you never felt that ?' she
said.

Vernon's voice dropped low, and he looked
with fixed eyes at her.   'That,' he said, 'is
what I feel with you.   I could speak to you
of my aims and hopes as I have never spoken
to any woman before.   My inmost thoughts,
at present, are like dim spirits in prison.   At
your spell they would come forth and embody
themselves.   You would touch my lips, I
should speak ; and there would be a new

world born in me. I feel your power now—
here, as we are floating on together. Some
of my thoughts you have set free already;
they can breathe, they have acquired shape,
they may take a part in guiding me. Do I
speak now like a merman?—do I speak like
a cold sea-creature?'

Vernon was far from conscious of the
directness of the declarations he was making;
but he was conscious certainly of the passion
with which he made them. There was a tone
in his voice which, had his words been merely
about the weather, would have winged them
like fire-tipped arrows to the woman they
were addressed to. She would be unable,
and he felt this, to miss their appealing
earnestness. He looked at her as he spoke,
to see the effect he made; but her expression
baffled him. Of one thing only he could be
certain; and that was, that he had not confused her. Then suddenly the thought flashed

across him that this was a woman who was used to be made love to. In an instant the air was peopled with hosts of phantom rivals, with whom she shared secrets that would be hid from him for ever. The hands of another man had lain clasped on hers; on her lips were the memories of another man's kisses; perhaps her heart was already in the grave of some dead lover. These imaginations fired him with a new longing for her. He would snatch her, he felt, from the arms and the lips of others; she should be his, and his only.

He drew his oars into the boat, and sat himself in the stern beside her. He was doubtful how she would take this, but he was reassured in a moment, for she moved a little to make room for him. Still she did not speak, she only softly looked at him.

'Miss Walters,' he said, 'Cynthia—why

are you silent? Are you angry because I
tell you how you have helped me?'

She gave a strange smile which seemed to
have something of pity in it. 'Once upon a
time,' she said, 'perhaps I might have helped
you; but I can never do so now. You have
known me too late for that. And yet I am
wrong. I can help you in one thing; I can tell
you to beware of me. I say this for my sake,
and for yours. I might so easily bring such
untold evil on both of us.'

Vernon put his hand upon hers, and
said in a whisper, 'I am going to ask you
one question.' She turned her ear to him,
and pressing her hand hard, almost painfully,
he said, 'Are you married to some one else?'

She drew back as if relieved, and shaking
her head, murmured 'No.'

'Then,' said Vernon, his voice once more
getting stronger, 'what harm can our nearer
friendship bring us? Harm!—it can bring

only good.' His hand was still upon hers, and now in silence he drew her towards himself, and he could hear her heart beating. For a moment she yielded passively to him; she was then again reluctant, holding her head averted, whilst her breath came quickly. Then again, and another change came over her. He felt her yield once more like a branch that breaks slowly. Her hand was on his shoulder, and his lips were on hers.

Whoever once had kissed them, he had made them his own now; such was the thought that thrilled him. And yet in his caress there was no warm vehemence. It was passionate, but its passion was tempered by a gentle earnest reverence, and a sense of solicitude that he could not account for. She seemed to have lost herself far more wholly than he. It was she, however, who first found her voice again. She slowly drew back from him, as if she were waking up from a dream, and looked at him with reproachful eyes.

'Oh, why,' she murmured, clasping her hands tightly, 'why have you done this to me?'

'Done what?' he said. 'Surely I have done no wrong to you. Is it doing a wrong to you if I can make you love me?'

'If you could do that,' she said, with a faint, unnatural laugh, 'it would be yourself you were doing a wrong to. But'—and her voice softened—'you have not done that; no, you have not done that.'

'What!' exclaimed Vernon in bewilderment; 'and do you not love me then?'

He turned to her in expectation of her speaking, but she said nothing. She was looking straight before her with her eyes fixed on the distance, lost in some self-questioning. Then her lips quivered a little, and she shook her head slowly. That was her only answer,

and for a time there was complete silence between them. Presently, however, a sudden
change came over her. A new smile lit her face
up, like the gleam of a spring morning; and
with a soft expression of passionless, pure affection, 'Oh,' she said, 'but I do indeed wish
you well. I do wish all that is best for you.
God has given you many gifts; I wish you
not to squander them. I wish you strength
and endurance, and a clear, unclouded faith,
that you may act up to the brightest light
that is in you. And if the thought will be
any help to you that by doing yourself justice
you are giving me pleasure, that help I may
indeed venture to offer you. Come,' she
went on, 'bend down to me once more. No—
not your lips, but your forehead; and I will
kiss you once there, as a sister or as a mother
might. The touch of my lips, like that, can
do no wrong to you. And now—take your
oars. It is late; let us row back.'

The two said nothing more till they were again floating into the boat-house. Vernon's mind meanwhile was in a state of dim commotion. He had partly the sense of a delightful rest in loving; partly a sense of hunger only half pacified. 'She must be more mine than as yet she is,' was one of the thoughts that shaped themselves; and with many variations this kept on recurring to him. But below all there lurked another of a somewhat different character, which, only half-perceived, gave its special tone to the rest. This was, 'Let me love her never so well, our tie will still be slight enough. She has told me she could never unite her life to mine. I need have no fear that she will ever prepare a yoke for me. No, we will not unite; we will meet on some neutral ground, in some lonely, sacred grove, far from the home of each of us. She shall be my spiritual mistress.'

He little thought how soon this mood was to change in him.

They walked back towards the Château, and the first pale glimpse of it keenly suggested parting.

Vernon paused in his walk, and turned to her. 'And is a sister's kiss,' he said, 'all you can ever give me ?'

'All,' she said. 'You must ask for nothing more.' She moved a pace away, and stood still, confronting him. 'Do you see me,' she went on. 'Will you please to take a good look at me. My eyes are clear ; my lips and my cheeks look young enough. You perhaps think me a good woman. Well, shall I tell you the truth ? To make me fit to give what you are asking for, you would have first to cast seven devils out of me !'

Vernon was well accustomed to feminine self-reproaches. 'Hush,' he said ; 'it is foolish

to talk like that. We have all done wrong,
and it may be right at times to acknowledge
it. But exaggeration of that kind must be
always morbid.'

'I do not exaggerate. I have already
ruined one man's happiness, as you will
perhaps realise some day, without my telling
you. If you were to count upon my love,
I should ruin your happiness also.'

'Nonsense!' said Vernon, with a quick
but tender sharpness. 'Of course, for all I
know, you may have behaved ill to some one,
but you have not ruined your nature, you
have not stained your heart, by it. I can see
you better than you can. It is wrong, it is
unreal, to talk of yourself as if you were a
Mary Magdalene.'

'You are right,' she said, with a cold
calmness that surprised him. 'You are
right,' she repeated ; and then hiding her
face in her hands, 'I am worse,' she ex-

claimed, in a whisper choked with sobs, 'I am worse, far worse, than any Mary Magdalene.'

All kinds of conjectures as to her possible past history had floated through Vernon's mind. But to think of a thing as a possibility, does not always prepare us for hearing it at last as a fact; and he, as he heard, stood for a time petrified, feeling his temples grow deadly cold, and the skin on his forehead tighten. For a long time he could do no more than look at her—at that form pure as a snowdrop, drooping her head so near him, her hands still hiding her face.

At last he said in a low tone, 'Speak to me!' But she gave him no answer. Then softly and gently he tried to remove her hands. At that moment, however, a sound was heard from the house : it was the sound of a window closing.

'Come,' she said starting, 'this has lasted

long enough ;' and she began to move quickly forwards, with her face still turned from him.

Lady Walters was already gone to bed, and a footman was busy putting out the lights in the drawing-room.

'Is the hall-lamp burning?' said Miss Walters. 'Mr. Vernon's greatcoat is there. The lamp is out? Then give me a candle, and I will open the door for him myself.'

She tried to hold the candle so that its light should not fall on her face, and she still refused to look at him; but when it came for her to unfasten the door, it was hard to avoid doing so.

'Don't make me look at you!' she said, as they stood together. 'How shall I ever be able to meet your eyes again? Don't you hate me? Don't you despise and loathe me? Tell me you do! Let me at last have justice done to me! I can't bear being thought good, when I am worse than the worst of women.'

Vernon took the candle from her hand and set it down on the table. 'Look at me,' he said, 'and see if you think I hate you.'

There was a tone in his voice by which she seemed conquered; for with a helpless resignation she let him put his arm round her, and draw her towards himself. Then timidly she raised her face to him; it was like a poor, piteous child's; and he, with all the tenderness of a compassionate elder brother, stooped and kissed her.

Her eyes filled with tears, and she faintly faltered, 'Thank you.'

'God bless you!' he said. He pressed her hand and was gone.

CHAPTER II.

HE following morning Vernon sent a line to Miss Walters, to say that, unless she would not receive him, he would call at the Château in the course of the afternoon. The note in its wording was altogether common-place; and alleged as his excuse for coming his desire to see her picture. She wrote him no answer, and he appeared accordingly. The servant's manner at the door at once showed him he was expected, and with a beating heart he was ushered into her own sitting-room. There she

was, standing before her easel, calm and
graceful.   Again his fears of a painful meeting were dissipated.   She had recovered all
her self-control and luxurious air of worldli-
ness ; whilst the pallor in her cheeks and
her expression of languorous melancholy
might have passed as the effects of a late
ball, not of sorrow.   Her hold over Vernon
was increased by this new aspect of her ; the
touch of her hand acquired a new charm for
him.   He stood with her by her easel, and
they discussed her picture.   The feeling and
power displayed in it made a genuine impression on him, quite apart from any thought
of the artist ; but connected with her it had
a special and startling meaning.   It was but
a single figure, that of a kneeling nun ; who,
despite her attitude, seemed less in prayer
than in meditation.   There was a crucifix on
the wall above her ; a devotional book of
some sort lay on the ground beside her ; and

tightly grasped in her hand was a species of small scourge.

Presently came a silence. She had moved a few steps away, and Vernon was still looking at the picture.

'Well,' she said at last; 'and do you still think I am worth speaking to?'

He turned from the picture instantly, and went towards her. She had seated herself in a chair, and her face was bent downwards. He bent down over her, and, taking her face in both his hands, he made her look at him. 'Do I *still* think so?' he exclaimed. 'I care a thousand times more for you than I should ever have done otherwise. I see your goodness and your truth a thousand times more clearly. Only you mustn't talk of yourself again in the way that you did last night.'

He smiled a little, and she smiled in answer. Then she said sadly, 'But it was quite a true way.'

He drew a low seat forward, and sat down beside her. 'Listen to me,' he said, 'my Cynthia, if you will let me call you that. What we all live by, what we all live down to, or live up to, is our own conception of what we ourselves are. If we subside into thinking that we are altogether lost and wicked, we are sure sooner or later to become what we think we are. To revive our goodness, we must realise that it is not dead. We must see it still in ourselves, and see that it is still breathing. But sometimes, if we trust to ourselves only, this becomes impossible. Our goodness gets so placed that we can no more see it, than you can see your own back hair in your looking-glass. What we should then do is to turn to another, and see our own reflection in the looking-glass of another's judgment of us. We may thus discover a truth we could never have taught ourselves. We may find that we are worthy of our own reverence still, and that what is best and highest in us is not killed so easily as we had thought it was. Let me be the glass in which you will study your own condition. Learn in my reverence for you how pure and noble you are; and only in my sorrow for you that you may have ever shadowed your purity.'

She looked at Vernon with a curious, mixed expression. In her eyes was an earnest gratitude, but on her lips a faint smile of compassion. 'Even yet,' she said, 'I think you know very little about me.'

'Surely,' he said, 'I know all that I need know. I have no wish to trespass on your secrets, or to stir up memories that I wish to be laid to rest for ever. Believe me, I can see you more clearly than you see yourself. A woman may err and yet not ruin her nature, nor are those the holiest women who need no repentance. None in God's eyes have renounced what is good and pure, who still

even from far off long for it. Certainly you
do that.'

'Yes,' she broke in, 'you are right there!
Oh God, how I have longed and prayed for it!
I don't suppose you could find a woman who
had a clearer sight of what is good than I
have : and yet no one can have shut herself
out from it more hopelessly. You say those
are not the holiest women that need no repentance. It may be so ; I am not even sure
of that. But, at all events, good women when
they need repentance, repent. They do the
one thing that I cannot do.'

'All can repent,' said Vernon, 'except
those who have made peace with evil.'

'No ; for we may love what we have no
power to return to. Is not that what Judas
did ? I am not, I think, in any danger of
hanging myself : it would not be a graceful
death. But in my bed-room upstairs—this is
perfectly true, what I tell you—I have a

bottle of laudanum ready, in case I should find any day that I was unable to endure myself. No doubt,' she went on, ' I could repent, if I were only my own mistress. But I am not. You see, that makes all the difference. I am the property, heart and soul, of another.'

A sick sensation came over Vernon. He looked at her in silence, with an expression of horrified inquiry. She, however, had still complete command of herself.

'We are each of us,' she continued, ' as we live on, building up within ourselves a second self, like the frightful monster in " Frankenstein," over whose actions we have no control, but for which we are still responsible. Out of my own past I have built up such a monster. It is my tyrant. It dogs me; it strides after me. Though I hate it, I cannot escape from it.'

Vernon listened with a quick sense of

relief.   Her words did nothing now but increase   his   pleading   earnestness.   'Hush,
hush!' he said.   'You must, indeed, not
speak like that.   It is weak, wicked, foolish.
Listen to one thing which will force you to
see how wrong you are.   Since you have
known me, you have done an angel's work.
You have breathed a new life into me.   All
my better self has gained strength again—
and through your influence.   Do you think
a corrupt tree can bring forth good fruit?'

'I——,' she said, 'and have I been of
help to you?'

'Yes,' he answered, 'and I only knew it
last night—last night when I parted from you
and found myself alone.   Do you know what
I did then?   I prayed for you—upon my
knees for a long time, and half the night as
well, as I was lying wakeful.   I have always
been accustomed to say a word or two of
prayer every morning, but these latterly have

been cold and brief. They have seemed only to keep up a sort of bowing acquaintance with a God that I could hardly speak to. But last night, when I had you to pray for, my words and my feelings rose as they have not done since my boyhood: and for the first time since then I felt that my prayers were answered.'

She raised his hand to her lips, and gently kissed it.

'I was awake,' he went on, 'at the dull gray daybreak. I saw

The casement slowly grow a glimmering square;

and oh, my child of the morning, my whole soul went out to you. I have become a new man for your sake in one short evening.'

'Don't talk like that,' she exclaimed, 'or you will make my heart break! Leave me to myself. You can do nothing, nothing for me.'

' I can,' he said, ' and I mean to.   I am
not to be frightened off so easily, nor does
what you say discourage me.   You talk of
your past, and you say that it is your master.
It is so in some degree—such is the case with
all of us.   But the greater its power is, the
more should that encourage you.   For what
is the past ?   Are not you every day, every
moment, creating it ?   And if your bad deeds
as they drift behind you become a monster,
will not your good deeds and struggles turn
behind you into a legion of angels ?   A bad
past is like a snake, whose head is the present.   Bruise the head, and the coils will no
longer crush you.   Just consider ; by next
year this year will be your past.'

' What use,' she said, ' would be one year
of good against so many years of bad ? '

' It will be the David,' said Vernon, ' that
will kill the Goliath who pursues you.'

She shook her head, and at the same time

smiled faintly. 'Some animals,' she said, 'when they are caught in a trap, cannot be induced to leave it, even when the door is open. I am told you cannot get horses out of a burning stable. As you said yourself, one may have a wish to do the thing and yet be without the will.'

'You have roused my will,' said Vernon; 'I will rouse yours. I will put my arms round you, and carry you off by force. We will have a moral elopement.'

'You talk of eloping; but who can elope from self? Will you ever give me strength to outrun my own memories?'

'Yes,' he said; 'that is the very thing I will do. Let me help you to form a new present, and whilst that is forming let us consent to bury the past. Then by-and-by, when we again go back to it, and roll the stone away from the door of the sepulchre, you will find no festering corpse, but only the grave-clothes purified, and two white angels keeping watch over them.'

He spoke with a mixture of so much fire and tenderness, that she seemed at last conquered by it. Her face softened, her lips relaxed and trembled, and her eyes, wide open, began to fill with tears. His, too, moistened. Then slowly she bent forwards towards him. 'Come to me,' she said. 'Come nearer to me.'

He slipt from his low seat, and knelt close to her. They might have passed, so far as grouping went, for a mother with her child praying. Like a mother too, with utter frankness and innocency she gave him a single kiss, and passed her hand over his hair.

'Thank you,' she said; 'you are very good to me. I will struggle, and hope against hope.'

Vernon resumed his seat, and, the little scene over, they were both calm again.

'I shall not,' he said presently, 'be a very

hard taskmaster.   You will let me walk and
talk with you; you will let me lend you books :
and, if you are sad and desponding, you will
let me raise your spirits.   Let us try a quiet
life together here, on these terms : and we
will see what comes of it.   If you want to tell
me more about yourself, tell me.   If not, I
will never trouble you with my curiosity.
And you too—you must do your part by me.
I want help just as much as you do, and you,
if you will, can give it me.'   He paused here,
and there was a debate in him of some
moments.   There was something he was
prompted to say by impulse, and withheld
from saying by judgment.   At last his eye
fixed itself on her exquisite hand and wrist,
as they lay before him on her dress of grey
velvet.

'Tell me,' he said, 'do you think that this
would be possible ; do you think that you
and I could ever make a life together?'

'Don't ask me now,' she said. 'How can I tell you what might happen some day?'

'Some day! What—must I wait for *some day*?' The feeling that had been a spark was now a flame already. 'Cynthia—tell me, my loved one—have you no love for me now?'

She looked at him mournfully for a short time, and in silence. 'Surely,' she said at length, 'you do not doubt my affection. I have said to you what I thought I should never have said to any human being—what I have not had courage as yet to say even to God. I would willingly think you had moved me to the deepest of all feelings for you. What may happen some day I cannot tell, but the special thing has not happened yet.'

'And yet,' he pleaded, 'you have kissed me as a lover might.'

'If I have,' she said, 'the more shame for me. I dare give you nothing at present approaching what you mean by love. It would be unfit for you to accept it of me. Take my friendship, my gratitude, my affection. They may not be worth much, but they at least will not dishonour you.'

'Well,' he said; 'I can wait. I will bide my time, and till I see some new sign in you, I will never again trouble you with my importunity.

CHAPTER III.

NOT many days had elapsed before Vernon wrote thus in his diary :—

'I am like a pinnace that has slid out of a storm into a water of glassy calm. I have a sense of shelter around me, as of crags and gleaming woods.

Hic fessas non vincula naves
Ulla tenent : unco non alligat ancora morsu.

I have at last found rest in finding something for which to labour, and in the literal sense of the expression it is a labour of love. Love—that hackneyed word!—a week ago what a wretched sound it had for me! and now, as I hear or speak of it, it throbs with meaning like an organ-pipe. The choicest lamb of all the flock had lost itself. My wanderer, my white wanderer, I am carrying you home to the fold. My holy and precious burden, you little know what you have done for me. I had strayed from the fold myself; I had lost all count of its whereabouts; but now, with you in my arms, I am finding my way back again. It is for your sake only that God begins to look on me!'

Vernon smiled as he re-read this, and then continued writing. 'During the present year I have made several expeditions with her aunt and her. I have been their guide, and have shown them some of the most striking places to be found within driving distance. We have seen old fortified villages, with their girdle of brown ramparts, rising on hilltops over their own grey olive-yards. We have explored for miles the windings of happy valleys, walled on each side with hanging pine-woods, and paved with meadows of the intensest green imaginable, and we have wandered under willows and alders, by the margin of snow-fed rivers. She is growing happy, she is growing at peace with herself. I have watched her violet eyes, and her cheeks like rose-leaves, and I have seen how

> **Beauty born of murmuring sound**
> **Has passed into her face.**

More than this—I have been twice with her to the chapel in the cork-wood, for Vespers and Benediction, and I have seen her praying. I too—had I only been alone, my God, I could have prayed too. My care for her has opened my heart again, has revived my faith again. Surely I know, and see, and with my whole mind assent to this, that what we are and what we make ourselves is something of infinite and eternal moment. Vice and virtue are as heaven and hell asunder. Space, with

its million stars, is as nothing to the gulf between them : and Thou, my Judge Eternal,
it must be that Thou art all in all. Soften
her heart! Cleanse her from all iniquity!
Let me bring her back to Thee! Mother of
Purity, she has knelt to Thee also. Oh
mother inviolate, consoler of them that
weep, refuge of sinners, pray for her!

'She is with me all the time I am writing.
I feel her in the air near me. She surrounds
me ; she is touching me whether her body
be there or no. I don't know exactly how to
describe what has happened. I could almost
believe, not in the transmigration of souls,
but somehow in the transmigration of bodies;
for, fanciful as the expression sounds, it seems
at times to me as if it were her blood that was
beating in my temples. A part of her body
seems to be mixed with mine. When I am
half asleep, if I put my hands to my face, it
seems to be her white hand caressing me ;

and sometimes I have started up in the night feeling almost certain that her lips were on mine, kissing me.'

Moods, motives, and affections are generally complex things. With Vernon in the present case they were so in a marked degree, as may be detected in the above extract. But any one who had judged him merely from what he thus wrote of himself, would have probably done him injustice. The passionate sentiments which he indulged himself in committing to paper, he committed to paper only. He kept his promise to Miss Walters, alike in letter and in spirit. He avoided all allusion, not only to the painful confession she had made to him, but also to his own feelings with regard to her. His one constant effort, in all his intercourse with her, was to direct her thoughts from anything that was personal to either of them, and to fix them on general questions and the wider interests of life. He made her dwell on such subjects as poetry, scenery, and pictures. He discussed various characters with her in fiction and in history, and the various tastes, qualities, and occupations that make men's lives so many-coloured. He tried to fill her mind with a yet graver order of questions—the various social problems that are perplexing the modern mind, and to extend by this means her ideas of individual duty. He often spoke to her also of the chief axioms of religion, and the history of the Christian theologies ; but he was careful to approach them on their intellectual side only, and to make no appeal to her feelings. Despite, however, the impersonal nature of this conversation, it became inspired, under his management, with a delicate, earnest devotion that is often wanting to more direct love-making. It would be indeed wrong in this case to say he was making love at all. An impression of love, he doubtless did convey to her, because, after its own fashion, his nature was then stirred with it; but he did not do this intentionally. What he intended to express, and what was always present with him, was an anxious, tender solicitude that whatever was best and purest should be what she most admired. He became almost morbidly sensitive to anything that had the least taint in its beauty, and he tried by his presence to inspire her with a repulsion for it. He seemed as subtle and insidious in suggesting good thoughts to her as the devil is supposed to be in suggesting evil. As to evil, especially of the kind she was in danger from, it was his wish that she should not so much condemn as forget it. The wound would heal better, he thought, if its progress were not examined; and every subject which they thought of or discussed together, he tried to administer to her as a sacrament of self-respect. He became too, in this way, a revelation to himself. Subtle moral instincts, which had been for years dormant, and as he thought dead, now woke to life again; and he found himself once more regarding the world with the solemn earnestness of his boyhood.

Beneath the surface, however, there were certain things that troubled him. Now and again her manner jarred on him slightly, though it was some time before he could explain why to himself; he had also two sources of a more defined uneasiness. One of these was the suspicion, which he could not be sure was false, that in speaking of religious questions he had assumed a stronger faith than he felt in order that her faith might gain strength from it. The other was the discovery, on his part, that she was singularly shrewd in her apprehension of religious diffi- culties—shrewder, indeed, than he conceived a woman had any right to be : and often, when she insisted on the grave nature of some of

these, he was tempted to borrow an answer
from Dr. Johnson :—' That may be ; but I
don't see how you should know it.' He
several times smiled to catch himself feeling
this ; and he at once translated his temper
into the thought that really had excited it—
' She has logic enough to see her way into
an objection, but not logic enough to see her
way out of it.'

These matters at times made his mind
misgive him ; but they could not embitter,
except for passing moments, the new life he
was leading. Every morning when he awoke
there was a day of duty before him, but it was
duty allied with the keenest form of pleasure.
His imagination wove for him a luxurious
world of enchantment ; and his conscience
looked down on it and said that it was very
good. He seemed to himself like a rapt
votary praying in a temple of roses, and he
several times repeated an expression that

Campbell had used to him : 'I am leading a consecrated life.'

He was in this condition, whatever view may be taken of it, when he received one morning a letter from Campbell himself. This was the first news of him since the day on which he had set out for San Remo. That was not a fortnight ago ; but to Vernon it seemed years : and yet, so much meanwhile had his own affairs absorbed him, that he had not had time to wonder at Campbell's silence.

'Well,' thought Vernon, as he surveyed the envelope, 'his post-mark is San Remo. That, at least, is of happy augury.' Here, however, he was not quite accurate, as the date of the letter showed him. He had misread the post-mark. It was Sorrento, not San Remo. The letter ran thus :—

'My dear Vernon,—I should have written long ago to you, could I have written with any certainty. I have been waiting till I could do that : but I may as well wait no longer. I am not yet in Hell ; still less am I in Paradise. You must think of me as one of those who are—not contented, but still hopeful in the flame. When I left you, I returned to Cannes to collect my luggage, and there, amongst my letters, I found the following :—" The plans of the person in whom you take an interest have changed since you were last told of them. She will not be at San Remo, and she is anxious that you should be told of this, as she has heard of your movements, and of course knows the cause of them. She is very anxious also about another thing, and one which I beg in advance you will not let discourage you. She is very anxious that at present you should not know where she is, and that at present you should not even try to see her. You could, no doubt, by taking some trouble, discover her : but if you regard her wishes you will certainly not do so ; neither will you do so if you regard your own interests. My only fear is that this note may not reach you, before you are already on her traces. It is for your sake I am writing, even more than for hers. Were I not sure that by pressing your suit now you would be ensuring your own disappointment, I should not be so urgent that you should yield to her strange fancies. She is a curious girl. I don't in the least feel that I know her : but this I do know, that, however she regards you, it is at least not with indifference. You have moved her in some way, and I think very deeply : so it is well worth your while to have a little quiet patience." I need not, my dear Vernon, quote you any more of the letter. The rest was only to tell me how the writer had heard of my movements, and that she herself was leaving Florence for Sorrento. Well—what I did was to go straight off to Sorrento myself, that I might learn more from my informant. I have not learnt much—at least not much that I can communicate. The details are all too slight to be conveyed by writing. But I have hope; I believe that I have hope. Ah, Vernon, the love of a woman who knows no evil, almost makes evil incomprehensible to oneself! Soft, tender, and innocent as my friend is, the thought of her is like a fire upon some of my past life. Tastes and habits, which I was long used to laugh over, now only fill me with indignant, burning shame. I don't quite know how long I shall stay here. I am awaiting more news. I mean to be patient, and not to attempt hurrying on things; and if nothing is to be gained by my remaining here, I may possibly find myself in a week's time on my way back to England. In that case I will propose myself to you for a day or two; or, if you should not be able to receive me, I could at all events get a bed at Stanley's *Pension.*'

This letter set Vernon thinking. But a few short days ago, the feeling expressed in it would have been a riddle to him ; and now, as though a sixth sense had been added to him, he saw it all clearly. 'And yet,' he reflected, 'between Campbell's case and my own what a difference !—more than a difference—what a contrast! He turns to another, and finds she raises him. I turn to another, and find I must raise her. Still,' he continued, 'here is one bright thought. Let me take it as a happy omen. If love has on Campbell the effect he says it has—the effect of a second cleansing baptism—*her* sins surely are fast being washed away. Her transgressions will vanish like a cloud, and like a thick cloud her sins. The shadow on her life will be as though it had never been. No—not so ; let me think this rather, that the fire of repentance will make the gold of her purity still purer.   And yet——' his train of thought seemed here to halt for a moment—' I do not yet know her thoroughly.   I know she has much to repent of.   I know she has much to purge away.   It is not that knowledge that troubles me.   I should love her far more could I bring her safely home again than I should have done if she had never wandered. What is it, then?   Or is it nothing—a fancy merely?   Is she not safe home already?   I cannot tell.   There is something in her still remote from me.   There is some " untravelled region of her mind " which I cannot get to.   When I am with her, when I am face to face with herself, I am conscious of it, I know not how.   I feel always as if there were some third presence watching us—some ghost that will not reveal itself.   Ah, Cynthia! will you never be quite open with me?   Must your eyes still have glances that I cannot tell the meaning of ? Must my heart still ache, and still be anxious as I think of you ? '

He was wandering in his garden when the above thoughts invaded him, with the leaves of Campbell's letter still fluttering in his hand. The uneasiness he felt was a surprise to him, dimming all his prospects like an unlooked-for driving mist, and he was trying to rouse his spirits by the morning air and sunshine. At this juncture a note was brought him from Miss Walters. ' I have got,' she wrote, ' a small piece of news to tell you. It is not very tragic, but still I am sorry for it. My aunt and I are going away for a few days, to stay at San Remo with Mrs. Charles Crane. She's a connection of that slangy little woman that you seemed to find so amusing ; but is not in the least like her. She is related to my aunt in some way, and is a very old and a very true friend of mine. She's somehow related, too, to poor

Jack Stapleton, whom I know you dislike so; but that's neither here nor there. Well—it can't be helped. Go we must, and that either to-morrow or next day. I want to know if you will come over this morning, so that we may make the most of the little time that is left to us. You needn't go to the house; but you will find me, at about eleven, by the little bay with the tunnel—the place where I caught you trespassing. Ah, those happy days that I have spent with you! I hate to think that there is to be even so short a break in them! Dear, dear friend—come to me. I do want you so.'

Vernon's anxieties, though somewhat vague in their nature, had had one effect upon him more intense than themselves. In proportion as they seemed to divide him from Miss Walters, they made his desire to be close to her more keen and more absorbing than ever : and the above note struck on his life like a flash of returning sunlight. The time

she had named for the meeting was but half-
an-hour distant; and there wanted still ten
minutes to it when he found himself at the
trysting-place. Early as he was, however,
she was there before him. She was sitting
on a rustic bench, with an open book on her
lap; but she seemed not to be reading, only
watching the sea-water. The sight of her at
once took him out of his solitary thoughts,
and as if by magic set him down in a new
world. The change was wonderful, and gave
him an intoxicating sense as though he were
being carried through the air rapidly to some
untold distance. She rose to meet him with
a bright, soft smile; and every movement of
her lips and figure charmed him with an
insidious magic. She had on a new dress, of
a delicate shade of brown, which fitted her to
perfection. Her hat, her gloves, and the
border of her pocket-handkerchief were all of
the same colour. From the worldly point of
view she had never looked more fascinating.

She read his admiration in his eyes, and she met his glance with a more than usual tenderness. She held his hand too, in greeting him, with a more lingering pressure.

'I'm glad,' she said presently, 'that you like my frock. It's my maid's handiwork.' And then turning her back on him, 'Does it fit well? Tell me.'

The temptation was too much for Vernon. He put his hand on her shoulder, and let it slip down to her waist. She made no struggle; he felt her yield to his touch; and, still holding her, he led her back to the seat.

'You are looking beautiful to-day,' he murmured.

'I'm glad of that,' she said. 'I should like your last impressions to be nice of me. Don't you admire my rose too?'

It was in her button-hole, and Vernon stooped forward to smell it. As he was slowly drawing back, her breath stirred his hair. He raised his eyes, and his lips were close to hers. Neither of them spoke : they each drew a breath sharply : in another instant the outer world was dark to them, and their whole universe was nothing but a single kiss.

It might have seemed natural, when they again woke to daylight, that Vernon should now renew in words his former declaration of affection. But for some secret cause he was not moved to do so. The occurrence just narrated had not put him in tune for it : and the only sign, when they spoke, of what had just passed between them, was not in the subject spoken about, but in the peculiar tone of their voices.

Vernon said, ' Had you been long waiting, when I came ? '

' About twenty minutes. I was out earlier than I thought I should be. I brought a book with me and read a page, and since then I have been watching the water. The little bay is like a pool of crystal. Those rifts in the rocks—I have been fancying them sea nymphs' grottoes! And the open sea outside—how broad, and blue, and free; and how gaily the sunlight dances on it! Do you see what I have been reading? It is the translation you made for me from the Odyssey, of the journey of Hermes to Calypso. This is just the day, and this is just the place, for it. Read it over again to me.'

She closed her eyes to listen, and Vernon read.

The Slayer of Argus on Pieria's crest
   Pitched for a moment, then from off the steep
Dropped like a diver to the sea's broad breast,
   With feathered ankles, and the wand of sleep;
And as a sea-gull fishing skims its way
   Over the seedless fields where none may reap,
Wetting its white wings with the puffs of spray,
   So went the God, breathing the breeze and brine,
Until at last he reached the isle, that lay
   Very far off, in strange seas sapphirine.
There on the beach he lighted, and he went
   Straight to the cave where dwelt the nymph divine
With the renownèd locks-luxuriant:
   And in the cave he found her. At her side

A great fire burned of smelling wood that sent
  A fragrance of split cedar far and wide ;
And she meanwhile with lips of melody
  Sate singing, and a golden shuttle plied !

Miss Walters here interrupted him, with a smile. ' I think,' she said, ' I should have made a very good Greek nymph. I should have looked very pretty in the water. How delightful to have winged one's way as Hermes did, and to have felt the sea-wind blowing over all one's limbs, and to have been at peace with nature ! Calypso could yield herself to all the beauty round her. She had no feud with the gladness of the violet-coloured sea, and the sunshine, nor with her lawny uplands of green parsley and violets. Had I been a Calypso, I might have sheltered you as a Ulysses—for you know you are a wanderer—if you would not have been too proud to share a cave with me.'

Vernon glanced at her for a moment, and her look certainly was curiously in keeping

with her wishes.   But his eyes did not dwell
on her.   He abruptly folded his arms, and
subsided into complete silence.   Presently
his brows contracted ; his face assumed a look
of distress and pain, and then again this
softened into sadness.   At last he turned to
Miss Walters, and spoke very tenderly.

' Cynthia,' he began, ' there are certain
subjects about which we agreed to be silent
for a time.'

She interrupted him.   ' I know there are,'
she said a little wearily ; 'but don't let us talk
about them now.'   And as she said this she
moved a little nearer to him.

The sense of her touch was like a dissolving charm.   It might have been Calypso
herself that was pressing so softly to his
side—Calypso acclimatised to the air of the
present century.   He felt a thrill pass from
her body to his, and a strong impulse was
rising in him to fold her once more in his

arms. But impulse was this time thwarted, and will gained the victory.

' Don't be afraid,' he said. ' I am going to talk of nothing that will pain you; but I want to ask you one simple question—perhaps two.'

His eyes, as he spoke, were full of a pure, grave earnestness, and, as she caught their expression, she gently drew back a little. He now put his hand out to her, but she would not take it. She only said, still speaking wearily, 'Well—ask what you want to ask me.'

'Do you remember,' he began, 'that when first I knew you, you told me you were unhappy. I want to ask if you are at all restored to happiness now?'

' I have been very happy with you,' she said, 'very, very, very! I never thought when I came here that I should ever be so happy again. Then all the world was blank, and dark, and hateful to me ; and now this place—these delicious gardens—I have grown to love them ; and it is you who have made me do so.'

When Vernon next spoke, he did so with more embarrassment. He even blushed a little, and his words came slowly. 'Tell me this too,' he said. 'Do not you find that the memories and the thoughts that troubled you have passed away like a dream? They have been no real part of your pure, high nature. You have had but to shake your wings, and you have soared away from them.'

'Whilst you are with me,' she said, 'such things never trouble me. You always give me a sense of safety and protection, as though your arms were round me. I can venture to take a happy interest in all that I once cared for ; and the shadows that used to threaten me are obliged to keep their distance. Even when I am alone at night they know that I am going to meet you in the morning, and that now, when I wake up, I have something each day to look forward to. It is your doing —yes, yours—the whole of this.'

'I am glad,' he said hurriedly, 'if I have been of any help to you ; but this new peace of mind surely does not depend upon me ? What I want to feel sure of is, that you have recovered your old trust in yourself, and that you are again reconciled with your best and purest nature.'

'You have taught me,' she said, 'to love what is best and purest. I shall go on loving them if you are there to encourage me. I shall love them for your sake.'

'What on earth,' he said, 'have I got to do with it ? You hardly, I think, understand my question. Good is good, no matter what I think about it; and you had loved *it*, and hated its opposite, long before you had ever heard of my existence. Isn't that so ? '

'It is,' she said. 'By nature, I think, I was a very good person.'

'Well then, what I want is that you should recover your own nature. It is this that I have asked of God, in my prayers for you. I wish you to love goodness for its own sake and for yours. Do you think virtue is virtue or purity is purity to us, if we value them only as the taste or the toy of another? What I want you to say to me is not "I love virtue because you love it;" but "I love you because you love virtue."'

She hung her head for a moment as if lost in thought, and he watched for her answer. Presently there broke from her a little, soft murmur of petulance. 'Why do you vex me?' she said; 'you are spoiling our last morning.' And then raising her eyes she fixed them full upon him. As he met their gaze they seemed to expand and deepen, and soften second by second into a liquid tenderness. Her lips parted a little, a flush stole over her cheek, she opened her arms as if to call him to herself, and at last, in a breathless whisper, she said 'Come!' She saw that he did not stir, and she moved her head imperiously. 'Come,' she repeated, 'come closer. I want you here. There is something I wish to tell you.'

He did as she commanded; he moved quite close to her, and in another instant her fair arms were round him, pressing him to her breathing bosom. Her lips were close to his ear. 'My own one,' she said, 'I love you;' and still holding him, and almost in the same breath, 'you must pay me,' she said, 'for having told you that. Kiss me—kiss me on the mouth, and say that you love me too.'

In lovers' ejaculations there is considerable sameness probably. It may be enough to say that Vernon's response had all in it that could mark the most earnest feeling; and for a few delightful moments her embrace brought perfect peace to him. He had no thought except that she was holding him.

'My own one,' she went on presently, 'this has come at last; but it has been growing up in me ever since I saw you. My first dislike of you at Monte Carlo was only the other side of attraction. I wanted you for myself—I'm sure it must have been that really, and I couldn't bear to see you in unworthy company.' At last her arms released him, and the two exchanged glances. 'Tell me,' she murmured, 'are you happy now?'

'Yes, and no,' he said; and there was then a long silence. 'Cynthia, even yet you have not answered my question.'

'What question?' she said. 'Do you mean if I love goodness? Oh, if I do not yet' (and she pressed his hand to her lips), 'you shall teach me to. You shall teach me everything. You shall do exactly what you

will with me. I will follow you like a dog.
I will breathe your breath, I will think your
thoughts, I will only live through you. Every
thought of my mind, every passion of my
body, shall be yours, and yours only. You
shall fill my being so completely that there
shall be no room in it left for evil.'

'My beloved,' said Vernon, 'you want a
better guide than me.'

'You are quite good enough. You are
all I should ever long for.'

'But suppose I died by the way : what
then ? What I am anxious for is, that you
should have a securer helper. I hope I do
not vex you; but let me talk on a little.
What I want to be assured of is that, supposing I were to be taken from you—suppose
I were die, for instance—you would still have
the same incentive to be true to your highest
nature.'

'If you were to die,' she said, 'I think I

should. I should wish to follow where you had gone before.'

'Well, put death out of the question. Suppose, simply, that somehow I did not care for you?'

'In that case I don't know what would happen. Why do you ask? Cannot you be content to let things be as they are? I love you, and you help me to love goodness; but without your help I don't know that I could be sure of myself. Why should I pretend what is not true? My memory is still full of the past; no magic can alter that; and if you went from me, and made a vacuum in my present, the past would probably rush in and fill it up.'

'Listen to me,' said Vernon, with a sudden coldness in his voice. 'Let us suppose I am very fond of the smell of eau-de-cologne. Do you think that if I had none left in my bottle, I should dip my pocket-handkerchief in the next drain as a sub-stitute ?'

'I think you would be very silly if you did,' she said, her voice growing cold also.

'Then would you not be equally or even more silly, if, on losing a comrade in the search for the thing you loved, you were to try to console yourself by seeking the thing you hated ?'

'Only the worst of it is, you see,' she said with a slight laugh, 'that the things that would console me are not things I hate. If it were so I should not be what I am. When drunkards have not got wine, they will drink stuff out of the next spirit-lamp.'

'Cynthia,' he exclaimed, with an intensity that was half anger, half earnestness, 'I will not have you speak like this ; you do not mean it, and I cannot endure to hear you.' Then his voice softened. 'What is it—tell me—what makes you so distrust yourself ?

Forgive me if I just now spoke a little roughly. It all comes from my intense care for you. My Cynthia, let me take your burden, if you will not be afraid to trust me. Surely it is not that ——.' Here he hesitated and looked in her eyes pleadingly. 'It is not—is it—that you love that other man still ?'

She flushed scarlet, and she turned her face away from him. ' No,' she said ; 'good God, no !'

'What, then, is it ? You are a complete mystery to me. If only I knew the truth, I could be of so much more help to you.'

'Don't ask me,' she said. 'Why harp upon this one subject ? Is there any use in trying to stir up all the dregs of my nature ? In all conscience I have told you enough already. Do you know,' she went on with a smile of expiring tenderness, 'you must be, I think, a very innocent-minded person, or you would have understood it pretty well by this time.'

' Is that so ? And have you nothing more to tell me ? '

She bit her lip, and said, in a low tone, ' Nothing.'

Vernon rose from his seat, and walked away for a space or two : then he came slowly back again, and stood confronting her. She did not look at, or seem to notice, him, but she began to trifle with a bunch of charms upon her watch-chain. When Vernon spoke he did so very quietly—with a quiet, indeed, that was not unlike apathy.

' Then in that case,' he said, ' I suppose I have done all I can do. I am sorry for it, for at first I was more hopeful. I thought at first I might have come to really know you ; but it seems I have overrated one of two things—either my own power of understanding you, or your wish to be understood.

Still, even thus, I have one thing left to ask you. Give me credit for at least good intentions; and believe that I have never wished to vex or pain you needlessly. I have never asked you a question out of any idle curiosity, nor do I wish to do so now; and now that I have come to a part of your character to which you can give me no clue, there is nothing let for me but to cease troubling you to no purpose.'

There occurred at this moment an unforeseen interruption. A servant made his appearance through the arch of the little tunnel, and announced to Miss Walters that Colonel Stapleton was in the drawing-room.

'Tell him,' she said, 'that I am coming up immediately. I will be with him in a few minutes.'

She waited till the man was out of sight, and then she rose to go. 'Good morning, Mr. Vernon,' she said coldly as she swept past him. 'I suppose I shall hardly see you again to-day—or, indeed, for some time to come—as we may possibly go to-morrow.'

She was already on the first step that led up to the gardens, when he had overtaken her and had grasped her hand. She turned round and faced him, with a stare of cold inquiry. 'Cynthia,' he said to her, speaking between his teeth, 'you shall not go up and see that man.'

'And pray why shall I not? Colonel Stapleton is one of my oldest friends. Have the kindness, Mr. Vernon, to let my hand go.'

'Cynthia,' he said, still detaining her, 'for God's sake do not be angry with me.' He looked on her flower-soft cheeks and longed bitterly that she would again touch his with them. 'I only speak for your good; that is the one, one thing that I long for. I can't bear that your sacred lips should talk to a man like that, who is everything—who is everything that a man should not be. His friendship can do you no good. It is no real friendship, and I hate to think of your enduring it.'

'Nonsense!' she said indignantly. 'What harm do you suppose this man can do me?' She stopped suddenly, and then with an angry flush—'You don't suppose,' she said, 'do you, that Colonel Stapleton could be the ——, the —— ?'

'Good God, no!' Vernon broke in, interrupting her. 'Little as it seems I know you, I know you too well for that.'

She seemed hardly to hear his words, but went on with a scornful laugh: 'If I could have got any harm from his company, I should have got it, you may be sure, long ago. If my morals, that you seem so anxious about, are ever in danger again, it will be from some new friend, not from any old

one. The women that men make love to
are those they have only just seen. I believe
you, Mr. Vernon, can bear witness in that—
not those they have been familiar with for
seventeen years.'

'You mistake me,' he said; 'I am not
jealous of Colonel Stapleton in the common
sense of the word: I am only jealous
of him in the way that God might be. I
love you so well that I am jealous of the
very tone of your mind: and is there one
thought that you really wish to cherish, in
which this man could sympathise, or which
you could so much as utter to him ?'

Words could not have been spoken with
more piteous earnestness ; but she showed no
sign of relenting. Rather, the more he
pleaded, the more did she seem to harden.

'Really, Mr. Vernon,' she said, in the
same unrelenting tone, 'if one is to cut
all one's acquaintance who do not come up

to such a lofty standard as yours, one would be obliged to go into a convent. I have far too much need of indulgence myself not to extend some to others: and I believe that your own young lady friends are not above suspicion. Including myself, I have seen you amusing yourself with three of them, and I can't say that of these any one has been a model of virtue. Come,' she went on abruptly, 'do you not see I am waiting? I cannot wrench my hand from you, if you still persist in holding me; but I believe I am speaking to a gentleman, and once more I must ask you to let me go.'

Vernon released her without a word. ' Good morning,' she said with perfect cold- ness and self-possession, as she turned away from him. But he stood silent, and only stared at her; nor, as she disappeared, did he make any attempt to follow her.

CHAPTER IV.

VERNON returned to his house in a state verging on stupor. He found his late breakfast waiting for him, among the dishes of which was a mayonnaise of lobster ; and the very sight of it turned him sick. But though he could eat nothing, he made up for the want by drinking, and he got through the better part of a bottle of fine Chambertin. From drink he had recourse to tobacco, and from his cigarettes he again went back to his Burgundy. He had not the least wish to drown thought in intoxication. All he wanted was somehow or other to sustain himself. He was battered, bruised, and crushed. He had not known a shock of this kind before, and he staggered under it in lost bewilderment. He ached through and through with a forlorn sense of desolation; and he sometimes muttered to himself in the words of Lear :

> Down thou climbing sorrow,
> *Hysterica passio*, down !

The wine by-and-by began to have some effect upon him ; he went out of doors, in the hope of getting rid of this ; and he turned with unsteady steps towards the hotel gardens. He wandered about there for he knew not how long, abjectly, like a wounded animal, or like a scapegoat, and bearing a kindred burden. At last, however, his wretchedness took the shape of resolution, and, returning in-doors, he wrote the following note to Miss Walters :—

'Cynthia, I must see you. If you are

really resolved that we are to part for ever, you shall at least not part from me as you did this morning. Something more I must say to you, and say it before the day is over. Do not refuse to hear me. I beseech you give me an opportunity. You have never been out of my thoughts since that moment when you turned away from me. Your last words have been bruising me, they have been weighing me down ever since. I could have borne it better that you should have beaten me with a horsewhip, than that you should have spoken as you did then. I could almost think that till to-day I had never known sorrow. It is not for myself I am sorry; it is for you, for you only. If you are tired of me, send me away; but oh, do not send your own soul away from your own self. It seems to me now that I have no feeling left but one, and that one has swallowed all the others. It is an intense desire that you may become true to yourself. As for me, think what you will of me. I am asking you for nothing on my own account. And yet I am wrong; I am asking for one thing. Do not be angry with me; if I have done anything to pain you forgive me, and see me if for only one half-hour, and let me say what I have to say to you. Come to me to-night in the garden. Be at the seat we know of—will you? Write me one line to say yes or no. I shall have no peace till I get your answer.'

The servant who took the letter brought back to Vernon word that an answer would be sent in the course of an hour or two. At last it came. It was only a pencil scrawl. 'Why,' it ran, 'should I be angry with you? Yes, come if you like. I will be there at ten this evening.'

The tone of this did not altogether re-assure him, and when he reached the rendez-vous, his heart was still aching. She was not yet there, and his spirits sank still lower. As he waited the moments seemed like hours to him, and a clear presentiment shaped itself that she would never come at all. The night was soft and lovely, the fountains splashed and glimmered, all nature was full of the same luxurious languor that had so well accorded with the earlier stages of his passion. But now all was changed. His passion had passed from romance into hard reality. There was nothing now in it akin to the scent of flowers, or the splash of fountains, or the glimmer of moon-lit seas ; and the human anxieties that could be affected by things like these now seemed to him but silly toys and child's-play. He waited in weary impatience for he knew not how long, and still she did not come. At length through the quiet he heard a faint, far sound. It ceased for a few minutes, and then again he heard it. It was now sharper and more clear, and he recognised it as the sound of carriage-wheels. Presently a gleam of white was visible, slowly gliding amongst the orange trees ; and in another moment Miss Walters was before him—softly perfumed—daintily dressed as ever.

' I thought,' he exclaimed, ' that you were never coming ! I thought you were drifting altogether away from me !'

' I couldn't come sooner,' she said softly and calmly. ' Forgive me for having kept you waiting.'

Her tone and her expression were both ambiguous, as though two minds were being balanced in her, the one against the other.

' Has *he*, then, only just left you ? ' asked Vernon coldly.

' If by *he*,' she said, ' you mean Colonel Stapleton, he has only just left us. I was obliged to wait till he was gone. I could hardly, you see, ask a guest to excuse me, on the ground of having an assignation in the garden.'

'I am not vexed with you,' said **Vernon**, 'for having kept me waiting. I am **only** grateful to you for having come at **all**. **Sit** down by me, Cynthia, for a little, and **let me** talk to you.'

She folded her hands before her, and **fixed** her eyes on the ground. 'I am **listening**,' she said. 'Please begin, will you?'

Vernon, however, was for a good **while** silent. He seemed to have some **difficulty** in finding either his words or voice. **At last** he began, speaking very low and slowly.

'Do you know,' he said, 'why I **have** begged you to meet me here? I have **had** one reason, and one only. It is because I **see** into your character—see down into the in-most depths of it, and because I **see how** noble, and pure, and beautiful it **really is.** My Cynthia, you are akin to all that is **best** and holiest; and if my death could **help** you, I would very gladly die for you. **Till** this morning I thought you were safe, and that I had no more cause for anxiety. You looked at peace ; and myself, I had seen you praying. I watched your eyes in the chapel, as they were fixed on the altar. I listened to your voice, as it said to God's mother, " Pray for me." My own one, I had hoped that all was right with you. But now, suddenly and without warning, you tell me I was quite deceived. You said very little to-day, but the little was like a ghastly flash of lightning. It revealed an unsuspected cavern that I have not explored—that I knew nothing at all about. I do not understand you yet. Cannot you bear to trust me ? '

'What more can I tell you ? You know too much already.'

'Too much and yet too little.' There was a long pause.

'I am sorry,' she said at last in a constrained voice, 'that I ever told you anything. It was very foolish of me.'

'For God's sake,' he exclaimed, 'don't say that! Surely I have been some help to you, even thus far. You are less unhappy now than you were when first I knew you.'

She gave a low, bitter laugh. 'Certainly,' she said, 'I could not possibly be more so.'

'You make it very hard for me,' said Vernon, 'to say what I wish to say; you perplex me so that I get almost bewildered as to my own meaning. Will you bear with me for a minute or two, and let me try to collect my thoughts? I am so miserable that I feel as if I were turning silly.' He was silent for some time, leaning his forehead on his hand. At last rousing himself, and with a wretched look in his eyes, 'Listen,' he said; 'I think I can speak now. You told me when first we met that you were very unhappy, and what I have been trying to do

has been to show you that you were not just
to yourself.   I have been trying to force you
to see the good that I see in you.   My
Cynthia, I see it now ; for your soul's garden
is still white with lilies which, with pure hands,
you may place upon God's altar.   It is this that I
have been trying to show you.   And I thought
you had seen it too, just as one sees a thing
when one wakes up from a dream, and finds
one is not drowning, but is safe in bed.   I
thought that whatever wrong you may have
done, had become to you "but a sleep and a
forgetting ; " and that you were reunited to
your own taintless nature.   But now you tell me
that you are still not sure of yourself, that the
very thing you hate has still some mysterious
hold upon you, and that it is I only —a chance
support like myself—who keep you where
you are.   If I were taken from you, you
might again be false to your true self, you
say.   And yet how ?   Where is your danger ?

All other affection, so you tell me, is dead in you.'

'My meaning,' she said, looking straight before her, 'is, I think, simple. If a woman has some one to lean upon, who will fill her life with affection, and will not only show her what is right, but will give it a living meaning for her, then she will love the right and be true to it. Her human love will make all other love clear to her. But suppose she is left alone—with no one to guide her, or even to care whether she is guided! But why should I talk? You are not a woman. You can never know what to a woman affection is. You talk of losing affection as you might talk of putting down one's carriage, or getting rid of an extra footman; whereas in reality it is like tearing out half one's sinews. No——; if I were left alone, I could certainly not answer for myself. When a woman has once found pleasure in a way she ought not, misery will always, if it comes to her, lay her bare to temptation. It is not a new affection by which such women are tempted. It is simply by the hunger for distraction.'

'But what I can't endure,' he said, 'is to think that what sullies you, can distract you even. It wouldn't distract you—at least not in the way you mean—to stand in the street and let a mob pelt and spit at you. Why should it distract you, then, to let a far worse insult be put upon you ? Cannot you understand the state of mind I wish for you ?'

'Perfectly,' she said ; 'it is an extremely simple one : indeed, no one by nature could have had it more strongly than I had. But you could as easily give a tumbled plum its bloom back, as give that back to me. One may recover many things when one has lost them ; but one will never recover that. If I live to be old enough I may perhaps be childish ; but I shall never again be innocent.'

He rose from his seat, and began pacing slowly up and down before her. His abstraction and prolonged silence seemed to chill and harden her.

'Well,' she said, 'and do you understand me now ? It was better to be honest with you, even if I have made you think me too depraved to be spoken to. I at least love truth, if I have no other virtue ; and I would far sooner that you did not care for me at all, than that you cared for me under false pretences.'

'You are not depraved,' said Vernon, 'and I do not think you are.'

'It is foolish of you,' she said, 'to eat your own words in that way ; nor is it the least comfort to me to hear you do it. If I were not a lady, I could describe my own character far better and more tersely than

you have done ; only, unfortunately, the only
word I could use is not generally found in
a well-bred lady's vocabulary.'

Vernon sat down by her and was about
to begin speaking ; but she did not give him
time.

'Come,' she said, 'am I looking well to-
night ?   Why don't you kiss me, and tell me
how soft and pretty I am ?   Isn't that what
you say generally when you talk to girls
like me ?   By the way, I have found a word
that will at least describe what I might have
been, had circumstances only favoured me—
an *hetaira*. If I had lived at Athens, I
should have performed that part capitally.   I
was made for a life of pleasure, I think, if
——, if ——.' She stopped abruptly for a
moment, and then broke out once more—' If
only there were not something in me that had
made all my pleasure a hell.'

Vernon had been listening to her hitherto

aghast, silent, and motionless, but he caught at this last sentence, and eagerly bent forwards to her.

'My Cynthia,' he said, 'my poor, unhappy loved one, do you think people really bad are unhappy in the way that you are? I am torn as I think of you by two conflicting impulses—to worship, and to pity you.'

The word *pity* stung her. 'Thank you,' she said, 'but I have no wish to be pitied. I am as much too proud for your pity as I am too depraved for your worship.'

Her voice, as she said this, had an icy coldness; but just at the last word or two it trembled ever so little, and in another moment her face was hidden in her hands, and she was sobbing violently.

'Oh, can't I do anything to stop this?' she gasped. 'If I can't I shall die. I have been often told so by the doctors. My heart is all wrong, and I might die at any moment.

And yet why should I not? It would be
the best thing for me. Then at last—then
at last I might be at rest.'

Vernon took her hand, but it was cold
and limp, and wet with tears that had fallen
upon it. He spoke to her with the most
tender kindness, and said all he could to
comfort her.

'Oh, why,' she said, 'are you so hard
upon me? Why do you send me away from
you when I tell you I am only good for your
sake? Oh, you have been cruel—you have
been cruel to me. If you only knew, when
a person is in my condition, how easy it is
to wound them—how the least hard word
can be like a dagger to them!'

'Indeed,' said Vernon, 'I did not mean
to be hard on you. If I had hurt you by
the way I have spoken, I'm sure I may say,
like the schoolmaster when he whips the
boy, "It hurt me most."'

'Yes,' she said, 'you might say that just like the schoolmaster, for it would not be true,' and she looked up at him timidly with a little faint smile of humour. This to him was like a gleam of returning sunshine: and now her voice softened and she began to speak pleadingly. 'Why,' she went on, 'if you really wish me to be good, won't you let me begin with thinking that you are pleased with my goodness? Let me do that first; and I will learn afterwards to love goodness for its own sake.'

'Yes—and for your own sake also; for the sake of your own self-reverence. I wish you to shun and to flinch from evil as you would from a wound, or from hot iron. And surely you do now, if you only knew yourself. Surely you wrong yourself by your own fears, don't you? Tell me, my Cynthia, my love with the saint's eyes, is what I say not true?'

She had ceased sobbing now, but her eyes were still damp with tears. As he said this she suddenly collected herself, and with a forced firmness in her voice, said, after a pause, ' No; it is not true.'

' Cynthia ! '

' Don't speak in that tone—please don't. If you don't wish to kill me, please be kind and patient with me. Oh, God, how my heart is beating ! Will you listen ? ' she went on, gasping. ' I have several things to tell you, which perhaps will make you think a little more kindly about me. Ever since I knew you—since that night when we drove home together, and you spoke to me about your having wandered from your true self— ever since then I have been struggling, battling with my evil. Then afterwards, when some impulse moved me to confess to you, I have tried yet more earnestly ; and I have had temptations fawning upon me which you little knew about—yes, during the last fortnight, since we have been at the Cap de Juan.'

'Temptations!' echoed Vernon.

'Yes,' she said; 'but I can't tell you what or whence. I can only say they were from some one that you never saw or heard about. And oh, how I prayed, and prayed, and prayed, and received no answer! You little thought what a poor creature there was, within a few hundred yards of you. Well! what do you think has helped me? My only hope and help has been the thought of you. Roman Catholics pray to dead saints. Why should I not get help of the same sort from a living friend?'

'You shall!' exclaimed Vernon; 'all help that is mine to give you. But there is one thing that I must once more beg of you. Don't go on yielding either in word or thought to these extravagant self-accusations.

Let me only whisper to you, Go, sin no more ; and, if I may venture to use the words, Neither do I condemn thee.'

She looked him in the face wistfully. 'What I say of myself is not at all extravagant. I know you think so ; and each time I see you do I feel that I am still deceiving you. You think, I believe, that there is some pretty story connected with me. You think no doubt that I am some sort of Juliet : not, I am sure, that poor Juliet had much to tax herself with. But I must shatter that bubble if I can. And yet how can I ? How can I begin ? Oh, me! the wretchedness and the shame of it all!'

' My darling,' said Vernon, ' if to tell me is any relief, tell me. But if not, let things rest as they are. I can trust you without forcing your confidence.'

' That is the very thing,' she said. ' You trust me too much. It *will* relieve me to tell the entire truth to you—that is, if I can only manage it. And don't be afraid I shall break down over it, and make a scene again. I am quite myself now, and my heart has done throbbing. Would you mind walking a little with me? I think I could talk better then.'

Her manner was perfectly calm now, yet without hardness. They rose at her last request, and walked along the path together. Vernon offered his arm to her, but she gently refused to take it. 'No,' she said, 'not now if you please. I mean you first to know better who it is you are talking to. Well— to begin with, you know this much already, that I am only received in society because the world knows nothing about me. I am there upon false pretences. That is hardly a pleasant sense to have always with one. However, we will let that pass. I have two things besides that to tell you: one is how I have treated a certain man ; the other, how a certain man has treated me. I can tell the first story easiest, and I will begin with that. Rather more than a year ago I made a retreat with a friend of mine—it is the very Mrs. Crane we are going to visit at San Remo—at a quaint little watering place between Genoa and Spezzia. For me it was really a retreat—a retreat in the religious sense. I was very unhappy about myself, and I had been trying to take up with religion. Didn't I tell you that I very nearly became a Catholic ? Well—Mrs. Crane there made friends with a man, who having nothing better to do fell deeply in love with me. Love is hardly the word for it. He simply worshipped me. He thought me a saint. He told me that I had saved him from all kinds of evil courses.'

'Did you care for him ?' said Vernon.

'Yes ; I liked him. I had an intense re-

spect for him. I was trying to be good myself, and I respected all goodness then. But I
did not behave well. I encouraged him. I
made him think I cared more than I really
did for him, and at last he asked me if I would
marry him. I had dreaded for a day or two
before that this might be coming. I told him
No. I had really not the least love for him,
and yet it was difficult to give him too hard
a denial. I suppose I had become so de-
moralised that I couldn't bear losing an admirer. Well, in course of time he had to
return to England, and I managed to put
him off with some indefinite hope, which I
believe he still indulges in and regards as his
most sacred treasure. If ever a woman played
with a human soul, I have played with his.'

She paused. 'You have shown me,' said
Vernon, 'how right I was in what I have
said to you. You look on your own misdeeds
in far too gloomy a way. God knows that we

should be all of us more careful than we are
in matters such as these. But there are
many good women who might make much
worse confessions.'

'Perhaps,' she said; 'but you must remember when I knew this man I fancied
myself to be going through the most solemn
religious experiences; and yet even then my
wicked vanity was misleading me. However,
it is not for its own sake that I tell you this
incident. It is for an accidental reason, and
one that is personal to yourself.'

'To me!'

'You,' she said hurriedly, 'to you. But
we won't stop to talk about that now. I must
get through the task I have set myself, and
the worst is not over yet.' Here her voice
failed her. She caught hold of Vernon's arm,
and gulped down a spasmodic sob.

'Don't go on,' said Vernon, 'if it gives
pain to you.

'I must,' she said. 'I will be brave and get it over. Only two months after this man had left me, I was staying at Nice, with some rather fast friends I had. One reason why I hate Monte Carlo so is because ———.' Once more she stopped. Then tightening her hold on his arm, so as almost to give him pain, she put her lips to his ear, and spoke in a quick whisper. 'I used often to go over there with a very bad person—a man. I used to gamble there—anything to drown thought. He used to bank with me, and I won a lot of money. I couldn't touch it— not a penny of it. I gave it all away to charities. Do you understand what I have just said to you?'

'I do,' said Vernon sadly. 'My poor, poor Cynthia!' Presently he added, 'I must beg your pardon for one thought, which did cross my mind this morning. I mean about Colonel Stapleton; for I know, from what he has told me, that at that time he was away in Palestine.'

'He was,' she said. 'I had not seen him till the other day for a long time.'

'Well——,' said Vernon, as if he expected her to continue.

'Haven't I told you all? I believe I don't quite know what I'm saying. I wish, for one reason, that you were a worse person. You would understand me so much more easily. What I have to tell you is——. God help me, I am sorry I began this. It is nothing that can be said exactly in so many words. It's a question rather of what I am, than of what I have done. Stay——,' she exclaimed. 'I think I know one way of enlightening you. Come with me into my sitting-room. The window is open. There will be nobody about by this time, and I will only keep you a moment.'

He followed her into the house in silence.

She went to a large despatch-box that stood
on one of her tables by a lovely vase of roses,
and she slowly opened it.

'What I am going to show you,' she said,
'I have myself only glanced at; but the very
fact that such a thing should be sent me will
throw some light for you on the character of
the sender, and the sort of character which I
have let him impute to me. It comes from
the person I told you of.'

She put into Vernon's hands a small
oblong something, which in the dim light he
did not at first see clearly. 'It is locked,' she
said. 'I believe there is a key somewhere.'

But she was stopped in her search by two
sounds behind her. The one was an exclamation from Vernon, the other was the fall
on the floor of the object she had just given
him. It lay there at his feet. It was the book
of photographs that had been shown him by
Colonel Stapleton.

There was a pause of some seconds, while the two stood staring at each other. At last Vernon said, in a low distinct voice, 'I have seen that book before. I know too who it has come from.'

Then his voice failed him. He sank back in his chair as if dizzy, and his eyes were fixed on the ceiling in a dull stony stare. As for her, she had sunk helplessly to the ground, pressing her face against the low cushions of a sofa. So far as human life went, the room was a ghastly silence. The only sounds heard were the tick of the small carriage-clock on the chimney-piece, the croaking of the frogs outside, and the faint splash of the fountains. Silence seemed to both the only thing possible. There was nothing in either mind that could lead to a wish to break it. Suddenly, however, there was the noise of a door slamming. The effect was as quick on Miss Walters as the kiss on the Sleeping Beauty. 'Quick,'

she said to Vernon. 'It is Braham coming—
our butler. I know his footstep. Get into
the garden till he's gone; but don't go away,
unless you mean quite to leave me.'

Vernon went as he was bidden. He
could hear Miss Walters' voice as she was
talking to the servant. He heard a door
closing, and then she re-appeared at the
window.

'I am coming out,' she said. 'Don't let
us go back into the room again.' She spoke
very solemnly, and there was a strange calm
in her face. 'I shall not keep you long,' she
said. 'I am come to say good-bye to you.'

Vernon answered nothing, he only stood
and looked at her. 'Am I not fit,' she said
at last, 'to have even a good-bye said to me?'

Again he gave no answer, so far as words
went, but he drew a little nearer to her, and
softly folded her in his arms. Her face as
she looked at him was full of astonished

gratitude, but there was no trace of a smile on it ; it seemed even more sad than before.

'Oh,' she murmured presently, 'you are very, very kind to me. You are being kind, as it were, to a person upon her death-bed ; for of course now it is all—all over between us.'

'All over !' he echoed.

'You can never,' she said, 'be my friend now you know me, especially now you have found out how I have been lying to you. But oh the shame of it all ! I was always so afraid you might guess it ; and I couldn't bear to think you should know who the person was.'

He took her hand and placed her arm in his, and they moved away towards the shadow of some orange trees. She was quite passive ; she went exactly as he guided her : but she seemed reassured a little by all his tender treatment. Presently she began again, and her voice sounded like a child's.

'I was so young,' she said,' 'when he made me bad first; and at one time, long, long ago, he had been really good and nice to me. I don't know when he became different. I suppose when I got prettier. I had hardly left the school-room, I remember, when he began to lend me horrid French novels. I didn't understand them; that was one thing; at least not till a long time afterwards. I have had—' and she gave a little nervous laugh—' I have had, you see, to live up to my education.'

At last Vernon spoke. 'By-and-by,' he said, 'when I have gone away from you, I shall pray Almighty God to damn that man's soul for ever.'

'Hush! hush!' she said. 'It was my fault as well as his. I knew what was right then as well as I do now. But you see by

this time, don't you, that I can never again
be what I once was? I know you are
horrified at me; but I can't help it.'

'I believe,' said Vernon, slowly and with
effort, 'that some feelings of moral revulsion
are pride in its hardest form. I might be
pleased perhaps to think you had never sinned;
but God would condemn that feeling, and I
condemn it also. The shepherd loves the
lost sheep when he finds it, even though it
is lame and wounded by its wanderings; and
surely he knows best what is loveable. You
will be a far finer character when you come
to your soul's home again, than you would
have been had your never left it.'

'*When!*' she repeated. 'Yes, you may
well say that; but that *when* is never. I can
still see the gates of that very home you
speak of, but I see them

With dreadful faces thronged and fiery arms.

There is no way back into Eden.'

'I was foolish,' said Vernon, 'in the way I talked this morning. I don't ask you any longer to become an innocent girl again. I ask you to become a holy woman instead ; that is far better. Amongst the highest saints in heaven, will be faces deepest scarred by the battle. You are right, very likely, that there is no way back into Eden ; but—I am not a great quoter of texts, yet I still remember this one : "We all die in Adam, but we may all live in Christ." '

She looked at him with a piercing eagerness, and said, 'Do you really believe that ? '

Vernon was embarrassed, as he had been once before already, by her direct questioning.

'I believe it,' he said slowly, 'and you will help my unbelief.'

She dropped her eyes, reflecting. 'Sit down,' she said, 'on that seat for a moment.'

It was strange how, through all her sorrows, the feminine fascination of her

command still continued. Vernon obeyed
silently. No sooner had he done so, than
softly, like a shadow, she sank on her knees
before him. 'If you will not mind hearing
me, I am going to say a prayer,' she said.
With a movement of kindness that was then
almost mechanical, he laid his hand upon
her shoulder; her hands were folded before
her face. Vernon was glad that she was
not watching him. He felt that his thoughts
were wandering far from hers, and that his
face, rigid and melancholy, would at once
have betrayed the fact. Presently a low sound
broke from her, and he caught the familiar
accents, as of a little child's 'Our Father.'
He meanwhile, in a bitter and blank wonder,
let his eyes stare at the stars and the palm-
branches, as he thought, 'Does prayer mean
anything?'

That night he slept a heavy, dreamless
sleep. He had not yet had time to settle either

into hope or misery; and his last memory as he sank to sleep was simply one of Miss Walters' parting words : 'Will you see me to-morrow morning? If we go to San Remo that day, it will not be till the afternoon at any rate.'

CHAPTER V.

THEIR meeting next day began with a low-toned quiet, that came of intense exhaustion. The first things said referred to the Walters' movements, and Vernon learned that they were actually going, in the course of the next few hours.

'For one reason,' she said, 'I am rather glad. There are so many things I can write far more clearly than I could say them.'

Vernon meanwhile had had time to be struck with one thing ; and this was a curious change in the style of Miss Walters' dress. In place of her usual dainty toilette, what she wore now might have been almost called dowdy, but for the unconscious grace which her figure and bearing gave it.

' I never saw you,' he said, ' in that frock before.'

She smiled faintly. ' Thereby hangs a tale,' she said. ' I used to wear this dress when your friend Mr. Campbell knew me.'

' Campbell ! ' exclaimed Vernon. ' Do you mean Alic Campbell ? '

' Didn't I tell you ? ' she said. ' I meant to have done so ; but I was so confused last night.'

' Are you, then, the person that has changed his whole life for him ? Good God ! why, but a fortnight back he was here in this very place, and he was telling me all about you ; only he never said your name, neither did I mention yours. He was with

me only a night, and then went on his way,
little dreaming he had been so near you.
Do you know where he was going? To
a friend of yours, that he might hear news
of you.'

Miss Walters gave a long sigh of relief.
'What an escape!' she said. 'I knew he
was coming abroad to hunt for me; but I
got my friend, Mrs. Crane, to contrive me
some respite. He has been at Sorrento, I
know, with her, talking night and day about
me. Perhaps, now, you wonder less why I
reproached myself.'

'He thinks you a saint, poor fellow; and
has been trying all he can to become worthy
of you.'

'I know he thinks me a saint,' said Miss
Walters; 'and that was what I could not
bear. It is more crushing to be thought
better than it is to be thought worse than
you are. Yet I should not be surprised at

Alic Campbell's misjudging me. He only thought I was what at the time I was really trying to be. I seemed to him to be a very simple person. Yes—this is the dress he knew me in : I think almost the only dress. I really did hate the world just then ; and I tried in every way to mortify my vanity. I wore the same dress this morning, as a sign of the same spirit. I couldn't bear to put anything on that should make my wicked body seem beautiful.'

Vernon answered her in an oddly absent manner : 'And has the spirit of that time come back to you ?'

'Do not you know it has ?' she said vehemently ; 'and if you will only help me it shall never leave me again. Oh, please be kind to me, and let me lean on you for a little while longer, and don't refuse me your support, because I tell you I can't do without it. It's quite true—I shall go straight to the dogs without you.' But Vernon gave no answer : he was simply staring into vacancy. 'What is it?' she asked, half frightened. 'Is anything the matter with you?'

Then he fixed his eyes on her. As he did so she seemed to divine his meaning, and her lip quivered with a sort of expectant terror.

'You told me,' he said, 'about your unhappy time at Monaco; and at that time Colonel Stapleton was in the Holy Land.'

He spoke very slowly, and her cheeks turned from pale to scarlet. With a sudden effort she regained command of herself; the flush died from her cheeks, and she said to him in a sad clear voice, ' Do you think such affection as Colonel Stapleton gives a woman is of a kind that is likely to keep her faithful during his absence?'

'Cynthia, my dear, Cynthia!' cried a voice in the adjoining drawing-room, 'is that you? and are you talking to Mr. Vernon? Ask him to stay and have breakfast with us. It is ordered at twelve o'clock.'

' It is my aunt,' exclaimed Miss Walters. 'Yes, Aunt Louisa, we will be with you in another moment. Come '—and she turned to Vernon—' our conversation is over now ; and now—at once—I can speak the utter, utter truth to you. You have got now the lowest dregs of my cask.'

' Must we go yet ?' Vernon whispered. ' Only one word more with you ?'

' No,' she said. ' *I* must go, even if *you* need not. It is twelve already. Come, will you have breakfast with us ?'

She was about to push the curtains aside, and go into the drawing-room, when Vernon caught her by the arm, and forcibly drew her near him. ' God bless you !' he murmured. ' God guard and save you !' And, instead of kissing her, he made a hasty sign of the cross upon her.

CHAPTER VI.

THAT afternoon, left to his own thoughts, he did what he had not done for a fortnight. He called upon Frederic Stanley. He found him in his little bare sitting-room, apparently deep in thought at a table strewn with papers; but Vernon's entrance brought a pleasant smile to his face.

'It is a long time,' began Vernon, 'since last I came to see you.'

Stanley detected Vernon's feeling, and adroitly disclaimed the apology. 'Had I more room for visitors,' he said, 'I would have asked you to come before now. I fear you will think that I affect to be very inaccessible.'

He spoke in this way out of a quick sense of delicacy. The emotion betrayed by Miss Walters, when he dined at the Château St. John, he had set down to a feeling on her part for Vernon; and though this particular conjecture was wrong, it had led him more or less to the truth. He had gathered that between the two there had arisen some special intimacy, which he hoped might result in good; and it was little surprise to him that he was himself lost sight of. What did surprise him most, however, was the dejection of Vernon's aspect, which was but ill concealed by his constant efforts at talking. Indeed, at last he ceased to attempt concealment.

'Stanley,' he said, 'the last time I was here—the day I came with Campbell—I asked a favour of you. I wonder if you would now

repeat it.   Will you come and dine with me
this evening, and name your own hour?   I
am out of spirits for many reasons, and to
give me your company would be an act of
Christian charity.'

'You look worn out,' said Stanley.   'You
have had, I trust, nothing much to trouble
you.   I will certainly come to dinner.   Shall
we say six thirty?'

The rest of that afternoon was to Vernon
a vigil of misery.   The painful excitement of
the last two days was ended, and he now for
the first time grew conscious of the effect those
days had had on him.   It was as though he
had been bruised all over in an accident, and
the bruises one by one were becoming distinct
tortures.   Every movement of thought or
memory made him feel what his condition
was.   Several times, as he dwelt upon Miss
Walters, tears too quick for repression filled
his eyes and fell from them.   In another

moment, as he still dwelt upon her, sorrow gave place to loathing ; and loathing in its turn to intense attraction. At one time it was, ' Can I ever touch her again ? ' at another, ' Why did I not make her my mistress ? ' And then again sorrow obtained the mastery. The *hysterica passio* had its own way with a vengeance ; tears blinded him, and he let them fall helplessly.

The sum of his sorrows, however, did not end here. He had the thought of Campbell also to prey upon him—Campbell, the friend whom he had supplanted, or towards whom at least he had played a supplanter's part. But this sorrow was of a somewhat different order. It did, it is true, but add to and complicate his wretchedness ; but it braced, it did not unnerve, him. It demanded his judgment even more than it roused his feelings. Finally, there was an image that did both equally. It was the image of Colonel Stapleton. When he had run the round of his other wretched reflections, he found fierce relief in his hatred of this man. At first he was busied with various schemes for fighting him ; but, considering the pretext, this did not seem possible. He would be blasting a reputation, most likely, in the very act of avenging it. Nothing was left him, at any rate for the time being, but to fan his anger by the most elaborate expressions of it. 'May he die slowly, and may the Spirit of God curse him ! May he cry for eternity for a single drop of water, and may none be given him ! May my own death be sweetened by the sound of his shrieks in Hell !' Such were a few of the ejaculations in which his anger embodied itself ; then anger in its turn would again collapse into sorrow. 'My angel, my angel,' he would say, 'what has this devil done to you !' And the procession of tortured thoughts would begin once more where it started from.

Such excitement, however, brings its own relief, and by the time Stanley came Vernon was wearied into a sort of quietude. But though the waves had ceased to lash themselves, there was only night over them, and with their spent force they were still murmuring disconsolately. 'The meaning of life is still blind as ever to me,' was the thought that was now filling him. 'God will not answer; all the heavens are silent. In the infinite hush of space is but one solitary sound—the tides of human history, as, without any purport, they moan like a homeless sea.'[1]

Vernon did not season his dinner with this forlorn philosophy; but its results were visible in his sad and spiritless conversation, which was relieved only by an occasional show of irritation at the mention of two subjects. These were none other than Campbell

[1] 'The moanings of the homeless sea.'—TENNYSON.

and Miss Walters.   Stanley, as was not unnatural, spoke often about them both—of
Miss Walters guardedly, of Campbell with
more freedom; but Vernon's answers were so
short and listless, that it was plain there was
something wrong with him.   Stanley could
not guess what, though he tried many solu-
tions.   By-and-by, however, he thought he
had found a clue.

'May I ask,' said Vernon, with a tone of
reviving interest, 'what sort of work it is with
which you are always occupied?'

'I am writing a small volume,' said
Stanley, 'on the teachings of Saint Thomas
Aquinas.   I am doing so at the suggestion of
the Archbishop, who wishes to issue a series
of primers, containing each an account of some
great Catholic theologian.'

'Happy man,' said Vernon; 'how I envy
you!'

'Do you mean you envy me because of

the kind of work? Or do you envy me merely because I have work at all?'

'A little,' said Vernon, 'because you have work at all, but chiefly because it is work that subserves a cause you worship.'

'I know,' said Stanley, 'that you do not worship my cause; if you did, you would belong to it. But your envy has a moral that may apply even to you.'

Vernon drank a glass of wine and stared blankly at Stanley. 'I wish to goodness,' he said, 'I could find out how that was.'

'Well,' said Stanley, speaking now a little drily, 'if you will not be offended with me, I will try to tell you. A man of your powers, and in your position, may have either the fullest of lives or else the emptiest; and if he does not achieve the first, he will probably have the second thrust upon him. I am not speaking of religion; I am speaking of common happiness.'

'Well,' said Vernon, 'go on. I am listening.'

'A fool, if he be rich,' said Stanley, 'is occupied very easily. There is no saying what trifles may not content him. But a strong man's mind is like a corrosive acid. It eats through countless interests that suffice to absorb others. It even takes the gilt off vice, and it makes gambling vapid. What it asks is, "Give me something to work for that I can feel is worth the work." Now for the bulk of mankind there is a ready answer to this. They must work to live, or at least to live in comfort; and all that they need do is to make a virtue of necessity. But the rich man's task is by no means as simple as this. He has not to make a virtue of necessity, but to make a necessity of virtue. By an act of will and choice he must take that yoke upon him, that the larger number are born with. He must choose some line of action ; he must devote himself to something. What makes a man is the sense that he has committed himself.'

'True,' said Vernon ; 'but the struggle lies in choosing. In choosing a life's work it is just the same as in marrying. Life *might* be lived with a hundred different women ; it *can* with consistency be lived with only one ; and however charming might be the choice I pitched upon, her one welcome would be drowned by the ninety-and-nine farewells. It is all very well to say *choose* ; but what is to make one choose ? '

'No doubt it is often difficult,' said Stanley. 'It is one of the rich man's trials. That is the very point I am urging. But such choices, or, if you like to put it so, such renunciations, are made daily. Every one makes them who meets with any success in life. The soldier does, the statesman does, even the man of fashion does. Every one

of these men, in some sort, takes the veil.
He chooses one part, and he renounces
others. Let him once do this, and his life
is thronged with motives. He walks firmly,
with firm ground under him. For the first
time he becomes, properly speaking, a man.'

'He may gain his manhood,' said Vernon,
'but he says good-bye to his youth.'

'Well,' said Stanley, in a slight tone of
contempt, 'would you keep youth beyond its
time? Belated youth is sillier than second
childhood. You ask me what is to drive you
to your choice? I should say many things
might do so. Ambition might, or common
sense, or a natural interest in the welfare of
others; or, as to the point of marrying, natural
affection. You see I am putting religion, for
argument's sake, quite out of the question.'

'Yes,' said Vernon; 'and, so far as I am
concerned, that prevents you from understanding me. Given religious faith, all the

rest becomes simple. Things worthy of your self-devotion at once surround you on every side, and you welcome—you do not deplore—your sacrifices. Happiness comes to you then by a very different process—by supernatural sight, not by artificial blindness.'

'I think,' said Stanley smiling, 'you are paying religion a somewhat misplaced compliment. It, no doubt, does bring us happiness, but it does not bring it to us ready-made out of a bandbox. You don't have a good cry and then get a sugarplum. Indeed, too many tears, I believe, and too many sensations of peace, are less often signs of religious depth, than of shallowness. One of the worst spiritual signs we can detect in ourselves is, that we are touched with the pathos of our own condition. I remember a young Catholic who once told me of the doubts he was tempted by, and who had resolved very rightly to submit reason to faith. "Of course," he said at last, "I can never forget my difficulties, but" —and the tears filled his eyes—" I will wear them round my head, as an intellectual crown of thorns." I advised him to do so, but not to talk about it : "If you suffer patiently God will bless you ; but do not suffer before the looking-glass." Religious life, Vernon, you may depend upon it, has, when it is worth anything, a very prosaic side to it.'

'I,' said Vernon, 'connect religious life with emotion less, perhaps, even than you do. Faith would redeem me not through the heart, but through the intellect. To do our work in the world we must suppose that men are lovable, and worth working for; but it would quite content me to believe the fact without feeling it. Love in this case is like gold, and belief is a sort of paper currency. If the bills of faith were only endorsed by the intellect, I should be quite content, and should be in no hurry to cash them. The only wages I should ask for my work, would be to know that my work was not wasted. That knowledge, my dear Stanley, would guide me through the shadows, though I have not the least expectation that it would conjure me into the sunshine.'

'Surely,' said Stanley, 'you don't want faith to tell you that you could at least do something that would be of some use in the world. There are certainly some whose lives you could make easier.'

'I measure,' said Vernon, 'my fellow-creatures by myself. If I have no soul, they have no souls either; and if I am a fool to be pleased by the best of the world's play-things, they are even greater fools if they are pleased by worse ones. If I consider myself not worth working for, how can I find satisfaction in working for inferior re-plicas of myself?'

'Of course,' said Stanley curtly, 'you can never know till you have tried. But I am wrong; you have tried. You were very kind to the lame child here. You would find it easier than you think to discover some path of duty.'

'Listen,' said Vernon; 'you speak of that child. You may say, if you like, that what I did for her was a kindness. Very well, then; consider this. A certain old peasant woman has an extremely dirty daughter. This fact, even were the daughter healthy, would hardly make me radiant. Why should it do so, because I have made her but half a cripple? The result of my kindness at its best is something that is less than uninteresting.'

'Why did you do it, then?'

'Out of good nature, I suppose. I have plenty, I think, of that. My dear Stanley, we are talking openly, so, perhaps, I may say

to you what I should say to no one else. I
have tried philanthropy on a more extended
scale. I happen to have about nine thousand
a year. Of this I give a good two-thirds to
entirely unselfish purposes—I do so at this
moment. But I get no pleasure from this;
or if at times I do, my reason very soon
steps in and destroys it. It acts, as you
said most justly, like a corrosive acid upon
it. But you were only thinking of frivolous
pleasures. I assure you I find them all
equally destructible.'

Stanley looked at Vernon in perplexed
surprise; and then with a faint smile, 'You're
a curious man,' he said.

'Excuse me,' said Vernon, 'I am not at
all curious. I only have a habit of applying
logic to everything.'

'Yes,' said Stanley; 'and natural love to
nothing.'

'I could love well enough,' said Vernon,

'if ——.' Stanley stared at him. He had stopped short abruptly; his eyes were fixed upon the ceiling; and he was biting his lip as if in acute pain. Presently, with a visible effort, he recovered himself.—'If,' he resumed, 'if I could be sure of two things— that the woman I loved had a soul to give to God, and that she cared to give it. But even then, you see, an assent of the reason is needed. Belief should precede, or at least accompany, feeling.'

'If you would listen to me,' said Stanley, 'I should tell you that love was far more likely to produce belief, than for belief to produce love.'

'You are speaking, I think,' said Vernon, 'of the love of man for woman. Surely for you, then, that is a somewhat singular doctrine. As far as I can understand the Catholic view of life, its chief aim and object is the love—not of woman, but God.'

'You are perfectly right there.'

'Very well,' said Vernon; 'rob life of its aim, and begin your amours then. A woman, then, is a mere animal like yourself; and if your desires are very strongly set on her, she will be far more likely to quench your religious longings than to excite them. So far as I can see, there is but one single way in which human love can be allied with divine love, and blessed by the Christian Church; and that is by treating it as a mutual exhortation on the part of those concerned in it to the service and love of God. In so far as it is more than this, in so far as their attention fixes itself not on God, but on their own two personalities, it seems to me that it must be, from your standpoint, a concession to human weakness, not an element of Christian strength.'

'You are wrong,' said Stanley. 'You are confusing two things—the characteristic error of the whole modern school. Let me explain to you how the Church regards the matter, and you will find that her view is a more liberal one than yours. The Church teaches that, sin only excepted, God made everything. He made man and He made man's affections, and He implanted in each of us, what Saint Thomas calls an *interior instinct*, by which, when developed, we recognise His existence. From my point of view, as you call it, that is a fact, is it not, as much as the law of gravity ? '

' I have no doubt of it.'

' Very well, then ; the fact remains, whether or no we believe in it. Apples fell to the ground before the days of Newton, and souls may be moved to God even before they know of His existence. One of the chief ways in which they are thus moved is through the affections. These human affections are the expressions of God's will, and, rightly exercised, they are in themselves good.

There is something holy in the love of a brother as a brother, or of a wife as a wife ; but these are not to be confounded with the love of God, any more than they are to be divorced from it. They are so like it however, that they prepare the way for it.' Stanley looked at Vernon and saw how worn his face was. 'Do you see,' he added gently, 'what my meaning is ?'

'Partly,' said Vernon ; 'and yet it does not meet all my question. Still, I shall think it over.'

He said this sadly, and with an absent air as if his thoughts were wandering.

'I hope,' said Stanley, who had been watching his face anxiously, 'that you did not mistake my meaning when I spoke about religion and emotion. Emotion, that is affection, is the very heart of religion ; and the surest way to be for ever cut off from God, is not to be misled by the intellect, which does but divert your eyes from Him ; but to quench your powers of loving, which is putting your eyes out.'

'He says the same thing that Campbell said,' thought Vernon when Stanley had departed. 'After all, I suppose there is something in it. Something!—why, once, when I had faith like Stanley's, I might have said the same myself. A pure human affection is the calix of Divine faith. But what is my condition? Stanley has not touched upon that. What haunts and threatens me is the foregone conclusion that Divine faith is a lie.' This set of thoughts seemed for a long time stationary, occupying his mind like the figure in a kaleidoscope. But at last a touch came, and the figure changed. That touch was given by the image of Miss Walters, as, with her 'pale, predestined face,' she came gliding like a ghost across his imagination. 'My own !' he exclaimed aloud, as he started from the sofa he was lying on, 'you may at least reach God through me, though I may never reach Him through you.' This passionate thought filled and overmastered him, and the listless bitterness he had felt all through the evening disappeared before it. 'I must write to you,' he said, 'even though I cannot speak to you.'

His pen moved rapidly; he never paused to hesitate. 'You entirely fill my thoughts,' he began. 'Your image haunts me; your eyes are looking at me. My white angel, my pure lily of Eden! Yes, you are that by nature. For God's sake, my own one, be true to yourself. For God's sake, I say;— well, and for mine too, if you like it—for mine too. All my life is turned into one long, mute prayer for you, that you may put away from yourself every taint of evil. Hate it; learn to hate it! Let it revolt you as it once revolted you! I will do all I can; but don't trust to me only. Help me too; try to see with your own eyes. My sight is very feeble; I am but a poor guide to God. I am like a blind man leading the blind. I only discern a glimmering, feeble light, and I am trying my best to feel my way towards it, carrying you with me. Will you not try to open your own eyes also, and give me a little counsel—a little assurance? My head is heavy; my eyelids ache with sadness. Did I not love you, I should have only asked to possess you. Your lips and arms could have given me all I longed for. But love is stronger than passion, and its demands are limitless, not for the lover, but for the loved. I am not trying to use fine language when I say that I am *consumed* with care for you. Scales have fallen from my eyes; I see now what I never saw before, and that is the meaning of Christ's love for men—His longing for their salvation. Oh, Cynthia, could I only die for you—could

I only take your sins on my head! Pierce my hands with nails—let me hang on the tree in agony—if only I might bear your sins and leave you once more spotless! I would be scourged, and spit upon! I would let my whole life be broken!

'Cynthia, my knowledge of you has indeed worked a change in me!'

BOOK V.

CHAPTER I.

VERNON'S state of mind next morning was little changed; he was still possessed by the same sorrow and solicitude. This, it is true, was not utterly unrelieved. The woman who had thus so completely filled his imagination, had confessed—had insisted on her love for him. In this fact certainly .there was food for satisfaction; and flying gleams of the most delicious happiness would at moments illuminate all his mental landscape with

The light that never was on sea or land.

But these did but serve to make his gloom

gloomier; and his heart ached with pain whenever it beat with pleasure. In this sombre condition he betook himself out of doors, to chew the cud of his disquietude. First he paced his garden, but its bounds seemed soon too narrow for him, and he strayed into the public road. Not far from his own gates were those of the Château St. John; and as he was passing these, he could not but pause. He leaned his forehead against the bars, and looked up the winding drive. It was a green vista of eucalyptus and of orange-trees, with here and there a cloud of foamy lilac-blossom; but its soft beauty did but fill Vernon with bitterness. The one thought that kept on repeating itself was, ' My Cynthia, could I save you, I would die for you.' Once a carriage passed, which had two well-dressed strangers in it. At the first sound of wheels he had suddenly faced about, in the fantastic hope that it might be

Miss Walters coming back again: but after an instant's glance he turned away impatiently. He could not endure the sensation that he was stared at. Not long after he heard more wheels approaching; but this time he had no impulse to look; he tried not even to listen. Listen, however, he soon found he must, when the following sounds struck on him.

'John'—it was uttered in a voice that, though somewhat raised, was like velvet—'is this where Lady Walters lives, do you know?'

'I believe it is, your Grace.'

'Is it worth trying, I wonder?'—this was addressed to another person. 'Shall I go and leave a card on her? Come—get up for a moment; you must be sitting on my card-case.'

In answer to this injunction came a slight leonine groan; but it was quickly drowned, for the velvet voice welled forth again,

'Upon my word,' it said, 'if that is not Mr. Vernon!'

Vernon at this was compelled to turn and show himself, and there face to face with him in a large open carriage, were the Duchess, Lord Surbiton, and a smart-looking young lady of some sort.

'Well,' said her Grace, 'and you are a nice young man, you are! I have been here for two whole days, and you have never once been to show yourself.'

Vernon replied that he had not known of her arrival.

'The fact of the matter is you're a great deal better employed. This is far more romantic, isn't it, than red fans and restaurants?'

'What is?' said Vernon absently.

'What? to be looking through a gate up a lovely young lady's avenue—especially when it's a young lady you have already carried off in your carriage. However, Mr.

Vernon, you go further than the gate, I suppose, sometimes.'

The Duchess did not laugh; but her voice when she was amused had a certain subtle quality which not only expressed her amusement, but transmitted it. It passed now into Vernon like an electric shock. He was instantly confronted with an absurd image of himself, and to his own intense surprise, he heard himself burst out laughing.

'Certainly,' he said, 'I was not waiting to take her another drive, for both she and her aunt are away at the present moment.'

'Very well then,' said the Duchess, 'there is one question solved. We will put off leaving our cards, and will go straight home again. Wait a bit, though. Lord Surbiton, you had better get out and walk, or else you'll be having indigestion again, and be unable to eat your dinner. Come, out you get—I know exactly what is good for you.

And listen,' she added, when Lord Surbiton had at last descended, ' you may as well give me my boa back again. You won't want it, you know, when you're getting warm walking.' Then turning to Vernon, 'And now,' she said, ' since you're not waiting for anybody, suppose you come back with us, and let us give you some tea. Whenever I see anyone now, I am dying to show my mansion to them.'

Vernon mechanically accepted this invitation. He took his seat opposite the young lady, and was vaguely conscious of being introduced to Miss Ethel somebody. ' Mr. Vernon,' the Duchess said—'a philosopher, and a great admirer of every species of beauty. Miss Ethel's eyes were sparkling, and they watched the Duchess continually, as though every instant she was expecting some amusement.

' Has Lord Surbiton,' she said presently,

' got indigestion ?   What a very unromantic thing for a poet ! '

' My dear,' said the Duchess, ' it is no wonder he has, considering the way he feeds himself.   When he arrived the other day to stay with me, what should you think he had brought with him ?   A cold plum pudding, if you please, wrapped up in his carpet-bag ; and he actually eats slices of it at six o'clock in the morning.   What did he do, Mr. Vernon, that time you were good enough to entertain him ?   One thing I know he did not do—and that was to give my orders to the gardener.   What I told him to say was that I could have no ants on the walks, and that they were to be all killed with boiling water.   Now I ask old Surbiton if he made this quite clear to the man, and that when I give an order I mean it ; and all I can get out of him is that Countess somebody—I don't know her name or nation—has the

finest ankle he ever saw. I told him ankles
were all very well ; but it's not so nice when
you have ants biting them.'

'Yes,' smiled Miss Ethel, 'but didn't
Colonel Stapleton give your message ? '

'As for Colonel Stapleton,' said the
Duchess, 'he's even worse than Lord Surbiton. He seems to have spent his entire
time with Miss Walters, till the wind was
taken out of his sails by—who should you
think ? The curate. It strikes me, Mr.
Vernon, that you have not been doing all
you might have done, if you let your special
young lady fall into other people's hands like
this. I assure you our fat Colonel is full of
her. I was going to have asked him over to
stay with me, only I was afraid Mrs. Grantly
would have his eyes out. However, he shall
come for my fancy ball. That will be quite
safe. There will be no time then for
quarrelling.'

'I think,' said Miss Ethel, 'Colonel Stapleton is very amusing.'

'Do you know him?' asked Vernon with an odd blank abruptness.

'Oh yes. He has stayed with us twice for Ascot-week. We have a small house near the racecourse.'

'Amusing!' said the Duchess. 'Oh yes, of course he is: and so useful, which is far better than amusing. He's going to order me all my Chinese lanterns, and my blue and red fire, and——I forget what else. Oh, some Strasburg pies, and some specially dry champagne. I quite delight in the Colonel. He's a most unselfish creature.'

Vernon listened to all this, as though it were a noise in a dream, making little effort himself except at some random smiles. Presently under the wheels came the crunching of new-laid gravel, and in another moment or two they were at the door of the great hotel.

Vernon had been in the building several times before; but when he now entered, he saw such a metamorphosis, that for the time being at least he was surprised into common attention. Where there had hitherto been a bleak solitude, there was now life and luxury. The large entrance hall was green with palm-trees, and gay with flowers. The white marble floor was strewn with oriental carpets, and on the softest of these was a yelping Pomeranian dog. There were larger tables draped with bright-coloured heavy cloths, and covered with books, photograph-frames, and a thousand-and-one knick-knacks. A stout English butler and a spruce groom-of-the-chamber gave to the scene a dignity all their own, and busy under their direction were some footmen with red waistcoats. Hardly had her Grace entered when a variety of orders, in tones of silver conveying a will of iron, went flying in all directions. 'Put that plant nearer the wall.' 'Where are you going with those Venetian glasses?' 'How often have I told you that those doors are to be never left open!' In answer to which came the rapid but hushed response of 'Yes, your Grace;' 'No, your Grace.'

'Now, Mr. Vernon,' said the Duchess, 'you must come and look at the drawing-room; or rather, to be *quite* accurate, I should say one of the drawing-rooms; for I assure you our splendour here is quite palatial, and we have five or six of them. There!' she said as they entered, 'it's getting to look liveable; but there are still some screens and things that I want a little advice about.'

'My! Mr. Vernon, and is this you again?' exclaimed a lady, slowly raising herself from an exceedingly deep arm-chair. It was none other than Mrs. Grantly, looking the picture of piquant languor, and arrayed in the most charming of tea-gowns. 'I guess, Duchess,' she said, 'I'm just tired out. I've been around for the last two hours showing Barnes where to place the flowers. Well, Mr. Vernon, and how are you by this time? Are you getting along pretty well out here?'

Vernon made some answer to this, but one so little in his usual manner, that Mrs. Grantly was struck by it. 'Duchess,' she exclaimed, 'here is Mr. Vernon quite out of sorts. He thinks, like Lord Surbiton, that all life is hollow.'

'That's a great deal more than Lord Surbiton himself is,' said the Duchess, 'at least at six o'clock in the morning. I've been telling him, and I may now tell Mr. Vernon, that if they think life hollow, they had better go in as I do, not for cold plum-pudding, but for old furniture. Look, Mr. Vernon, there is my last purchase—those six *Louis Seize* chairs.

I bought them at Grasse, out of the house of a certain notary. Four thousand francs is the sum he has done me out of; and now his daughter, I hear, is going to law with him, because she declares they are an heir-loom.'

Vernon praised the chairs with as much interest as he could muster, and then forced himself to say something *à propos* of the fancy ball.

'You'd better,' said the Duchess, 'be getting a dress ready, for I can tell you, we shan't allow any idle make-shifts—none of your black dress coats with a bit of pink satin tacked on to them.'

'I have a dress,' said Vernon. 'It is a Spanish pedlar's. It makes me look rather a blackguard, but I suppose that doesn't matter.'

'Oh, dear no,' said the Duchess. 'It will only make you popular.'

'And when,' said Vernon, 'is this festivity to be?'

'As soon as we can manage it. I don't quite know yet who will be in the house, but I shall know more presently, when the post comes. I mean to ask about a hundred from Cannes, and about half that number from Nice.'

At this moment tea made its appearance, and with the tea a large budget of letters. 'You must excuse me,' said the Duchess, as she tore open envelope after envelope, 'but these are all from our expected guests. I think,' she went on presently, when the work of inspection was over, 'I think we may manage the ball towards the end of the coming week. Montey Moreton comes to-morrow, who will of course lead the *cotillon*, and I must have a talk with him about it.'

The sight of the post's arrival made Vernon restless. He longed to go home to see if there were no letters for him; but the Duchess loved conversation, and he was un-

able to get free.   At last, however, a sudden
rescue came.   Captain Grantly entered the
room, with the 'Sporting Times' in his hand.
In an instant the Duchess turned to him, and
a sudden gust of the spirit sent her thoughts
in a new direction.   'Well, Captain Grantly,'
she exclaimed, 'and what about the City and
Suburban ?'

Vernon saw his opportunity, and at once
made use of it ; but when he was at the door
he was again recalled for a moment.   'Mr.
Vernon,' said her Grace, 'come and dine with
us to-morrow.   We shall be a larger party by
that time.'

He had no excuse to plead, so he accepted
and went his way.

This plunge into the common noises of
life confused him at first as a sudden fall
from a cliff might.   It made him feel for the
moment doubtful where he was.   Perhaps in
some degree this was a slight relief to him,

but the shock soon wore away, and his former cares returned to him. When he entered his own house, however, he at once found food for excitement. Lying on his table was a letter from Miss Walters. It was dated 'San Remo.'

'We arrived here,' she wrote, 'at about six o'clock. There was such a lovely sunset —such spaces of clear primrose, fading behind violet hills. I don't know why—but as I looked at it, it made me think of you. Perhaps it is because I associate you with everything that is pure, and suggests withdrawal from earth.' As Vernon read this he raised the letter to his lips and kissed it. 'The post goes at ten,' it went on; 'and I have very little time; but I must, I must write to you. I have been so saddened this evening. Mrs. Crane has been talking to me about Alic Campbell—only for a few minutes, it is true; but she will begin again to-morrow. It is so hard—I was going to say so tiresome; but this is not the thing that I want to write about. It is you—it is only you. I want to tell you how good, how forbearing you have been to me; and yet words can never give my meaning. No, my own, and nothing ever can, unless some day or other my life does.—I was miserable when you knew me, but it was with a hopeless misery. There was no germ of any amendment in it, and the only effort I made was a lazy effort to kill it. Don't you remember what I said to you that first morning in the garden, about my thinking that the Church laid too much stress upon purity? I tried to persuade myself that we daily—even the best of us—did things far worse than those special things that tormented me. But oh, I could not. I was but a very half-hearted liar to myself; and you at a touch put all my lies to flight. Had you not done that I should have gone on sinking deeper.

You found me not so much drowning as being sucked down in a quicksand; and you held out a hand to help me.   If you do not let me go, I shall by-and-by, I hope, free myself; but oh, I have one prayer to make to you. Do not be too hard on me.   Make a little concession to my extreme weakness.   Let me love you and love goodness for your sake, a little while longer, without asking me to do more than that.   Some day, if you will still help me, and hold me, and keep me pressed close to you, I may be able to say what I suppose you want me to say :—" I love God even more than I love you ; and yet for this very reason I love you more than ever."   But I can't say that yet.   Have patience: I shall learn in time.   I wonder, I often wonder— was God ever as kind to a sinner as you have been ?   Your own unhappy Cynthia.'

All this covered several pages, and from the middle of them there dropped out a small packet. The nature of this was explained in a brief postscript : ' I have found in my despatch box the enclosed little picture of myself. I hate it for what it reminds me of ; but if you can allow it to remind you only of me, perhaps you might like to have it.'

Vernon undid the wrappings of silver paper, and found within a small oval photograph, finished with extreme skill like a miniature. There Miss Walters was ; there was no mistaking her. She was in a white ball dress, with her fair shoulders visible, and a scarlet and silver opera-cloak clinging, but barely clinging to them. Her eyes looked full at you; her cheek rested on her beautiful clasped hands ; and round her fair hair was a wreath of the darkest myrtle-leaves. Vernon gazed at it fascinated ; it seemed to speak to him. There was in her cheeks a deeper rose-tint than, when he had known her, was habitual. He could have almost fancied that

they blushed because he looked on them.
What did the picture mean? Her expression
in it, her very attitude, was ambiguous. It
might be that of a Magdalen in sanctity, on
the brink of relapsing into sin; or a Magdalen
in sin on the eve of seeking for the Saviour.
As he continued looking, the Duchess and
her friends faded in his memory till they became nothing but irksome shadows ; and his
one impulse was to immure himself with the
image of this beautiful woman. The direction
his thoughts were taking became soon appa-
rent to him. ' If she will not be God's,' he
said, ' she must and she shall be mine!' He
looked at the picture again, and he noticed a
new detail in it. On her bosom there hung
a locket. His attention fixed on this, and it
seemed to him that it bore some inscription.
There was a small magnifying glass on the
table close at hand, and with its aid he de-
ciphered two initials. They were ' J. S.'

'Jack Stapleton!' he exclaimed, and seizing the picture he tore it into small fragments.

He was a sober man again. He now went back to her letter. He read it, and he re-read it. There was much in it, but not all that he longed for. The anxiety that had preyed upon him, the anxiety for another's sake, once more took hold upon him; and when night came he had still failed to be comforted.

The day following he wrote again to Miss Walters. His letter expressed the same solicitude as his last one, and his day was occupied with the same thoughts about her. As for himself, and his own private claims on her, these were cauterised, so to speak, by the fire of his unselfish longings. Her welfare, not his own satisfaction, was in literal truth the one thing that engrossed him —at least the one personal thing. There is that exception necessary. For with his wishes for Miss Walters wider thoughts would mix themselves; and he could no but identify the hopes of the human race, as a whole, with those he entertained or despaired of for one woman in particular.

Much to his annoyance a certain recollection haunted him—the recollection of his engagement to dine that night with the Duchess.

CHAPTER II.

IT was not to be helped, however. As eight o'clock was striking, the tall doors of the hotel were being thrown wide to receive him. Well-trained servants, with all the manners of London, were adroitly helping him to get rid of his great-coat. More doors were opened, and then, sharply and in an instant, came the sea-like murmur of the polite world conversing.

The Duchess's party had indeed increased by this time. The dim air of the drawing-room, starred with subdued lamp-light, seemed full of varied colourings, from the dresses of divers ladies. Vernon as he entered had almost a sense of shyness. His eyes were not dazzled, but he felt as if his mind were blinking. He was breathing an atmosphere that it seemed he had long been a stranger to. Here was the London world once more enfolding him with its familiar sights and sounds, and full of the memories of the pleasures it once gave him. He felt it to be all unreal. It gave him a giddy sense, as if he had just come off a steamer. Still he was obliged to exert himself; it was impossible to shrink into a corner. Before long he discovered an old acquaintance or two, and as he moved from one to the other, he felt himself getting more at home again. When they went into dinner, Miss Ethel fell to his share, looking exceedingly bright and pretty; and she reminded him with a slight tone of reproach, that she had met him

before in London. The long dinner table,
with all its gleam and glitter, gave Vernon
an experience like that of a saint's inverted.
He was being dazzled by a vision—not of the
next world, but this ; and it seemed to be
moving him to renew his old communion
with it. Miss Ethel's brightness began presently to tell on him. It was of a quiet,
almost a demure kind, but it possessed the
power of provoking men to respond to it ;
nor did Vernon prove an exception. Champagne too came to assist its influence, and
very soon he began to laugh quite naturally.
By the middle of dinner he had become so
mundane in his mind, that he turned round
and glanced at his neighbour on the other
side. He wondered when he had done this,
that he had not done so sooner. She was a
dark woman, singularly beautiful, with voluptuous long-lashed eyes. In a minute or two
these eyes met Vernon's, and said plainly

that she would be very glad to talk to him : and upon this he achieved one of the prettiest of all toy adventures—the breaking that dainty delicate ice-film which exists between guests in the same house, when they have not been introduced formally.

After dinner, when the gentlemen had rearranged themselves, Vernon found that sitting next to him was the Lord Lieutenant of his county—a peer of great distinction, and a Conservative ex-minister. Here was a new distraction. The noble lord at once plunged into politics and home matters ; and he soon gave them a flattering personal turn. ' I can tell you,' he said, ' you made yourself extremely popular in ——shire. I was talking the other day to one of the farmers from your part, who calls himself—so he told me—a Radical. Well, in spite of your politics, you had won his heart, I can assure you ; and I hear the same story of you in

various other quarters. The Workmen's
Conservative Club, which you did so much
to help forward, is getting on admirably. I
hope sincerely that you are still thinking of
Parliament. I've not the least doubt, for my
own part, that if there were a petition, we
should unseat Tom Bowden ; and in the event
of another contest, no one would have a chance
against you.'

All this discourse put Vernon in better
spirits. He began to feel he was waking up
in earnest. He waived the allusions to himself, although he was not insensible to them ;
but he plunged with interest into various
questions of politics ; and the image of Miss
Walters, which had been hitherto still watching him, seemed to melt at such magic words
as *land*, *labour*, and *capital*.

Meanwhile, there had been a change
made in the drawing-room. A large curtain
at one end had been raised, and displayed the

drop-scene of a charming miniature theatre. The gentlemen once more showed themselves; and, to the slight alarm of certain of them, it appeared there were to be some charades. Vernon was pressed to take part, but he refused stoutly. His sadness, banished for a moment, was already coming back to him. He found, however, that no denial would be taken ; and when he realised that he would be acting with his dark-eyed neighbour of the dinner-table, he consented with sufficient grace.

As the *corps dramatique* were retiring to mature their plans, he discovered a familiar presence, which had till now escaped him. This was Mrs. Crane, exceedingly well pleased with herself for being of the Duchess's party, and looking at him with a charity all her own. She informed him she was not going to act herself, but that she was ready to do her best in the green-room, and that she would rouge or powder anybody, provided it was not a woman. Nothing could have been less pleasant to Vernon than the apparition of this lady ; and though he tried to be as civil as he could to her, he left her on the very first opportunity.

The charades began. Vernon felt from the first moment that he and his dark-eyed beauty had some sort of attraction for each other ; and when the concluding act came, it was his part to make love to her. From old habit he could not help infusing a flavour of personal tribute into the tender things he said to her : and when, at the end of the scene, he had to lead her off the stage, he continued the process till he had brought her out of doors into the moonlight. There he remained talking with her, leaning against a great vase of geraniums. All his attentions to her were as unreal as a ghost's ; but for this very reason he did not attempt to check them, and they certainly to one observer looked marked enough. This observer was Mrs. Crane, who was leaning against the window-curtains; and, as she observed, the small passion broke in her, which, by straining a compliment, might perhaps be called her jealousy. It was a passion certainly of no very dreadful intensity. It might lead her to laugh from malice; it would never make her pale from rage; and instead of poisoning its object, she would be far more likely to play him a practical joke.

CHAPTER III.

THE events of that evening were
not without their after-effect on
Vernon. He carried away with
him from the Duchess's a certain amount of
excitement, which deranged his mind and
was very far from pleasing it. Since his intimacy with Miss Walters, it was as though
he had been descending deep into the hidden
places of life, and the world on the surface,
with its laughter, noise, and sunlight, had
faded away to a mere shadowy memory. His
only companions had been thoughts of sin.

and holiness, and the awful gulf between
them ; and his only lights had been tapers at
shrines for prayer. But now the darkness
seemed to be slowly parting, and the day and
the things of day appearing like grey clouds
through it. Sounds which he thought he had
said good-bye to for ever, once more assailed
his ears, and mixed themselves grotesquely
with the voices to which only he had of late
been listening. He felt as though two worlds
had come into collision, and he was surrounded by the dissolving fragments of both of
them. The world of prayer, of penitence, and
of aspiration, where sin was the one calamity,
and communion with God the one success
worth striving for ; the world, on the other
hand, of balls and duchesses, of private
theatricals, and the gossip of Mayfair—
these two worlds seemed to have struck and
wrecked each other, and each seemed equally
unreal.

So Vernon felt when he lay down to rest; so he felt too when he awoke next morning. But next morning there was a new symptom in him. The world which had thus come back again, he now felt had brought with it a breath of grateful air. He had been amused for moments, and had forgotten the burden that was bound to him; and it was on his lips— only he checked himself—to say in so many words, 'I have climbed up out of a charnel house, and have breathed the air of heaven.'

He was first conscious of this change of disposition when he began to write to Miss Walters, which he did that afternoon. His words and thoughts would not flow freely as hitherto. The intense solicitude which had racked him for days into misery was more or less relaxed. It was not that his intention for a moment wavered. He was still resolved, as much as ever, to help her; but he was now master of the resolve, the resolve was no longer master of him. He was not happy, he had not become light-hearted. He was in some ways more wretched than ever; but a vision of happiness, a vision of gay spirits, had, like a gleam of sunshine, once more broken across his life. 'Ah, Cynthia, Cynthia,' he thought, 'why do you compel me to be serious? Could I only be sure that you had recovered your own natural strength, that you were strong and confident in your own self-respect, how happily we might walk together! Our fears, our hopes, our anxieties need not be kept always on the stretch. What could I not give to be able to laugh again without an aching heart!' The consciousness of such feeling in himself had, so far as he knew, one effect only. It turned his moral devotion to Miss Walters from an impulse into a duty. Because he found some difficulty in writing to her, he only wrote more earnestly, and with intenser consideration.

He had just completed this task—it was then about four o'clock—when two male figures passed the windows of his library. A moment after these were announced and entering. They were Lord Surbiton and the Conservative ex-minister. The visit, it appeared, was one of more than ordinary compliment. There was something like business at the bottom of it, and of a very flattering nature. The ex-minister had just received intelligence that a relation of his own, who sat for a certain borough, was to accept the Chiltern Hundreds, and it was now suggested to Vernon that here was a new opening for him. The conversation lasted for some time, and then Vernon was left to consider the matter over. The new range of prospects that were now presented to him stirred his mind like fresh bracing sea-wind, and he wandered out of doors to digest the sudden excitement. He paced nearly the same ground that he had paced two days ago, but with different thoughts to busy him. He passed again the gates of the Château St. John, but he did not stop now to peer through the bars and meditate. Instead of that, he again had recourse to **Stanley.**

'My dear fellow,' he exclaimed, as he broke into the priest's sitting-room, 'I have come to have another talk with you.'

Stanley stared at his visitor. It was hardly the same Vernon. A new light danced in his eyes, there was a happy smile on his lip. 'Stanley,' he went on, 'I have taken your advice at last. I am going to commit myself, or at least I shall try to do so. There is another chance of my getting into Parliament, and if matters turn out as I think they will, I shall be going home **directly.'**

'I am very glad to hear it,' said Stanley. 'You will find,' he went on, smiling, 'that to have a useful purpose before you, will change your views about many things.'

'It not only will,' said Vernon. 'It has already done so. I have a little property in the East end of London. A project has revived in my mind with regard to that, which I had a year ago, but which I have since let drop. It is for a kind of workhouse arranged on a new principle, which shall give more relief than such places do at present, and yet be without what I consider their chief drawbacks. I made the plan for the building myself, and had arranged nearly every detail. I thought, for a sort of motto above the door, to put this : "Come unto me, all ye that travail and are heavy-laden, and I will refresh you."'

'And who was the "I"?' said Stanley. 'Did that mean *you*? Take care, Vernon, take care! Have we not already agreed to distrust too eager emotion?'

Vernon, however, was not to be disheartened. All his serious thoughts, all his anxieties to find something in life worth working for, forced themselves into the mould of this new excitement; and Stanley, as he heard him talk, began to feel stronger hopes of him. Vernon indeed at this moment drew vigour from three sources. First there was the thought of Miss Walters. She was a beautiful woman, she had a strong hold on him, and it seemed in his power to redeem her whole character. Then there was this prospect of active life suddenly breaking in on him; and lastly there was the pleasant world at the Duchess's, which was stinging him back into common social consciousness. This last influence indeed so far increased upon him, that on the following day he proposed to give a luncheon-party: and the idea being approved by everyone, arrangements were made accordingly.

The life of Miss Walters meanwhile had been outwardly less eventful, but not less so inwardly. Whenever she could she retired to her own bedroom, the view from which was beautiful : and at a table by the window she pored over Vernon's letters. The first that reached her from him, after she had left the Château St. John, was the one to which she recurred the oftenest. The strength of the feelings it stirred in her may be gathered from the very first words of her answer.

' My belovèd,' she wrote, with the accent duly inserted—a fact which made her smile herself after she had written it, ' I should be indeed ungrateful if I did not live for you, since I know you would die for me. As I read your letter, it was as though you were close to me—as though your arms were round my waist holding me. Will you ever know

what to a woman that sense is of being held,
of being clasped, of being supported? It
seems to draw the very soul out of one.—
If you were here I could fall on my knees and
worship you. Between these two last sentences
do you know what I have done? For a good
ten minutes I have been leaning forwards,
with my face upon your letter, thinking,
thinking, thinking about you. It was very
silly, no doubt; but oh, my darling, could
you only know what my thoughts were! You
need have no fear for me, as long as you fill
my being. There is no room for any evil
then. But I won't bore you with my affection any longer. I will tell you what has
been boring me. Dear Mrs. Crane has been
at me again about Alic Campbell. She is
always asking me if I don't like him; and I
believe if I have ever said a word in his
favour, she has written off and told him of it.
I do like him in a way. But he treated me

like a saint, and a simple saint into the bargain, which you know I am very far from
being. That is one thing in him which was
always jarring me. But he is your friend.
I would like him for your sake, if he only
would not love *me*. Well, Mrs. Crane has
heard from him, and he is coming, it seems,
back from Sorrento soon. What shall we
do ? Poor fellow, I am very sorry for him.
He will want to come to you, at least for a
day or two. You told me he would do that.
You must think over what had best be done
about it.'

The next letter she received from Vernon
contained the full news of the arrival of the
Duchess's party, and of his own intercourse
with them. This, however, was very soon
told ; and he then passed on to graver subjects, repeating his former advice, and his
former wishes for her welfare. ' As to mere
affection,' he said in concluding, ' I cannot

express myself properly. But you must remember me as I have been, when I have been speaking to you; and with the aid of this memory you must read between the lines when I write to you. If I did not care as I do for you I could pour out fine expressions by the page; but to be really serious makes me silent.'

This letter crossed that of Miss Walters's which has just been given above, and, though she tried to avoid the impression, it struck her as a cold return to it. It seemed to blow like a chilly air over her; it produced in her a sense of isolation; and though she succeeded in concealing its exact nature from herself, she could not avoid giving it some expression. This took the form, when she wrote that day to Vernon, of begging him to come to San Remo. 'We are planning an expedition,' she said, 'into the mountains behind here. They are so beautiful—a world of woods and gorges, where every valley has its snow-fed river in it, and every height its village and its domed sanctuary. We think of going next Friday. Oh, if you could only come! We want it to be Friday, because on Saturday the other Mrs. Crane—the one you know, will be here for a night or two, and I would so far rather go without her. Try and come. It is a very short journey, and hour by hour I feel I want you more. I told you,' she went on—her pen was now running away with her, 'that I felt as though your arm was round me. Do not withdraw it; I might so easily fall away again. To see you even for one day would be a kind of sacrament to me. Come to me—oh, do come—keep my life full of you, or something else will fill it. I can throw a new light, I think, on the way in which you have helped me. You have made me believe again in the possibility of goodness in men.

Before I knew you I thought they were all bad. The Duke of Wellington said that the cause of panic in an army was the belief on the part of each soldier that the others had lost confidence, and would not obey orders. I was suffering from a kind of moral panic. Human nature is not logical, and the feminine nature, I suppose, is the least logical part of it. It is for that reason that example helps me so. I am not logical, my love. All my trust in goodness, and all my strength for it, is founded upon you.'

The letter went, and before she could get an answer to it, there came another from Vernon. In this there was more description of the various doings at the Duchess's, and a long account of the suggestions made to him *à propos* of standing for Parliament. ' If this plan,' he wrote, ' really comes to anything, it may require me to return very soon to England. If I were not anxious for you,

I should go happily; but how can I be happy when every step I take, my heart is almost broken with anxiety for fear a poor wounded child I am carrying may be in pain?'

As Miss Walters read this, she was conscious of a painful agitation. She repeated an action which she had already described to Vernon. Her head drooped, she leaned heavily upon the writing-table, and her face rested blindly on the letter that lay before her. 'Going'—she thought—'going back to England! and so little said of his sorrow for leaving me!' These were her two thoughts, and long as she remained motionless, there were none but these that occupied her.

By-and-by, however, a revulsion of feeling came. She reproached herself and said, 'I am selfish. Why should I be always troubling him?' And she set herself then and there to write to him in a changed tone. 'I have been wrong,' she began. 'I have been crying to you like an unrestrained child, and I believe I have fostered my sense of weakness by thus going on deploring it. Surely it is time that I now felt confident ; and your last letter, I think, has given me some reason for being so. It has made me feel that I can take an unselfish interest in the career which I hope may be opening to you. And what a relief to fix one's thoughts on something utterly apart from one's own condition—one's own bad or good, and to project one's interests outwards ! When you come on Friday, as, my love, I know you will, what joy it will be to me to talk all this over with you ! Did I not tell you that I could at least do one thing for you—that I could stimulate you to make the very best use of your powers ? Even now I foresee that when you come over here, there will be a new light, a new gladness in those eyes of yours, whose looks I know by heart ; and which so many a time I have known full of sadness only.'

In this account of herself, undoubtedly there was a certain amount of truth ; and she did her best to bring her feelings into accord with it altogether. She took Vernon's letter in her hands, as if she would grasp her nettle, and went out of doors with it. The house was fronted by a long strip of garden, which had a pleasant terrace as its boundary, overhanging the public road. Beyond the road was the railway ; beyond that moved the glossy blue of the sea ; and the view for the saunterer was framed by the fronds of palm-trees. It was to this terrace that Miss Walters took herself ; and attempting to compose her thoughts she paced it to and fro slowly. Her dress was still of extreme simplicity. She was very different from the Miss Walters whose entrance had been so noted in the restaurant. Still, since the day that Vernon had marked the change, she had become more *soignée* again in some ways. Her dove-coloured velvet hat, it is true, was old and faded. Her dress, of the same colour, was faded too, and was of a common stuff; but by some magic on her maid's part or her own, its simplicity savoured more of the world than of the cloister; and she was gloved and shod daintily now as ever. She had studiously avoided lately much contemplation of herself in the glass; but to-day as she went out, she could not avoid noticing that she looked beautiful, and that the faded tints became her; and in spite of her sorrow, there went through her a thrill of vanity. In an instant this was cast into the treasury of her dominant passion; and she said to herself, with her heart full of Vernon, ' My body at least is worthy of your acceptance.'

Had she wished on the terrace to consult another looking-glass, she might have found one in the many glances that were turned to her from the road below. But of these she took little heed. So absorbed indeed was she in her own thoughts, that a servant from the house had overtaken her, without her having heard his footsteps. In his hand was a tray, and on the tray was a telegram. Her eye fell first upon the name of the sender. It was Vernon. Her face flushed with pleasure. She crushed the paper in her hand, and continued her walk at an increased pace, feeling that between her palm and fingers she was clasping tight a treasure. She would not read it yet; she would enjoy the throbs of uncertainty. 'Perhaps,' she thought, 'he may be coming even before Friday—this evening—this afternoon—perhaps by the next train.' This last possibility was suggested by the noise of a railway-whistle; and presently, like a black reptile, smelling of smoke and coal-dust, the train went sliding by. She watched the carriage windows, hoping to detect his face at one of them; but not having done this, she resolved to inspect the telegram. She half unfolded it; but then she stayed. Uncertainty still charmed her; and she looked at the unread paper with a smile of pensive tenderness. It was still not opened, when the sound of her own name startled her. It did more than startle her, for she knew the voice that uttered it. It was that of Colonel Stapleton. Instinctively she thrust the telegram into her pocket; and in a state of mind that was at first but blank astonishment, she stood stock still for a moment, and then went forward and greeted him. As she did this, there was a smile on her lips that came of long habit. It is impossible to make an entire change in one's manner to a person who is unconscious of any reason for a change. Some change in hers, however, there without doubt was, for the Colonel at once declared she was 'grumpy,' and 'out of sorts.' When this meeting took place they were standing near a small summer-house; and by a rapid move of the Colonel's in another moment they had sat down in it.

'Come,' said he, 'what on earth is the matter with you? You shouldn't treat me in this way, for I can only stay ten minutes. I've come over with some lawyer's papers, for Molly Crane to sign, and in another half hour I shall have to start for Nice again. I heard you were in the garden, so I couldn't help having one try at finding you.'

The news that the Colonel was going gave Miss Walters great relief, and brought a smile to her face that was perhaps more cordial than she meant it to be; for the

Colonel took her by the chin and turned her face towards him. At his touch, however, she started back abruptly, though the smile did not desert her.

' Remember, Jack,' she said, ' I'm going to have no more of your nonsense. We are too old, both of us, for that kind of thing.'

' *I'm* not,' said the Colonel, ' though I believe, at this moment, I'm in too great a hurry for it. However, I shall be back here to have another look at our Molly, in a couple of days. I've engaged a room—a first-rate one—at the Hotel Victoria. Such a view from it, I can tell you ! You must come,' he went on, fixing his gleaming eyes on her, ' and see it yourself one of these days —little cross, vindictive minx that you are ! '

When the Colonel said he was in a hurry, he really spoke the truth. There was a certain bal masqué at Nice that evening, to

which he was going to escort a select party of
friends; and so anxious was he that he
should not miss this, that he very soon was
taking leave of Miss Walters, though without informing her as to the joys that lay
before him.

As soon as he was out of sight, Miss
Walters took out the telegram, and now she
at once read it. It was not a lengthy docu-
ment; it consisted simply of this; 'I can't
come on Friday. I am asking a party that day
to lunch with me. I will explain by letter.'

The curtness and the coldness, as she
thought it, of this despatch had an effect as
sudden on her as that of a physical blow.
Her first outward expression of her inward
feelings was a rapid movement to the
parapet of the terrace, on which she leaned
her arms, and looked fixedly towards the
railway-station. 'What a fool I was,' she
murmured, 'to have driven Jack away!'

An hour after this she was in her bedroom kneeling, for the most part silent, but now and again whispering, 'How wicked I am! Shall I never make myself good for anything?' The same night she began another letter to Vernon.

'I don't know,' she wrote, 'if I shall send you this. I shall see as I go on. I don't like to trouble you, and to make you wretched; but nothing that I could tell you could make you half so wretched as I myself am. You tell me to say my prayers; you tell me to love God. I try to do both. I have tried each night to do so. But I feel more or less as you do. It is not a man's privilege only to find his reason at war with his faith. A woman sometimes can have the same greatness thrust upon her; she, too, can doubt the reality of all that she thinks most valuable. I have had bitter experience of this, these days I have been away from you. All the holy things that we were brought up to long for, and for which, till I had ruined myself, I did long——what do you think they now seem to me? Like one of those fabulous rocks in the middle of a great ocean, which sailors see sometimes, and which then disappear suddenly. What tricks are played one by the various faculties of one's being! Yes; I believe one five minutes, and I disbelieve another. You know my opinion about the Catholic Church. I have often told you how impossible it is to me to believe in its teachings literally. Well—what do you think I have done, and done in real good faith, more than once lately? I have prayed to Saint Mary Magdalene! What does it all mean, my friend, this *bizarre* confusion of emotion, thought, and judgment? If I had no faith, I should not be so miserable as I am. That is what seems so hard to me. I have enough faith left to make me miserable, but not enough to make me hopeful. My faith has lost its courage; but like other cowards, it can still bully. My life is bitter with the lees of a belief whose finer spirit is evaporating.

'Do you not see how, when one is in this state, the desire for self-respect becomes of the same nature as one's belief and faith? Self-respect, it is always being whispered to one, is nothing; neither is there any need for any self-condemnation. It is our judgment of our past, not our past, that fills us with self-reproaches.

'My friend, out of this chaotic mind of mine your love might call peace and order. But now—what shall I say to you? I begin to feel, or at least to fear, that your love is getting——. But no. I will not finish the sentence. I will wait till I hear what you say to-morrow morning. My darling, I dread your letter.'

Vernon's letter arrived. It was full of regrets that he could not come to San Remo on Friday. It was full too of little details and incidents that he judged would amuse Miss Walters; and it begged for her sympathy in his hopes of a new career. It was impossible to say that it was not written most affectionately. But for all this, her instinct observed a want in it—not a want she could blame, one only she could shudder and wonder at. It did not put *him* in a different light before her, but her own relation to him. Her answer expressed this.

'Dear,' she wrote, continuing her last night's letter where she had left off, 'I have got yours of this morning, and I think I will send you what I have already written. I am sorry you can't come on Friday, but I have no doubt you are amused better where you are. So far as I can gather, you are very gay. That must be pleasant. And now let me tell you that I *have* done one thing that you told me to do. I have been reading between the lines of your letters, and doing this very carefully ; and I feel that a change is coming over them. I can't explain to you what or where it is. You write still as kindly—even as lovingly as ever. But my instincts, as you know, are very quick ; and my instincts tell me this—that you, though you do not yet know it, are getting tired of me. I do not complain. I know I am not worthy to keep you : and yet you cannot wonder if I feel it a little bitterly, when I see my last hope in this world, and for aught I know in another, slipping so soon—so soon away from me. My aunt and I are coming back in a day or two.

'A letter has been sent on to us from your dear friend the Duchess, to ask us to come to her fancy ball. I think we shall go. I have a dress with me which I once wore in

Florence; and I shall have it done up at Nice, where we stop for a night on our way back. Of course you will go. I expect you will find it very amusing.

'I am sorry to have to write as I have done. It took me some time to bring myself to do so; but it is best to be quite honest, at least with the people one is fond of.'

What reply to expect to this Miss Walters did not know. The effort she had made in writing it, and in acknowledging to herself what she had said in it, left her in dull dejection. At luncheon, however, this was somewhat broken in upon by an unwelcome and unexpected sight. When she went down into the dining-room her aunt and Mrs. Crane were already seated: but they were not alone. Miss Walters perceived that there was a beautifully dressed visitor with them, whom in a moment more she recognised. It was the other Mrs. Crane.

This lady was fresh from the Cap de Juan, and was full of accounts of the Duchess and her doings. Many smart people were shy of Mrs. Crane; but Mrs. Crane was never shy of them. Everyone of a sufficient position was spoken of by her with a familiarity that implied anything but contempt, though it continually took the form of it : and an immense amount of gossip was rattled off by her during luncheon about Algy *this* and Mabel *that*, with their proper style and title sometimes added in a parenthesis. Vernon's name occurred several times. He was going to give a luncheon-party, he had written a charade, he had taught a young lady to play lawn-tennis, he had frequent private conferences with the Conservative ex-minister. All this, however, was being only dropped by the way, amongst the other flowers of information that Mrs. Crane was scattering, till Miss Walters said with affected carelessness,

'Mr. Vernon seems to be contributing much to the general amusement, and I have no doubt to his own.'

There was something in her tone—a certain pain or pique in it—that touched as it were a spring in Mrs. Crane's being. Mrs. Crane had amused herself so well at the Duchess's with a certain young guardsman, that Vernon's coolness to her had quite escaped her memory. But when Miss Walters spoke, it somehow or other came back to her, and seemed in common justice to demand some slight punishment. Memory and imagination at once came to her aid, in friendly struggle as to which should be most active.

'Mr. Vernon,' she said, 'may amuse other people well enough, but he amuses himself even more. Perhaps, however, it is ill-natured to say that, for there was one other person at least who I imagine has been as well pleased as himself.'

Miss Walters, as she heard this, drew a sharp breath, and her hand closed tightly on a fork she was idly trifling with. Her eye fixed on Mrs. Crane with a helpless stare of attention, and she was struggling for self-possession to make some common remark on the matter. Her aunt, however, saved her the trouble.

'And is Mr. Vernon,' she said smiling, 'a great admirer of young ladies? What should you say, Cynthia? You and he are such friends.'

Mrs. Crane shrugged her shoulders a little. 'As for young ladies,' she said, 'it depends what we mean by that. Mr. Vernon likes them married. There's one who just suits him at the Cap de Juan now, and he sits in her pocket every evening.'

Miss Walters at last contrived to force a

smile to her lips, and to utter three words, while it was still on them. 'Who is that?' she said.

It was the lady with the dark eyes, to whom Vernon had made love in the charade. 'She's one of my best friends,' Mrs. Crane said, 'so of course one can allow for her little eccentricities; but we all know that dear Lily is not bashful.'

Miss Walters discovered after luncheon that Mrs. Crane was going to stay at San Remo for a day or two, and for the first time in her life she sought her company voluntarily. She proposed that they should go a walk together. During the course of this *tête-à-tête*, Mrs. Crane was brought back to the subject of Vernon's doings, and induced to give more particulars, which she did on the following principle. Mr. Ruskin has observed that one of the commonest faults in painting is the representation by the painter of more than his eye sees. He thinks he has seen distinct leaves, whereas really he has only seen green shadow. Mrs. Crane was afflicted with exactly the same delusion. She saw shadow, and she thought she had seen kisses. The little scene on the terrace, after the charade was over, was presented in this way to Miss Walters, and a number of other incidents of something the same nature.

The following morning when Mrs. Crane met Miss Walters, 'My dear child,' she exclaimed, 'what a lovely frock that is of yours! You weren't looking half so well yesterday. Indeed, I did think you were wearing the willow for a certain friend of ours, whose little doings we talked about. But this, I suppose, is put on in honour of Colonel Jack; as to-day, I believe, he is going to honour San Remo.

CHAPTER IV.

VERNON'S time meanwhile had been passing pleasantly enough; but though his conduct here and there might have been such as to explain, it was in no case such as to justify, Mrs. Crane's conception of it. The letter, therefore, that Miss Walters had sent to him, when she received his telegram, was an unexpected and inexplicable blow. Its immediate result was to rouse his anxiety for her to a greater intensity than it had ever reached before; and he proceeded at once to write to her, with even more than his accustomed earnestness. He

was full of wonder at the impression he
had given her; he was hurt bitterly at
having hurt her. But next day, when he
thought the matter over again, he could not
deny that there was some foundation for her
charge, even though there might be no direct
truth in it. The brightness of the world certainly had attracted him. It had come to
him like fresh air and sunshine; and it had
been little short of rapture to him to be able
to laugh gaily and talk lightly again. He
could not deny, too, that amongst the fair
guests of the Duchess there were several
whose good graces he had found some
pleasure in winning. He had felt himself to
be popular; he had felt himself to be fit for
the world. He had felt himself to be *liked*
by many; and he had found this a refreshing
change after having been *loved* by one. He
acknowledged all this to himself; but was
there, he asked, any wrong in it ?

What answer, he wondered, would this letter of his elicit from her? He had to wait a day before it elicited any. It reached Miss Walters the afternoon of her walk with Mrs. Crane, and that evening she was unable to write anything. But by the evening following her answer was written and posted. Vernon at last received it.

'My dear, dear friend,' she said, 'I have received that last kind letter of yours. You will think that my answer to it is very strange. I am intensely weary; there is the same languid heaviness in my mind that there is in the air before a thunderstorm. I cannot tell, but I think, perhaps, that this may be a good condition for me to write in. I am not perturbed for the moment by any violent feeling.

'You know how little sanguine I have been about my own case. My mind misgave me all the time, that I needed more help than I had any right to expect of you. The intense, the tender devotion that you have shown for me, and for my welfare—I know how true it has been. I do not for a moment doubt it. I am not one of those unjust women who say that a feeling cannot be true because it does not last for ever. We do not judge of bad feelings in that way. Why should we judge so of good ones ? No ; I believe that you have had at heart my welfare in the truest and best of ways. I believe that you have loved, and that you do love me. Were I other than I am—were I only now what I once might have been, we might have been happy all our lives together. It is my fault, it is not yours, that what has happened has happened. I am speaking deliberately, and with the conviction that I speak truth, when I say that the only love, the only devotion that could have saved and redeemed me, would have been a devotion too sad and sorrowful for your bright nature to have endured it.

Who breaks a butterfly upon a wheel?

—I am not applying that line to you, but somehow or other you suggested it. What I would say with regard to you is, who expects a swallow to carry a millstone? I in life should be a millstone hung about your neck. You could not lift me. There is nothing left for you but to spread your wings and leave me.

' Dear, the strongest *personal* hold I could have had on you, would have been through your lower nature. Had you had less self-command, less self-denial, I might have held you through that. I know it, though I ought not to know it. But you can command yourself; and I revere your strength, because I realise your temptations. I must explain myself. I say the strongest *personal* hold.

What is actually your strongest feeling for me, indeed what is practically now almost your only feeling for me, is your desire that a soul should save itself.   But listen to me.   It is *a* soul, not *my* soul, that you are anxious for.

‘ You remember the little lame child you so kindly carried to its home.   You carried it in your goodness ; but you were glad to put your burden down.   I am to you like that poor child.

‘ I have no anger against you as I write this.   I feel no bitterness or desperation ; though these may very soon come on me. But I am calm, just yet.

‘ I have not formed this judgment of you from your own letters only.   I have heard of you from a third person—a person I cannot endure, and who, I am sure, said what she did say out of a more or less defined ill-nature.   The person I speak of was Mrs. Crane, who tells me that she has been at the

Duchess's ; and seems to have kept a sharp eye on your doings. There are several things she told me which I, of course, do not believe for one instant. But, subtracting the falsehood, I could easily see the truth. I could see how, as the world and its brightness once more came back to you, your letters to me grew not less kind, not less purely intentioned, but shorter and less earnest. If a man would really redeem a woman, she must be all in all to him. That is a truth, dear friend, you have not learnt yet. I think—yes, I think that, had I been different, I might perhaps have taught it to you. But never mind. The dream is over. Had it been longer, the awakening would have been harder to bear even than it is. After all, what does it matter ? You know many women as bad as I am, perhaps even worse, and you think their company pleasant enough, and you never waste a tragic thought on them.

'Well, we have talked about the world. It will be in the world that we next meet. The fancy ball is the day after to-morrow, and we do not return till that evening. We shall meet again there. I wonder if you will recognise me.

'I told you Mrs. Crane had been over here. Someone else comes to-day. Ah me!'

She had added in a postscript, 'No, you are not all I thought you were. Surely were you what a man ought to be, you would be able to love in a more human way than you do. There is something wanting in you. You are good enough to make me wish for holiness; not good enough to make me able to attain to it. You are——.' But here she stopped, and tore off the leaf on which all this had been written.

CHAPTER V.

MISS WALTERS in her letter had
spoken no more than the truth.
Until the ball Vernon was not
able to see her, neither was there any chance
of writing to her. It is true that the ball
was to be the following evening, and the
interval of waiting was not long. But to him
it seemed long. He was perplexed, bewll-
dered, miserable. Miss Walters filled his
mind to the exclusion of all other thoughts.
They had been driven away by her letter, as
though by a scourge of cords. He could fix
his attention on nothing excepting her. His
grave plans for the future, his pleasant amuse-

ments of the hour or the moment, were all
ruined by her image. It shattered his peace
like a persistent street organ. It would not
let him alone. It forced itself on his consciousness. What should he think of Miss
Walters? What of himself? He could give
himself no answer. In forlorn hope of comfort he betook himself to Stanley, with whom
lately he had been having much serious intercourse, and talked long and earnestly with
him about our influence over others, and the
responsibility that influence lays on us.

His acquaintance with Miss Walters was
the first incident in his life that made such influence a reality to him. That opened his eyes
to the vast and appalling issues that might hang
on his own conduct. It seemed suddenly to
have placed in his hands the entire future of
another; and he trembled when he saw the
value of what he was thus unexpectedly
holding. He had resolved, however, with the

most intense sincerity, that he would do his utmost ; or rather, he had not so much resolved as been seized with a desire to do so. The desire had come first, and the resolve afterwards ; and the thought that here at least was one good deed made plain for him, had been a taste of the bread of life to one who spiritually was starving. But now, it seemed as if this bread was to be like Dead Sea fruit. It was turning to ashes in his mouth. And why ? How had he been false to his trust ? What on earth had he done that Miss Walters should write thus to him ? His first impulse was to tax Mrs. Crane with lying, and he trusted very soon to set the matter right again. But by-and-by he began to suspect uneasily that in Miss Walters' impression of him there might be some amount of truth. He might be wanting, possibly, in that *personal* solicitude which was the thing she seemed to hunger for, and which indeed he had himself professed; and this misgiving was haunting him when he went to talk with Stanley.

By the time, however, the conversation was over, he had worked off some of his more painful excitement, and went away once again prepared to be sanguine. But his hopes now were of an anxious and solemn kind. The night before the ball he spent alone, thinking over his life, his powers, and what he should really do with them; and his earnest purpose with regard to a single woman tinged with its earnestness all his other resolutions. As for Miss Walters he had fears about her of which he could not define the nature. The closing words of her letter, in especial, made his mind misgive him: 'I told you Mrs. Crane had been over here. Someone else comes to-day. Ah me!' Who was the someone else? What did it all mean? There were moments that night, as he tried to compose himself to sleep,

when he hardly dared to think of this; and
when after hours of weary tossing, his
eyelids at last closed themselves, he had been
forced to stifle arbitrarily all such doubts by
determination.

With the following morning, however,
they all came back again, and his excitement
before long had grown a physical pain to him.
One picture only was before his eyes all day.
That was his meeting this very night with
Miss Walters; and as he dwelt continually
upon this single prospect, he felt, or hoped
he felt, that the personal love she longed for
was growing distinct and strong in him.

Evening at last drew on. He had in-
vited Stanley to dinner. The priest's company was the only thing that soothed him.
He went upstairs to prepare himself before
his guest's arrival; and here he experienced
another jar to his feelings. His fancy
dress, now that the time had come for

wearing it, seemed a hateful and degrading mockery, and he several times thought of avoiding the ball altogether. How could he bear to be making a fool of himself outwardly, when his whole inward being was as dark as death itself, and concerned with as serious issues ?   But to remain away was even more hard than to go ; so he overcame his reluctance, and put on his costume.   It was a relief to him, beyond any of his expectations, that this was quiet both in form and colour, and required no alteration, or, as he would now have called it, disfigurement of his face. It is true that there should, by rights, have been a gaudy scarf about his waist, but he would not submit to this ; and he found himself, when his toilet was completed, all in black with the exception of some coarse stockings.   He was simply a Spanish pedlar— a familiar figure in every town on the Riviera. He looked so little fanciful, that he might pass unnoticed amongst any Southern crowd. He even found something in his appearance that actually harmonised with his feelings.

Stanley remarked, when he came to dinner, on the sombre aspect that this dress gave Vernon, and said with a laugh, ' I should feel rather afraid of you, if I met you on the Cap de Juan, in any of these dark lanes. By the way,' he went on presently, 'you have not heard, I suppose, about Alic Campbell.'

Vernon started. 'Heard what about him?'

' He is coming to-night, to sleep at my little *Pension.* I got a telegram from him a few hours ago. He is on his way back to England, but he only says a word or two.'

The mixed shock and pleasure which this news caused was not, in one way, a bad thing for Vernon. It brought him face to face with an anxious practical embarrassment, and acted on him as a species of moral shower-bath. His first fear was that Campbell would come to him that evening, before he was safe out of the house : and his wish was to write to him before meeting him. 'What time does he come?' he asked of Stanley. The answer somewhat reassured him. It could not well be before half-past ten.

Vernon abruptly rose from the table. 'Stanley,' he said, 'will you excuse me for a minute or two? I will write Campbell a note. I have something particular I wish to say to him; and I shall be more at ease when I have got it off my mind.'

He went into his library, and before long came back again. 'Perhaps,' he said to Stanley, 'you will give this to Campbell. Life is full of sad coincidences. This afternoon I received, sent back to me, a letter I wrote to him some three weeks ago, begging him to come and stay with me. There is something ghastly in having your own words sent back to you, especially when you have in many ways much changed since you wrote them.'

After this Vernon became more restless; and his eyes began to gleam with an unnatural excitement, which contrasted curiously with the worn look of his face. When dinner was over, he went to the open window, and remained there for some moments silent. The evening was warm, but the moon had not yet risen, and the sky was thick with stars. A soft breeze came blowing up from the sea, and brought a splash of waves with it. Vernon sniffed the air, as if it were a kind of smelling-salts, and proposed to Stanley that they should go outside and enjoy it. Stanley assented. No sooner were they on the gravel than Vernon began to step out vigorously. At an increasing pace they made the circuit of the garden; they did the same thing for the second time. Then the

garden bounds grew too small for Vernon,
and nothing would satisfy him but that they
should wander out upon the rocks. The
project pleased Stanley ; he was himself being
braced by exercise. The rocks in question
were part of the same reef as that on which
Vernon with other companions had been
clambering not so long ago ; and access was
to be had to them from his own garden, as
well as from the Duchess's. In a few moments more he and Stanley had descended
a winding path, and found themselves almost
on the sea-level. The long reef before them
was indented with miniature fiords, in which
the dark water swayed and gleamed under
the starlight. Here the breeze breathed
fresher, the noises of the waves came clearer,
and the naked skies and stars towered
over them in the treeless air.

Presently Vernon began abruptly, ' We
have often, Stanley,' he said, ' talked about

human affection; and even yet I hardly
know what to think about it. Is it more
than, or is it less than, a desire for another's
good ?'

'It includes that,' said Stanley, 'but it is
beyond doubt more than that. A desire for
another's good, and a wish or will to work
for it, is what we should have for every
human being; but if, in speaking of affection,
you mean that special personal longing
which is what we mean by the word usually,
then affection is more than a mere zeal for
souls. Indeed, it is almost impossible to
have the latter, unless you have at least the
capacity for the former. You must have at
least the power of being fond of some *one*,
or of some special *ones*, or you will never
have the power of being zealous, in God's
sense, for all.'

'To me,' said Vernon, 'that longing for
the individual seems sometimes but the

intensity of self-indulgence. Stanley, for
reasons which I cannot explain to you, this
has been brought home to me with a fearful
personal force. In following one's own
salvation, one may be stealing the salvation
of a friend.'

'I have no wish,' said Stanley calmly,
'to enquire into any of your secrets; but the
case you state I can very easily imagine. It
is by no means uncommon. The life of the
Christian is full of such paradoxes, and the
Christian philosopher accepts and is not
daunted by them. I have been studying
you, if you will let me say so, for some time
past; and in a certain way your condition, I
think, is singular. The most sensitive part of
you is the intellect, just as with many men it
is the senses; and there has fallen full on
your intellect the dissolving forces which are
at work in the world about us. They are
everywhere; in the air we breathe, in the

light we see by. Only on your mind the scattered rays have been focalized. The denials of the intellect have gone far, in your case, towards paralysing the affirmations of the affections.'

Vernon was picking his way carefully over the ledges of the rocks ; and this slow fashion of walking gave him full time to attend to Stanley. At last he said in a slow constrained voice, with his eye fixed on the sea :—

' That is just my stumbling block. The intellect *does* deny the affirmations of the affections. Against my will it annihilates them.'

'And why is that ?' said Stanley, with sudden vigour. 'Is it the fault of your intellect or your affections ? My dear Vernon, I know quite well that our intellectual difficulties are not things to be pooh-pooh'd, nor can they be in all cases set down as wickedness or perversity. But believe me, that in many cases intellectual denial is based upon moral trifling. The intellect is a mill. It will grind if you bring grist to it: if not, it will only turn and turn. And what brings grist to it? First and foremost I should say that love did. In that thing, so despised of you— a man's common natural affection for another human being—is the germ not only of all morality, but of all philosophy. To love another, is to affirm the external world; it is to create creation, it is to open the eyes to God. What can the senses do for you? Can they even prove to you that you are not alone in the universe, and that all its shapes and seemings are anything but modes of your own aimless consciousness? No—were it only for the senses, you would be unredeemed in dreamland. There is a passage,' Stanley went on, 'in the writings of a modern English physicist—one of the bitterest of the younger generation of English freethinkers—which seems to me very happily put, and which I know well by heart. *The inferences*, he says, *of physical science are all inferences of my real or possible feelings; inferences of something actually or potentially in my consciousness, not of anything outside it. There are, however, some inferences which are profoundly different from those of physical science. When I come to the conclusion that* YOU *are conscious, and that there are objects in* YOUR *consciousness similar to those in mine, I am not inferring any actual or possible feelings of my own, but* YOUR *feelings, which are not and cannot by any possibility become objects in my consciousness.'* [1]

'I agree with you,' said Vernon; 'that is very happily put. It is your first step towards redeeming yourself from dreamland to realise that you are not the only dreamer. I was trying some time back to write down my own feelings with regard to life; and my one

---

[1] *Lectures and Essays*, by W. K. Clifford, vol. ii. p. 72.

complaint was that I lived in a world of shadows, and that my fellow-beings had no living reality for me.'

' Exactly,' said Stanley ; 'that is the very point I am insisting on. To a man who does not love, his fellow men will be shadows. What gives them reality for you is the act of loving—of loving some other creature of a like nature with yours. Love truly is in that way creative. It is the passionate affirmation of a fact which your senses never can assure you of. It seems to be small, and to deal with passing and local issues ; but it contains in it the assent of your nature to the reality of the universe. Look at the stars above us —look at the sea about us ! It is but a commonplace of philosophy, which no school doubts of, to say that all the worlds are held in the hollows of our own minds. The only universe you would ever know, or dream or think of, would perish, so far as you could tell, with your perishing, were it not for one belief—that in that universe there were other minds like yours, which like yours reflected it. Doubt this, and you must then doubt everything; but if you love, you will be unable to doubt this. The man can never logically be a sceptic who can say what a man I know said to a woman who is now dead: "In your soul also, there is for me a universe. Time, space, and eternity—these are there also; so too is the infinite world of matter, from Orion and the Pleiades to that blue forget-me-not in your bosom." '

At this moment they were rounding a small headland that ran out between Vernon's garden and the large domain of the hotel. The reef of rocks stretched right ahead of them, brown and black, towards the open sea. The moon was still unrisen, yet the rocks looked more distinct than they would have done under mere starlight; and here and

there it seemed a wan colour flickered on
them. This was remarked both by Vernon
and Stanley ; and when they had gone some
paces farther, they suddenly came on the explanation of it. Far up, beyond a slope of
shrubs and cypress trees, were a thousand
lamps burning, and coloured fumes of emerald-
green and ruby were floating up into the clear
night air ; whilst in the midst of all stood the
great hotel itself, looking like some palace
of enchantment—a mystery of cloud and
marble.

The thought of Miss Walters came to
Vernon with a renewed intensity. He
turned to Stanley and said, 'I must go :
my time is come. I will go this way, I
think, through the Duchess's gardens, if you
can get back without having me to guide you.
Your companionship, my dear fellow, has
been more comfort to me than I can tell you ;
and there is one thing which, if it did not

trouble you, I should like you to do for me. I told you I had jotted down some of my thoughts on things—especially such things as religious faith and affection. I did my best to be honest, and I wish you would read over what I wrote. I left it on my writing-table in the library, in a blue envelope. If you go through the house you will find it there. And by the way,' he added, as Stanley and he were separating, ' if Campbell does not want to go to bed directly, I shall be back from the ball soon. He will find me in by half-past twelve. I am very tired. I shall be sure to be back by then. Last night I slept ill. To-night I am looking forward to sleeping better, and more calmly.'

CHAPTER VI.

WHEN Vernon parted from the priest,
climbed from the lonely rocks, and
at last entered the Duchess's brilliant portals, he was like a man just dead
coming to life in another world. Before his
eyes in gay confusion was a throng of moving
colours, amongst flowers, and lights, and palm
trees ; and on his ears in quick cadence
burst the measured crash of waltz music.

He was at first quite bewildered ; he
could recognise nobody. At last he saw the
Duchess, who was standing near the ball-room
door. He exchanged a few words with her,

and she rallied him on the severity of his appearance. But while she was speaking another sound startled him. It was the voice of Colonel Stapleton. Vernon did but catch a word or two, but these few words were enough. 'The fact is,' the Colonel was saying to somebody, 'I've been away from Nice for some days; and, of all the places in the world, at San Remo.'

The Duchess heard the Colonel's voice also, and at once called to him. 'Well,' said her Grace, 'and where is she? I'm dying to have another look at her.'

'Coming,' said the Colonel gaily. 'Something has tumbled out of her hair, and she's gone into the cloak-room to get it put straight again.'

'We're talking, Mr. Vernon,' said the Duchess, 'of your friend Miss Walters. If you haven't seen her yet, I can tell you, you should at once go and look at her. We had expected, you know, that we should have had you in attendance on her, instead of our fat friend here. Look, now—there she is, with a dozen men round her already. Go at once and talk to her.'

Vernon looked as the Duchess bade him, and there Miss Walters was; but for some time he was rooted to the spot. His limbs seemed to be giving way under him. He could not move an inch. What he had heard since he entered the ball-room had, to all appearance, petrified him; and he could only stare about him stupidly.

'Can't you see her?' said the Duchess, as she was turning away to speak to a new arrival. 'There she is; I believe she calls herself "A Snow-drop."'

Thus urged, Vernon moved mechanically towards the place where Miss Walters was. She was all in white. Her dress was trimmed with snowdrops, and she wore in her hair a wreath of the same flower. She had her usual calm manner, which seemed to show that admiration came to her as a thing of course; but through this calm more animation than usual showed itself; her eyes looked larger and more luminous, and her cheeks had a deeper flush on them. No wonder she was the centre of an admiring circle.

As he drew nearer he saw she was slightly rouged, and that the darkness under her eyes was not only that of nature. In the case of most women he would have thought nothing of this, but here it gave a strange shock to him. He joined the group, pressing his way into it with a something that, had he been less preoccupied, he would have felt to have been almost roughness. But he could think of no such trifles now. He moved like a somnambulist more than a waking person. In a moment Miss Walters caught his eye. She advanced in a marked way to meet him, and the others perforce had unwillingly to disperse themselves. 'Come with me,' she said, 'to that window for a moment. I can talk to you only for a moment now.'

'Only for a moment!' he exclaimed. 'Good God, Cynthia, tell me what is this that has happened to you!'

'Be in this window,' she said, 'at half-past eleven. I can't talk to you now—not with all these people about me ; and I can't get away before. But be here then, and we will go for a little into the garden. Remember the place—that door close by the ladies' dressing-room. I shall escape there on pretence of finding a smelling-bottle, and shall be with you, unobserved, in an instant. Don't talk to me to-night in public if you can help it. I don't think I could bear it. Now —go away, and amuse yourself. I know you have many friends here.'

They went back to the throng, and were

almost instantly parted in it. But Vernon
was utterly unable to collect his wits to talk,
and he could hardly reply coherently to the
commonest greetings or inquiries. Before
long he had found the scene unendurable,
and he escaped by himself into the garden.
The walks about the house were too bright
with lamps. What he wished for was silence
and darkness. He found his way into a by-
path, and slowly paced up and down in meditation, waiting wretchedly for the appointed
time to arrive. On Miss Walters herself he
could hardly bear to let his thoughts rest;
but the image, if not the thought of her, was
continually present to him. His thoughts,
however, found another object, and this was
Colonel Stapleton. His whole being grew
concentrated into a hatred of this man, and
signs of the feeling began to rise to the surface, in the shape of broken mutterings.
' May God in heaven for ever damn and

curse you! May I be cursed myself, so that I only secure your everlasting misery. Beast, the clay you were made of, was black and fetid with the vilest sewage of life! For your own filthy pleasure you have broken and trampled on the whitest and purest soul that ever looked out of the holy eyes of woman. God curse you, you dog! May I die to-night and awake in hell to-morrow, if only I might gloat for ever there over your everlasting agony!' Such were the sounds that came from his lips half audibly; and in this condition he wandered to and fro, for he knew not how long. He was roused by-and-by, however, by hearing a step behind him, and in another instant a hand was laid on his shoulder, and a rough voice was ordering him to be off and about his business. The stranger addressed him in a mixture of French and English—the former broken, the latter coarse. The mean-

ing of the incident presently became clear.
The man was one of the house servants, and
Vernon in his pedlar's dress had been seen
and mistaken for some suspicious character;
nor, when he cast a glance down at his gar-
ments, could he much wonder at what had
happened.   The servant departed with many
apologies, and some suppressed amusement
and Vernon, annoyed at the interruption, went
back towards the house.   He consulted his
watch.   Time had passed faster than he had
thought possible.   It was a few minutes after
half-past eleven.   He hastened to the appointed window, from which a flight of steps
led down into the garden, and there Miss
Walters was.   She had plainly been waiting.
She was looking about her anxiously.   He
ascended a step or two.   She came down to
meet him.   'You are too late,' she said in a
low tone.

'Too late!' he echoed.

'Yes,' she said. 'Someone else has discovered that I was about to escape into the garden. It is with difficulty that I have secured ten minutes or so, alone. He will be looking for me presently. I told him I would remain here. But come now, let us move away quickly. The time is short, for where-ever I go I know he is sure to find me. At the end of the straight terrace there is a bench—take me to that.'

They passed down the walk in silence, nor did either speak until they had sat down together. Then Vernon very gently put his arm round her waist, and tried to draw her to himself. But she would not permit of it. 'No,' she said passionately, 'that must never happen again. I am not fit for you. We know both of us—we have quite agreed by this time—that I am not fit for you.'

'Cynthia,' he exclaimed, 'tell me what all this means! Who is it that is coming here

to look for you ? I am not asking you out
of any captious jealousy. If it were anyone
who would be good to you, and for his sake
you chose to leave me, I would tease you
with no prayer to keep you.'

' That is just it,' she cried bitterly. ' I
knew you would let me go. That is just the
bitterness. You have the same care for me
that a priest might have or a doctor ; it is not
the care of a human being that loves me. It
is my welfare you care for, it is not me. I
am your penitent or your patient ; I am not
the one woman who could make life happy
for you.'

' You are wrong,' said Vernon ; ' for I do
love you. If you knew how wretched you
had made me, you would not doubt my
love.'

Her eyes softened, and she looked at him
with a despairing tenderness. ' You speak
the truth,' she said. ' You love me enough

to be made wretched by me, but not enough
—not nearly enough to be made happy by
me.'

'Tell me,' said Vernon in a whisper, 'who
is it that you say will come here to look for
you?'

'You asked me,' she said, 'if he was a
man who would be good to me. He is not.
He knows no more of goodness than he
knows of Hebrew; and he has no more com-
punction for the soul that he has crushed by
his kisses than he would have for a beetle
that he trod on, in his path, by accident.'

'What do you mean?' said Vernon. 'It
seems that my head is swimming. I must
know who you mean. I need not ask his name.
But for God's sake tell me—what have I done?
What horrid crime have I committed that you
should leave me for him? Surely, my own one
—surely, my angel, it is not too late to come
back to my arms again. He can never—

surely this is not possible—have recovered his old influence over you ? '

' Oh, my heart !' she exclaimed, pressing her hands hard on it. ' How my heart is beating.'

He put his arm about her waist, and she now made no resistance. She let herself be passively drawn towards him, and once again she was resting quietly in his embrace. As she yielded she fixed her eyes on him, and said with a quick painful gasp, ' He has recovered everything ! '

There was a long silence. Neither looked at the other. By-and-by Vernon again spoke to her, but her eyes were closed, and she would give him no answer. He took her hand, and then again he spoke to her, but there was still no answer ; and he now saw that she was unconscious. He tried to revive her by fanning her, but this produced no effect. He then bethought himself of a foun-

tain close at hand, and he hurried off to dip
his handkerchief in the water. On his way,
however, he heard footsteps; and he stood
aside for a moment under the shadow of a
cypress tree to listen. The sound came
nearer. It was a man's firm tread. He
was walking slowly; and presently Vernon
caught, whistled softly, a fragment of a
vulgar song, popular in London music-
halls. A moment later, and the man's figure
was visible. It was Colonel Stapleton. One
of the many pet dogs of the Duchess was
trotting by his side, and with a soft kind
caress he stooped down to pat it. The moon
that was now risen shone full on his face—on
the sleek blonde moustache, the well-trimmed
beard, and the waterish grey eyes, with their
somewhat puffy lids. It shone, too, on his
well-shaped hands, and glittered on his heavy
gold rings. At sight of him, Vernon was, as
it were, fascinated. His eyes fixed them-

selves on the Colonel ; his teeth were set,
and his hands clenched themselves till the
nails tore the palms.

The Colonel never dreamed that he was
watched.

> I'm getting a big boy now—
> I'm getting a big boy now—

Such was the burden of the ditty with which
he was enchanting the ear of night, as he
went past the cypress tree. At that instant,
from the shadow, a Spanish pedlar sprang on
him, and laid a hand upon his throat. It was
like the grip of a wild beast in its strength,
its rapidity, and its savageness. The Colonel
was utterly unable to free himself from the
grasp of his unrecognised assailant, who said
nothing, but whose shadowed face was fixed
on him. The Colonel knew in an instant the
strength of the grasp that held him. He
made no effort to free himself, nor did he
seem in any degree to lose his presence of

mind.   What he did was the work of a single
instant.   In a single instant from his pocket
there had flashed out a small revolver : a
sharp sound for an instant broke the silence,
and the form of a Spanish pedlar fell flat and
motionless across a bed of purple cinerarias.

CHAPTER VII.

ABOUT half an hour previous to the above incident, a battered and dirty carriage had arrived at Stanley's *Pension*; and Campbell, seated at supper in the little brick-floored *salle-à-manger*, was opening Vernon's letter.

'My dear, dear Campbell,' it ran, 'do you remember some idle words of mine, for which you reproved me? I said that my true *métier* would be that of wooer-in-ordinary to all my male friends. I would make love for them, and when once I had won the heart of whatever woman was in question, I would hand it over to the man who wanted it. I

remember also I said to you, Would you let
me do your wooing for you on these terms ?
Campbell—God, Destiny, or the Devil heard
me when I said that. Unhappily I have fulfilled my *métier*, only I cannot hand the heart
over to you, that I have won. Do you know
who my neighbour is, at the Château St.
John—the woman about whom I spoke to
you—the woman I drove home at night with ?
You need not tell me the name of *your*
friend. I know it ; she is my neighbour. I
could not help what has happened. I never
knew that I was fighting against you, till it
was too late. The event in many ways has
been to me a sad one. I have become much
changed since that day when last you left me.
If you can bear to do so, come and see me
directly. You told me that my face was
changed from what it was when first you
knew me. Perhaps when next you see me
it may have suffered one change more.'

Campbell had supped alone, as Stanley was upstairs busy; but when Stanley by-and-by came down again, he found Campbell with his face white as a sheet. He rose abruptly, and seized Stanley's hand. 'Stanley,' he said, 'do you know the news you brought me in that letter? Do you remember,' he went on in a whisper, 'what I told you about myself the last morning I was here? The woman I told you about was Miss Walters; and Vernon is going to marry her.'

Stanley started and remained quite silent, staring in Campbell's face. Presently he cast his eye down to some papers he had in his hand, and said, 'I have been just reading some of Vernon's thoughts. He wants you to go and see him. Will you come to-night? Can you bear it?'

'I don't know,' said Campbell, 'what I can do or bear! Then suddenly he exclaimed, 'Yes, I will go. I will face everything; and

you, Stanley—will you come with me ?
Come !'

The two men set out together, and they
went silently along the white moon-lit road.
On their way the silence was only once
broken. Once Campbell opened his mouth,
and said, ' I hope Vernon will be happy.'

They reached the garden gates ; they saw
lights in Vernon's villa gleam through the
leaves like glow-worms. When they got near
the door there were several men standing
about, and conversation of some sort was proceeding rapidly. ' Stanley,' said Campbell,
' I wish you would go in first, and see if he
has people with him.'

Stanley advanced, and the group at the
door eyed him. He was recognised in a moment or two by one of the servants, who at
once advanced to meet him, and said something to him in a very subdued voice.

Stanley was led by the servant into a

small dimly lighted vestibule at the back of the villa, and remained there for some minutes. When he came out, he set himself to find Campbell, and he at last discovered him in the library. He was reading. He had found open on the writing table Vernon's letter to himself, which had that same evening been sent back to the writer; and it had now at last reached the person it was addressed to. One or two of the passages arrested his attention, in spite of the perturbation of the moment, and in a dreamy dazed way he kept reading and re-reading them. 'What do I find has happened?'—this was one of the passages—'Something glad, strange, and altogether unlooked-for. Out of the ashes of my manhood has re-arisen my youth—my youth which I thought I had said good-bye to for eternity; and the divine child has again run to meet me, with its eyes bright as ever, and with the summer wind in

its hair.' There was another passage also—
'Oh, the sweetness and rest of this serene
self-possession.' He was repeating these last
words to himself when Stanley entered.

'Campbell,' said Stanley, in a strange unnatural voice, 'there is another shock in store
for you. Shall I break it to you slowly, or
can you bear it now? It has to do with the
most solemn of all human events.'

Campbell rose with a sort of desperate
look, and Stanley whispered a few words in
his ear. 'Good God,' gasped Campbell, and
he seemed to be almost tottering. Stanley
grasped him by the arm, and led him into the
vestibule. There on a sofa was something
like a human form, covered with an oriental
tablecloth, with gaudy arabesques on it, and
fringed with heavy gold. Stanley slowly
raised one extremity of it, and a face was
visible, calm and placid like a boy's, only
bloodless and with no colour in it.

Campbell stood over it as if petrified. Some words he had just been reading came into his mind. ' Out of the ashes of my man‧ hood has re-arisen my youth. Oh, the sweetness and rest of this serene self-possession ! ' Except for this, his mind seemed like an utter blank, till with a start he turned to Stanley, and said piteously, ' And she——— what of her ? Does she know of this ? '

Stanley looked into Campbell's eyes fixedly for some moments, and in the room there was a deathly silence. At last he said, ' She knows nothing, and she never will.'

In the Protestant part of the Cannes Cemetery may be now seen two headstones, not close together, for it was found impracticable so to place them ; but still not far apart. Under one of them sleeps Vernon, more soundly than he had done during the last three weeks of his life, with the leaves of his confessions clasped on his breast and buried with him. The other headstone bears this inscription, suggested by Alic Campbell,—

CYNTHIA WALTERS.

SHE DIED SUDDENLY OF HEART DISEASE,
APRIL THE 10TH, 1881.

' Blessed are the pure in heart, for they shall see God.'

THE END.

LONDON : PRINTED BY
SPOTTISWOODE AND CO., NEW-STREET SQUARE
AND PARLIAMENT STREET